SETTLE UP

ALLISON SPEKA

Copyright © 2023 by Allison Speka

All rights reserved.

No part of this book may be reproduced in any form or by any electronic or mechanical means, including information storage and retrieval systems, without written permission from the author, except for the use of brief quotations in a book review.

Cover Design: Allison Speka

Publisher: Speka Press

❀ Created with Vellum

For all the couples who once insisted they were just friends.

ONE

Jared

"Jared, we need to talk," Janelle said, her lips pinching together as she crossed her arms in front of her chest.

I groaned and reluctantly pushed myself up, shifting to the edge of the bed. My eyelids drooped, struggling to remain open and focused as they fixated on my hovering girlfriend. Clutching the mattress, I braced myself for the argument ahead.

I wished she could have the decency to wait until I had my first cup of coffee.

"What is it now, Janelle?"

"You're seriously taking that tone with me after how you treated me yesterday?" She glared at me and paced the worn wood floor in front of my bed.

My mind replayed the events of last night and the show my band had played. The bar itself wasn't anything to write home about. Still, sixty or so lively people showed up and sang along to almost every cover we played. Afterward, we were all high on adrenaline and decided to stay out and celebrate. Janelle had wanted me to go home earlier in the night with her, but I had brushed her off.

"I didn't do anything last night."

"Are you kidding me? You were flirting with every single girl that came up to you after the show." She stopped pacing and clenched her fists. This was *not* good for me. "Then, when I practically begged you to take me home, you insisted on staying out late. Again."

I ran my fingers through my tousled hair. "Janelle, for the millionth time, I was just talking to them. Nothing would ever happen. I'm with you."

"It's like this every time you have a show," she said, ignoring my comment. "It's like you can't get enough of the spotlight. I know you love it that girls are all over you."

"That isn't true."

Well, it wasn't entirely *not* true, but I couldn't tell her that and fuel the flame of this argument. How could I not love the attention of beautiful women—or anyone, really—telling me they think I'm talented?

But that was beside the point. I would never trash our relationship like that, even with our ups and downs. Loyalty ran deep within me, and it baffled me that Janelle seemed oblivious to this fact despite our yearlong relationship.

I stood up and reached for her, but she pulled away. My outstretched hand hung in the air between us.

"I only have eyes for you," I insisted.

"Yeah, right." If looks could kill, I'd already be six feet under.

"I don't know what you want me to say." Irritation crept into my voice. "We have this fight every weekend, and it's getting old."

"You're telling *me* it's getting old?" She laughed, and a

sour expression took hold of her face. "You know what's getting old? You and your Peter Pan lifestyle. It's time you got a real job and stopped trying to live out this ridiculous rock star fantasy."

"This *is* my real job. Between the band and bartending, I'm doing alright for myself, and you know it. The band is only getting more popular. We're so close to a breakthrough. I can feel it."

"You're thirty-one and in a cover band, Jared. Oh, and you're a bartender who doesn't even drink. It's embarrassing."

She knew how to deliver lashes that would sting. My nostrils flared, and I took a deep breath. Making jabs at the band was typical for her, but I hated when she mentioned that I didn't drink—like it somehow affected her.

"How could you even mention me not drinking in the same sentence as telling me to get my life together? You know I used to have a problem."

The problem being that I used to be a reckless drunk. After high school, I fell in with a bad crowd. Thankfully, my best friend Dean forced me to ditch them and get my life together, but I still hadn't gotten sober until recently. I had been so content with the band and the trajectory of my life that I didn't need the crutch of alcohol like I used to. Plus, with all the shows in bars, I would rather be safe than sorry. Returning to old habits was not an option for me.

She sighed. "I'm sorry. It's just that you used to go out with me and my friends. But lately, I feel guilty inviting you because I know you judge us when we drink."

"That's not fair. I would never ask you not to drink or judge you. I'm a bartender for fuck's sake. One minute you're harping on me about staying out late, and the next you're mad because I don't party with you? Make up your mind because these double standards are giving me whiplash."

"I just don't think this is working anymore." Her eyes flickered away from mine for a moment before returning to meet my gaze.

"What are you talking about?" A knot formed in my chest as concern replaced the anger I felt moments ago. "Are you-are you seriously trying to break up with me right now?"

She looked at the floor, not responding.

"Janelle, baby." I reached for her again, but she took a step back. "We've been together for a year. Please don't throw this away because of one stupid fight."

"It's not just one stupid fight. We fight all the time. Do you think this is what a good relationship looks like?"

I shrugged. "Yes?" It came out like a question. This was my first and only relationship, so it wasn't like I had much to compare it to.

"I don't think we're right for each other." She bit her lip and looked me in the eye. "You can't be who I need you to be."

Pain sliced through my chest at her casual tone. Her choice of words impacted me more than the actual sentiment.

"I guess if that's how you feel," I muttered.

"It's how I feel."

I watched as she moved around my apartment, gathering her few scattered belongings. My mouth hung open a few times as I almost begged her to stay. But the words never came. It was as if that last argument had sucked me dry.

It only took her minutes to pack up everything that was hers. I hadn't even moved from beside the bed when I heard the click of the doorknob.

I waited for an ache to overtake my chest, but instead, all I felt was the tension fly out of my body as she slammed the door behind her.

I KNOCKED BEFORE STUFFING MY HANDS IN MY POCKETS AND shifting my gaze down the long hallway. After waiting only a few seconds, I knocked again.

A petite brunette in an oversized black T-shirt opened the door.

"Hey, Al," I barely greeted my best friend's girlfriend before walking past her and slumping onto their couch like I had done a thousand times before.

"Um, everything okay with you?" She glanced at the clock on the wall. "I'm surprised you're up this early after a show."

"Janelle dumped me," I said.

The weight of that reality had sunk in on my commute over here, but still, all I felt was this weird lightness that had infiltrated my whole body. This was my first breakup, and according to every cheesy movie I'd ever seen, I should be wallowing in self-pity right now. I guess I did feel bad for myself, but mostly just because she had been the one to end it.

Al searched my face. "Shit. That sucks." Her expression shifted to one of sympathy, but I noticed the lack of disbelief in her tone.

"Why don't you seem more surprised?" I asked.

She bit her lip as she struggled to figure out what to say. Al was a woman of few words. Typically, I loved this about her, but at this moment, I needed her to give it to me straight. If I couldn't make sense of my breakup, the people that knew me best would have to.

"I don't know...it did seem like you guys had been fighting a lot recently."

"We hardly fought," I lied.

Al cleared her throat and shifted from one foot to the other. She glanced at a closed bedroom door, probably hoping Dean would swoop in and rescue her.

"Come on, Al. Tell me how you really feel."

She sighed. "You know I like Janelle. It just seemed like she was always trying to change you into someone you're not."

"Elaborate," I said, sitting up and staring at her.

"Well, she hated your band to start."

"I wouldn't say *hated*." I got up and stood across from her. "Maybe she was a bit resistant to the idea."

"She was also more into her friends than getting to know yours."

I tilted my head, considering this. While she had tried with my friends in the beginning, I had to agree that she had shown a considerable lack of interest in the past few months.

"Why didn't you voice these concerns earlier?"

"Um, I…" Her voice trailed off as a tall guy with just as many tattoos as me and dark, disheveled hair slumped out of their bedroom.

"Dean, thank god you're awake," Al said, her face breaking into a relieved smile.

He rubbed his eyes and blinked twice. "Jared? What the hell are you doing here this early?"

"Janelle broke up with me," I said.

"I'll make some coffee." Al raced to the kitchen, clearly eager to get away from my line of questioning.

"Well, shit," Dean replied, leaning on the back of the couch.

"You and your girlfriend could really use some sympathy training."

I had known Dean almost my entire life. We grew up a few houses down from each other in the same shitty neighborhood. He was my best friend. My brother, really. If anyone could tell me how to feel about this breakup, it was him.

Dean shrugged. "Sorry, it's just that you didn't seem all that happy together."

"What are you even talking about?" I paced the room. "We loved each other."

Dean only stared at me in response.

"What?" I demanded. "Say it."

"Did you love each other, or did you love the idea of each other?"

"What's the difference?" I glared at him.

Dean held up his hands in surrender. "Don't jump down my throat. All I'm saying is that sometimes it felt more like you loved the idea of having a girlfriend than you actually loved Janelle."

"We were great together."

"Were you?" Dean asked as Al entered the room with two mugs, handing us each one.

I took a sip as the past few months of my relationship replayed like a bad movie in my mind.

All of the times I invited Janelle to hang out with Dean and Al and she made up a weak excuse. All of the fights she picked anytime I was on a high after a show. All of the times she begged me to go out with her friends and have one drink even though I told her I didn't want to.

When was the last time we had fun together?

I decided to deflect instead of facing the truth that our relationship had probably expired a while back.

"I can't believe you both hated Janelle and I'm just now finding out about it."

Dean looked at the ceiling and shook his head. He wrapped his arm around Al, tugging her toward him.

"Come on. I didn't hate Janelle. I just didn't love how she acted like you were never good enough for her."

I leaned back against the wall, trying to process his words. He had a point. While I might come across as a confident guy—my bandmates would even say cocky—I did have a slight inferiority complex. I didn't grow up well off, and sometimes being around Janelle and her uppity friends made me feel like an outcast. I tried never to let it get to me, but in all honesty, it was the reason I had spent significantly less time with her lately.

A fact that irritated her quite a bit.

Sometimes it felt like I was on autopilot with her—just moving from one disagreement to the next, and trying my best to quell any issues before they turned into a fight.

"Look," Dean said. "I've known you pretty much your entire life. You've had a lot of ups and downs, and right now, you're the best I've ever seen you. You're doing something you're passionate about. You're reliable. You've got your life together. It felt like Janelle wanted you to give all that up to be some corporate jackass that will go to happy hour with her and her friends every other day of the week. Nothing wrong with that life, it's just not you."

"It's okay to grow apart," Al added.

"Right," said Dean. "Just because she was your first serious girlfriend doesn't mean she has to be the one."

"Exactly," Al said. "Now you'll know what to look for in your next relationship."

I sighed and assessed the two of them. "I can't believe I'm taking relationship advice from you two."

Dean's jaw clenched. "Why wouldn't you? We're happy."

"I know. You're disgustingly happy. But remind me again how much relationship experience the two of you had before getting together?"

They both eyed each other and refused to meet my gaze. They both knew full well that neither of them had a significant relationship before falling head over heels for each other.

"Right, that's what I thought. And don't make me remind you about how you almost messed things up before you even got together."

"Alright, that's enough." Dean glared at me, but Al laughed.

I raised my hands, smiling. "Alright, alright. I'll stop."

"Not trying to be a dick for pointing this out, but you really don't seem that upset for someone who just got dumped," said Dean.

"I guess you're right."

"So, I think you probably know deep down that you two weren't meant to be." Dean walked over and smacked my shoulder.

"Now you can find someone that better suits you," Al said.

I stroked my chin.

"I think what might better suit me is not sticking to just one if you know what I mean." I smirked, and Al scrunched up her nose.

Dean rolled his eyes. "Good to see you're recovering from your heartbreak so quickly. I don't think I'm mentally prepared for single Jared again."

"Too bad because he's here to stay."

TWO

Evie

"I'm sorry, Evie. I wish I could help you out, but my grandson wants to move in next week."

I sighed and looked down at the older woman's apologetic expression.

"Isn't there any way he could wait just a couple more months? I'm already planning on leaving then, and I really need a place to stay."

She shook her head and peered up at me through her half-circle glasses. "His new job starts sooner than that. Is there any way you can move your trip up?"

My face fell. "I already booked my plane ticket. It would cost me way too much money to switch it."

"I'm sorry, honey. You've been a lovely tenant. Sometimes I get weirdos that want to rent monthly, but you've been perfect. But I promised my grandson he could move in at the start of the month, and I'm so excited to have him close by."

Her face lit up at the mention of him.

I gave her a defeated smile. "I understand, Mrs. Emerson. I'll figure something else out."

She apologized again, and I assured her it was alright as I slowly closed the door to the garden-level apartment located underneath her modest home in downtown Seattle.

I tossed my keys onto the kitchen counter and rubbed my temple.

What was I going to do for the next two months? It was hard enough to find this place, let alone find something so last minute.

I couldn't really blame Mrs. Emerson for the late notice. She had difficulty keeping track of the dates, and technically we had no lease or official agreement in place. When I decided to come to Seattle for a while, I simply flew here, walked around, and found a "For Rent" sign posted in her window. The whole thing had been too good to be true, so I guess it was only fair that now I had to struggle to figure out a solution.

I decided to put my living situation on the back burner and get some work done. Slumping into my plush office chair, I placed noise-canceling headphones over my ears and watched back the video I had made earlier. I leaned into my pink microphone and took a deep breath before pressing record.

"This veranda I actually built using the third expansion pack. You have to modify the patio and use the indoor stair railings, but the end result is totally worth it."

My phone ringing interrupted my thought process, and I pressed pause.

"Shoot," I muttered.

Switching it off, I resumed virtually walking through the new Victorian home I had constructed in LifeCraft, a video game where you could create people, neighborhoods, and an entire simulated life.

I finished recording the audio and did some quick edits before posting it to my account for my hundreds of thousands of followers to view.

I had been streaming LifeCraft videos since I was sixteen, so almost ten years at this point. Growing up the way I had, this video game had been the perfect escape. When I discovered an online community of others that loved the game, I quickly became addicted to sharing videos of me playing. In my wildest dreams, I would have never thought millions of people would be interested enough to watch my videos. Thank god they did, or I might have never gotten out of my parents' house.

I removed my headphones and checked my phone—two missed calls from my cousin Cam. Pressing redial, I held the phone up to my ear while opening a new tab to browse apartment listings.

He answered after three rings. "Evelyn."

"How many times do I have to tell you it's Evie now."

"How many times do I have to tell you I've been calling you Evelyn my entire life, I can't change now."

I rolled my eyes. As soon as I left my parents' house, the need for a new identity flowed through every vein inside my body like lava bursting from a volcano. I shortened my name almost immediately since they had never let me while growing up.

"We named you Evelyn for a reason," my mother would say. "It's insulting to try to shorten it."

"Did you need something, Cam?"

"What, I need a reason to call my favorite cousin?"

"I'm your only cousin."

"Same thing. So, what are you up to?"

Although Cam and I were the same age and grew up less than an hour away from each other, we hadn't been very close growing up. Our moms were sisters but had very different outlooks on raising children.

Cam and I became close when I finally moved out shortly after my eighteenth birthday. Due to the nature of how I was raised, I didn't exactly have a ton of friends to call on. Cam let me crash in his college dorm for a few months while I figured out what to do with my life and my newfound freedom.

"Just apartment hunting."

I clicked around on the map view of my current neighborhood and winced at the prices.

"Aren't you leaving soon for your trip?"

"Not for two months, and my landlord is evicting me now."

"Throwing too many ragers, huh?"

I snorted. "Her grandson is moving in."

My original plan involved staying here for eight months before leaving on my trip around the world. I had been planning this for ages and had finally saved up enough to buy a one-way ticket to Bali and make it a reality. I had no plan other than to go wherever the journey took me.

"So, what are you going to do? Try out another city before you leave?"

"I might have to. I would need to sell my kidney to afford the rent on some of these places."

"Hmm. Where could you go next? I can't even keep track of all the cities you've lived in."

"Don't exaggerate." Although, truthfully, it wasn't much of an exaggeration. For the past six years, I had been jumping around to whichever city caught my attention. I had moved from New York to Charlotte, to Atlanta, to Austin, to LA, to Reno, to Portland, and now Seattle.

There was nothing quite like a fresh start in a new city—leaving behind any familiar comforts for the excitement of the unknown. The prospect of meeting new people and exploring every corner of a vibrant new city thrilled me like nothing else. The possibilities were endless, and I found it addicting. This lifestyle was the polar opposite of my upbringing, and I thrived on it.

"Any recommendations? Preferably somewhere affordable. I'm trying to save money for my trip, not blow it all on some short-term rental."

"Everything is expensive nowadays unless you want to move to the middle of nowhere."

I groaned. "You know I need a city."

"How about Chicago?"

My heart beat heavily against my chest as he suggested the city he lived in.

"That's a little too close," I said, knowing he would understand my meaning.

"It's nowhere near where you grew up. Just because it's driving distance doesn't mean anything. Rural Wisconsin is a completely different planet than Chicago. You've never even visited me here," he whined.

I brought my knees to my chest and hugged them as I swiveled around in the desk chair.

"I don't know…"

"What if I let you stay with me?"

I bit my lip as I considered this.

Cam took my silence and jumped on it. "You can have

the couch. It won't be fancy, but it will be cheap. Good luck finding free rent in any other city in America."

"It would be nice to save some money," I finally relented. "And it would only be for a couple of months."

"It'll be just like when you stayed with me in college. Oh my god, remember how cramped we were in that tiny room? This will be like luxury living compared to that."

I laughed at the memory. "It would be kind of fun to relive those days."

"That's it. I'm sending you flight options now. You're coming."

I smiled at my cousin's persistence. Even though we had only gotten to know each other well in our adult years, he had always been a massive supporter of mine and had quickly become one of my closest friends. My only close friend, actually.

We ironed out a few details before hanging up. Excitement buzzed through my mind as I stood up and paced my quaint, overpriced living room. Chicago hadn't been part of my plan, but the idea of packing my bags and leaving so quickly like this thrilled me.

Moving to the dresser, I opened the top drawer and took in my belongings. It wouldn't take me more than a few hours to pack up. I hadn't acquired so much as a desk lamp since I had left home. My computer, recording equipment, and clothes were basically all I owned.

The thought of moving to Chicago settled over me. The entire idea was spontaneous, random, and barely thought out.

Just the way I liked it.

THREE

Jared
───────

"You need to work on that bass line. It's falling flat." Our drummer Tyler pointed one of his sticks at our bassist Drew who glared at him.

"Why do you feel the need to criticize something every time you open your mouth."

I glanced at Max, our lead guitarist, and we shared an eye roll. Drew and Tyler bickered constantly. It probably had something to do with the fact that they were brothers.

"I wouldn't feel the need to criticize if you could just write a halfway decent part," Tyler said.

"Maybe if you kept a cleaner beat, I'd have more to go off of."

I sighed, and Max shook his head.

The two of us had started this band about two years ago. I met him at a local music store, and we hit it off immediately. Max was mellow and easy to work with. We started jamming at his house before deciding to make a cover band. We met Tyler through a mutual friend, and when he told us his brother played bass, we thought, *Hey, it's meant to be.* In a way, it was. They were both talented musicians, and our sound was top tier. Unfortunately for Max and me, this came at the price of our peace of mind. Our once relaxed jam sessions had turned into constant arguments. Drew and Tyler went at it as if they were still in middle school.

"Alright, alright. Chill out, guys." I stepped in between my bandmates and held up my hands. "There is no need for this animosity. Tyler, stop being hypercritical. Drew, learn how to take constructive criticism. We're all new to writing music, and we need to have thicker skin if we're going to make anything worth listening to."

Max nodded. "Jared is right. We're so close on some of these songs. 'Free To Be Me' is sounding so good with the new lyrics."

"Yeah," Drew agreed. "Jared should implode his relationship more often so we can get good material."

I smirked.

He was right. My breakup with Janelle had unleashed a flood of creativity that I'd never experienced before. Part of me felt guilty for not being more devastated about the end of our relationship, but I was too exhilarated by the prospect of pursuing my music and living life on my own terms. For months, I'd felt like I was under constant scrutiny. I hadn't realized how much her criticism and lack of support weighed on me until I felt the relief of being unburdened by it.

"I think the originals are going over well. Look." Tyler held up his phone. "We got twenty new followers since our last show."

I nodded. "That's pretty good, right?"

"It's okay." Max shrugged. "We should probably be putting more effort into our social media if we want to build a fan base."

"Who wants to take the lead on that?" I asked.

Three blank stares looked back at me.

"Come on," I pressed. "One of us has to do it. Max is right. Social media helps indie bands take off all the time. We should be using it to promote ourselves."

"We can't even decide on a name, let alone market ourselves," Drew pointed out.

"I thought we were going with Jared and Company—ouch." I rubbed the side of my arm where Tyler had thrown his drumstick at me.

"That's a stupid name, and you know it."

"I mean, I did bring the band together," I muttered before holding up my hands as Tyler readied his other stick. "Fine, fine. You're right. We need a name."

Over the past year, we had mainly played wedding gigs and referred to ourselves as The Wedding Band online to ensure we showed up in local search results. While we all appreciated performing, and a steady income, we were eager to branch out to other venues that allowed us to be original.

"Why don't you think of name ideas while you figure out our marketing plan," Max said.

"We need to hire someone. I don't know shit about marketing." I glared at my bandmates, irritated they were putting this pressure on me.

Drew snorted. "Good luck finding someone that will work for what we can afford."

A knock sounded at the garage door, and we all yelled for whoever it was to come in.

A tall blonde poked her head through the door and smiled when she saw me.

"Hey, Jared. Sorry to interrupt. Didn't you say seven?"

I glanced at my phone. Of course, practice was running late again. How could it not when we spent half the time arguing?

"Just a few more minutes, babe." I winked at her. "Why don't you wait for me in your car."

She nodded and smiled before backing out.

Max raised his eyebrows. "Someone's wasting no time moving on, I see."

I clutched my chest. "What are you talking about? I'm torn up. I need the distraction."

"I guess it makes sense that after a year of being forced into monogamy, you would be busting at the seams," Tyler said.

"There was no busting at the seams, thank you very much. I was a fantastic boyfriend." I slung the strap over my head and set my guitar in its stand. "Now that I'm single, it would be a disservice not to give every woman that's interested a piece of this."

Drew mimed gagging. "Do you hear yourself? How do you even pick up women with those lines?"

"I don't know, Drew, but considering you go home alone after every show, maybe you shouldn't knock my game." I winked at him before slipping out the door.

Jared

I KNOCKED THREE TIMES BEFORE CHECKING TO SEE IF THE door was open. The knob turned easily, and I pushed it open to let myself in.

Al lifted her gaze from the kitchen counter where she sat with Cam, sharing a plate of food. Cam was her old roommate and one of her closest friends. Despite his dry sense of humor and sarcasm, he never failed to attend one of our shows if I invited him, a fact that had not gone unnoticed by me.

Dean lay sprawled out on the couch watching something on TV.

He looked up. "Hey, man. What are you doing here?"

I flopped onto the couch next to him. "Just got back from a date."

"But it's not even eleven," Al said.

I shrugged. "The date was at seven."

"So, it didn't go well?" Cam asked.

"Oh, it went well." I turned around and winked in response.

Al scrunched up her nose in disgust as Dean shoved me in the leg with his foot.

"Then why are you here and not with her?" he asked.

"It went well, and then we went back to her place where it went even better—if you know what I mean—and then I left. Was I supposed to sit around and hang out with her all night? I thought the whole point of being single was that I didn't have to do that."

Dean rolled his eyes. "I forgot how annoying you are when you're single."

"Hey, thanks for the support," I replied. "You coming to the show tomorrow night?"

Dean looked at me and yawned. "Another show this week?"

"Come on, D," I whined. "I need my best friend there."

"I'll come," Cam said. "Is it at the bar downtown again?"

I nodded. "At least *someone* is supportive." I eyed Dean and Al, who looked guilty.

"Of course, we'll come," said Al.

"Yeah, yeah. We'll be there." Dean waved off my remarks.

"Also, while you're all riding the support train, can you follow the band? We're trying to drum up some interest on social media."

Dean laughed. "What do you know about social media?"

"Not a lot," I admitted. "But we've got to start somewhere."

"You always get a pretty good crowd," Al said.

"But it's usually the bar bringing in people. Our fan base is microscopic."

Cam raised his eyebrows. "Any chance you want some help with all that?"

I stood up and walked over to the kitchen. "Are you offering?" I asked.

He shook his head. "Not me. My cousin. She's literally moving here tomorrow. She's great with social media, and I know she could use the extra money."

"That's perfect." I grabbed his shoulders and shook them lightly. "Any chance she'll work for cheap to help out some struggling musicians?"

Cam hesitated. "I'm sure you can work something out.

Besides, she's insanely good at all that stuff. You'll get your investment back, guaranteed."

"I didn't know your cousin was moving here." Al looked interested. "Evelyn, right?"

"Yep, that's the one. She just decided a couple of days ago."

"You should bring her to the show tomorrow so we can meet her," she said.

"And so she can see the band play," I added.

"She'll be there," Cam promised.

"What's she like?" I asked.

"Um, she's a bit of a nomad. Always traveling and moving around. I can hardly keep track of her."

I nodded. "And you're sure she'd be interested in helping my band?"

He shrugged. "Why not?"

"I hope you're right. God knows we could use the help." I walked behind Cam and Al and proceeded to help myself to the hummus they were eating.

"Is this the cousin that escaped from a cult or something?" Al asked.

I coughed as the bite I had just taken tried to go down the wrong pipe.

Dean whipped his head around. "What?"

"Al!" Cam exclaimed. His face turned red, surprising for him since he was a hard person to fluster. "That's *not* what I said. Maybe I said my aunt and uncle were *like* a cult. And whatever you do, don't say that in front of her. Her parents were just…a bit intense. They kept her extremely sheltered, and she left home to stay with me when I was in college. That's the story I told you. There was no cult involved. And please don't bring this up when you meet her."

"Sorry," Al mumbled. "I swear you made it sound like—"

"Whatever. I don't care what I said, don't bring it up to her." He shot us both a warning glare.

I held up my hands. "Fine, I won't say anything. I'm sure we'll only be talking about the band anyway."

FOUR

Evie

"I'll be where?" I asked as I heaved my limp, exhausted body out of Cam's compact sedan. Despite my love for traveling, I could never quite adjust to red-eye flights. I hadn't managed to sleep for more than thirty minutes.

"At Jared's show." Cam's muscles bulged against his shirt as he grabbed my suitcases from the backseat.

"Could your shirt be any tighter?" I mumbled.

"What? I'm just supposed to not show off my hard work? Yeah, right."

"Who's Jared, anyway?"

"He's a friend of a friend. And he's in a band, and they might have a job for you."

I narrowed my eyes. "What kind of job?"

"They need more followers, and they suck at social media—I don't know. I told him you were perfect for it."

My tired eyes shot open. "Why did you do that? I don't know how to run a social media account for a band."

"Please, you have tons of followers, and you post all the

time. How hard could it be? I could have sworn you were just talking about how some extra spending money for your trip would be a dream."

I groaned. I had said that when we discussed my staying on his couch for free. "So you're using that to blackmail me into helping your friend?"

"Come on, it'll be good for you. Gaining new skills and making money in the process. Besides, you'll love them."

"Really?"

He bit his lip and shifted his gaze away from me. "Sure."

I rolled my eyes. Considering I usually met people in new cities by finding local game nights or book clubs, I doubted very much I would fit in with a bunch of guys in a band.

I struggled to keep my heavy eyelids open as we entered the lobby of Cam's apartment building—a high-rise with sleek, modern finishes and a doorman. Cam acknowledged the man at the front desk with a nod before using his keycard to unlock a door leading to a row of elevators.

"I'm so excited you're here," he gushed, pressing the button. "Wait until you see my view."

As he swung his arm around me, I leaned into his embrace. Being in the same city as my only close family member comforted me in unexpected ways. While I had met countless people during my travels, nothing quite compared to the feeling of being around someone I had known my whole life. It truly felt like home.

One of my few memories of us together as children flashed through my mind. Our mothers, who were still on speaking terms at the time, had taken us to the local fair. Despite being only eleven, Cam had managed to persuade them to let us wander off on our own and try a few rides. While I'm sure they were keeping a watchful eye on us from a distance, it still felt like we were free. When we rode to the top of the Ferris wheel, it was the first time in my life I felt like the world could be big.

The elevator dinged, ripping me from my thoughts.

"Here we are." Cam gestured for me to step off first and led me down a short hallway. We arrived at a door that looked identical to every other one we passed.

"Welcome home," he said before opening the door and pushing my giant bag inside.

My mouth hung open as I took in the floor-to-ceiling windows.

"You weren't kidding about the view." I took a few steps inside, dropping my backpack to the floor. "This is amazing."

Lake Michigan sparkled in the sunlight next to a sea of tall buildings.

"Wait until you see it at night." He gestured to the plush sofa against the wall. "This is yours for now. Not the most glamorous. We can get an air mattress, but I didn't have time."

"No, this is perfect. Thanks again for letting me stay here." I walked over and gave him another hug.

"Are you kidding? I'm so excited you're here. We haven't been in the same city since you stayed with me in college."

I chuckled. "I remember. It was when you were going through your emo phase."

He playfully shoved my shoulder. "Don't you dare bring that up. If I recall correctly, you were going through a crochet phase."

I winced and thought of the crochet hooks currently tucked away in my suitcase. "Crocheting has actually gotten pretty trendy."

I was a bit of a compulsive crocheter. My mind and body needed near-constant activity. I tended to get almost painfully restless if I wasn't doing something with my hands.

He smirked. "I would have never come for your crafts if you didn't bring up my skinny jeans and straightened hair."

"I think I still have some pictures if your friends want to see."

"Don't you dare," he said before pinching my side.

I laughed and doubled over onto the couch. "Don't tickle me."

"Don't threaten me."

He paused and glanced at me. "So, this must be the closest you've been to home in years."

"I don't really refer to that as home."

"I know, I know. I'm sorry. I shouldn't have even brought it up." He hesitated. "I just wanted to see how you were doing is all."

Before I boarded the airplane, I had felt quite anxious about the proximity, but Chicago was completely different than my rural hometown with one stoplight. I may as well have been halfway across the world for how far away that life felt.

It was a bit strange to think about my parents being only a drive away, though. The fact that I could borrow a car and be at the house that once felt like a prison made me shiver. I would never go back. I knew I wasn't welcome there. My mother had made that clear.

"It's fine," was all I said. "I haven't even thought about that."

I tried to reassure him with a smile as I took in the view from the couch. I let the buzz of being in a new city wash over me. Despite feeling a bit weary at the prospect of attending a band's show tonight, the idea of exploring the city's nightlife exhilarated me. Typically, I didn't go out to bars much. The idea of doing it alone made me uncomfortable, and the people I tended to gravitate toward weren't the bar-hopping type. But with Cam by my side, I felt good about stepping outside my usual comfort zone.

"What time is this show tonight?"

"Starts at nine."

I sprawled out on the couch and yawned. "I need a nap if I'm going to make it."

Cam rustled around in the hall closet before producing a blanket and pillow and throwing them at me. I laughed as plush material connected with my face.

"Hey!"

"Get some sleep. I don't want anyone to think my cousin can't hang."

As Cam and I stepped out of the taxi, I took a moment to gaze up in awe at the vibrant lights that surrounded me. The palpable energy in the air sent my heart racing.

"This is so exciting," I said.

"For someone who moves around so much, you really need to get out more."

"I get out," I insisted.

Cam dipped his chin and looked down at me. "Going out in LifeCraft doesn't count."

"Shh," I hissed. "Don't tell your friends about that."

"It's literally what you do for a living."

"I know. And I'm not saying I'll keep it a secret. I just hate when it's the first thing people find out about me. Everyone has such a strong idea of what a gamer is."

"You build old Victorian mansions in a simulated environment. I don't think *you* have a strong idea of what a gamer is."

"I've told you before. It still counts even though I'm not wielding a gun and fighting some zombie apocalypse."

"Whatever. I won't say anything. I'll just say you're an emerging social media manager."

"That sounds fake."

"Only because I just made it up."

Cam grabbed my arm and steered me to the door before pointing at the long line of people snaking around the corner, patiently waiting for their IDs to be checked.

"This place is packed," I said.

When Cam said he had a friend in a band, I envisioned a few people in a crusty dive bar—not a packed venue downtown.

Cam shrugged. "They've gotten popular the past year. They've started to play here semi-regularly."

We stepped into line, and I bounced my foot up and down as I stared at the bodies in front of us. I tugged my dark green crocheted tank top down in an attempt to cover more of my stomach. I hadn't meant to make it a crop top, but I had gotten a little bored with the project and had rushed to finish it last week.

"Stop fidgeting." Cam grabbed my hand and pulled it away from my stretched shirt.

"This is taking forever."

"It's been thirty seconds."

I muttered something under my breath but stopped complaining and pulled out my phone to check the views on my latest video. Once I let my focus drift from the line, it moved quickly. Before long, we were inside the bar. The space was even more expansive than the outside made it look, and the high ceilings added to the spacious feeling. I scanned the crowd, trying to take in every detail of my first night here.

"I think I see some friends," Cam shouted, his voice almost drowned out by the loud music pumping out of the overhead speakers. "Come on."

He grabbed my arm and pulled me through the crowd. A petite, brunette girl in all black and a tall, dark-haired guy covered in tattoos waved us over.

Cam hugged the girl, and I noticed the familiarity between them. He turned to me, grinning.

"Al, Dean," he said, gesturing toward them. "This is my cousin Evelyn."

"Just Evie," I corrected him with a smile.

The noise made conversation difficult, but we shouted our greetings over the music.

"It's nice to meet you," Al said.

"Thanks for coming," Dean added. "Jared is really excited about you helping them out."

I side-eyed Cam before whispering directly into his ear. "You already told them I'd help?"

"What did you say?" He yelled, winking at me. I knew he could hear me, but I decided to let it go.

Why shouldn't I take a job helping this band? Maybe I had never done social media management before, but how hard could it be? I managed my own successful account. If I spoke confidently, I'm sure they wouldn't question whether or not I could do this job.

"We've got a spot saved upstairs," Dean shouted. "I can't take getting pushed around in this crowd anymore."

"Don't we want to be downstairs?" I whispered to Cam. "Seems more exciting."

"Only if you like getting jostled around by sweaty people."

On second thought, upstairs sounded nice.

I followed the small group to the stairs. We were about to ascend when Cam grabbed Dean and dragged him toward the bar.

"We'll grab some drinks and meet you up there," he called.

I nodded and followed Al upstairs to a small booth with a great view of the stage.

"They should be on any minute." Al smiled at me before glancing around. Her eyes shifted to the floor and then back to me. "So…Seattle, huh? I've heard that's a cool city."

"It was great. Highly recommend checking it out."

"Cam said you move around a lot."

"I'm a bit restless," I admitted. Who wouldn't be after spending their entire childhood in the same town?

"Right. He also mentioned you're just staying until a big trip."

I nodded excitedly, rattling off all of the countries on my bucket list.

Al's eyes widened. "Wow, sounds amazing. I haven't

been anywhere."

"Are you from here?" I asked.

She shook her head. "No, but close by. I moved here from Michigan. Where are you from originally?"

"I've heard the beaches in Michigan are beautiful," I said, deliberately ignoring her question.

Her eyes lit up. "They are. I grew up right next to one of the state parks. I feel like no one ever realizes how beautiful it is there."

"Too bad it's September, or I'd say we should check it out."

She smiled, and the tension in her shoulders seemed to relax. She definitely had a bit of a guard up. I could see why Cam had clicked with her. He loved people but let very few close enough to get to know the real him.

"Is Dean your boyfriend?"

"Yep. We just moved in together. I actually lived with Cam before that."

"Oh, you were one of the roommates, right? He told me he used to live in a house with a few other people."

"Right," she confirmed. "I'm so glad I found that house and Cam. He's been such a great friend."

"He's okay." I smirked.

She laughed. "Don't tell him I said that. It'll go straight to his head."

"So, did this Jared live in the house too?" I asked, still trying to piece together this friend group.

"No, he's Dean's best friend. They grew up together."

"Got it." I peered over the railing. Four guys were on stage now, setting up their equipment.

"Which one is he?" I asked as Al leaned over and squinted.

"The one in the dark green crew neck."

I evaluated the guy she pointed out. He stood up from plugging a cable into an amp, and I couldn't help but notice he was pretty tall. Long, tousled hair hung over his face. The ends of his dark brown hair were almost white, devoid of any color. Almost as if he had bleached it at some point but had since let it grow out. Tattoos peeked out from the collar of his sweatshirt and trailed up the bottom half of his neck. I followed the dark swooping lines to the smooth curve of his jawline. His face looked boyish and approachable despite the light bouncing off the silver ring in his eyebrow.

As he crossed his arms and scanned the crowd, his gaze locked onto mine, and he broke out into a huge smile that caused the skin around his eyes to crinkle. My stomach did an involuntary somersault when he waved.

Al shifted in her seat next to me before standing and waving.

Duh, he was smiling at her.

I gulped to try to remove the lump that had formed in my throat.

"He looks…intense," I said.

Al shook her head. "He's not at all. Don't let the tattoos and piercings throw you off. Jared is like a golden retriever. Overly friendly to everyone."

One of the other band members threw a towel at Jared. He caught it and laughed.

"He does have a nice smile."

"Don't tell him that. His confidence is already unbearable."

"He's cocky?" I removed my gaze from the stage and focused it back on Al.

"I mean, he's the nicest guy you'll ever meet. Just has a bit of an ego is all."

She glanced up to ensure Cam and Dean weren't coming back before leaning into me.

"He just got out of a relationship. I've never known him single, and he's *a lot*." She shook her head. "He was always a harmless flirt, but now that he's untethered, he's a bit of a handful."

I laughed. "I know the type."

I didn't really, but I had watched enough reality television and romantic comedies to catch her drift.

"Soda water?" Cam handed me a fizzy drink with a lime.

"Thank you." I took the glass from him as he scooted into the booth.

Dean went around the other side and tucked Al under his arm.

I continued to look on as the band set up. My eyes kept finding their way back to Jared. He must be the frontman with a face like that.

Cam nudged me in the side. "Not bad to look at, eh."

I glanced over at Al and Dean to make sure they hadn't heard him. "He's alright, I guess. If you go for that whole rockstar aesthetic."

"You should go for it. Probably a lot more interesting than the guys you usually date."

"Hey." I smacked his arm. "The guys I date are interesting."

He lifted his eyebrows. "Didn't you say the last one brought you to a comic convention?"

Heat rushed to my cheeks. "That was fun. Shut up, Cam."

"I'm just messing with you." He chuckled. "But seriously, I could totally see you and Jared. A bit of an opposites-attract situation."

"I thought you wanted me to work with him," I hissed.

Cam shrugged. "Why not get some benefits with the job? It's not like it pays a lot."

"You're ridiculous."

I tore my attention away from my cousin and moved it back to the stage. The band had taken their positions, and Jared approached the mic.

"Don't you all look beautiful tonight," he said, that adorable smile still on his lips. "I'm Jared and this is Max, Tyler, and Drew. Thanks for coming out tonight. Be sure to follow us if you like what you hear."

"Follow them?" I whispered to Cam. "How is anyone supposed to find them online? He didn't even say their name."

Cam pursed his lips. "I don't think they have a name."

"What kind of band doesn't have a name?" I asked before the opening riffs of Jared's guitar drowned out my words.

I leaned forward in my seat to assess them, my head bopping along to the music. They were good. Not just good, great. They had their sound set up perfectly. Jared's vocals weren't drowned out by the bass. He also had a natural stage presence. He moved around and interacted with each band member while also constantly locking eyes with the crowd. He made playing the guitar look effortless, and his voice had a nice rasp to it.

I pulled out my phone and pressed record on my camera app. If they wanted help with their social media I might as well start now.

FIVE

Jared

"Thank you all for coming, and goodnight," I yelled into the mic.

Sweat dripped from my forehead as I gave a final wave to the packed house. I held up my hand to Max for a high five.

"That crowd was unbelievable tonight," I said, grinning.

He nodded. "I can't believe that many people showed up on a Thursday."

I pulled the cables out of my amp and packed them away in the carrying case I had set nearby. "Let's hurry up so we can head out there."

"Jared, I'm exhausted," complained Tyler as he packed up his drums. "I can't stay out after every set if we're going to play this often."

"Jesus, man. Don't say that in front of anyone else," Drew said. "Nobody is going to think we're cool if we're calling it a night before eleven."

"Nobody gives a shit about that as long as we sound good," Tyler argued.

"Yes, they do. How are we going to get a fan base if we're at home binging a TV show?"

"I only watched three episodes last night. I had a headache."

Drew and Tyler continued to bicker. Max and I shared a look. He was my closest ally in the group. When we all played, we were so in sync, but sometimes it felt like Drew and Tyler chose to disagree on everything just for the sake of having something to argue about. It was exhausting and had inhibited our decision-making capabilities in the past.

"Guys, guys, guys," I finally intervened, stepping between them. "This isn't worth fighting about. Tyler, I'm not asking you to get drunk and stay out late. There's someone here tonight I want us all to meet."

"Who?" Max raised his eyebrows.

"A friend of a friend. Apparently, she does social media and marketing for a living. She might be willing to help us out." I glanced from Drew to Tyler. "That is, so long as we aren't a bunch of blubbering idiots when we go out to meet her."

"She better be cheap," muttered Tyler.

"Whatever the price, it'll be worth it if we can grow our accounts. Can you imagine how much we'd get to play if we actually had people demanding to see us? We could stop playing mostly covers too."

"We'd have to write more original songs to play less covers," Max pointed out.

"I'm working on it." I waved him off. Writing was coming more and more naturally to me. It was only a matter of time before we had a short set to work with.

I ushered them out of the back area and through a door that led to the main bar. The crowd remained, but now there was room to walk around.

"There," I said to Max, pointing at the balcony. "I see them."

I pushed through the diminishing crowd before being stopped by a tall brunette in a skintight black top.

"Hey there." She smiled at me, and I instinctively stopped and leaned into her.

"Hey yourself."

"It's Jared, right?"

"That's right." I grinned.

"You were great up there."

"Thank you. What's your name, beautiful?"

"Oh my god." I heard Drew's annoyed tone from somewhere behind me.

"It's Lauren." She giggled and licked her pouty red lips.

"So, Lauren. Any chance you want to hang out tonight?"

"Definitely." She nodded and looked up at me underneath thick lashes. A smack in my shoulder hit me like a bucket of ice water.

"What?" I scowled at Drew who had shoved me.

"Dude, are we meeting this girl or not?"

"Oh, right," I muttered before turning back to the beauty. "Lauren, I've got something to do real quick. Mind waiting around for twenty minutes?"

"I'll come find you." She winked at me before departing back into the crowd.

I gestured for the guys to continue following me.

"That's so unfair," said Drew. "Just because you're the

frontman, you get all the girls. You're objectively the least attractive one."

I glared at him. Not to be cocky, but I wasn't the least attractive. Not by a long shot.

"Fine, fine," Drew back peddled. "Maybe you're not the ugliest, but your personality should turn them off."

"Maybe I don't let them get to know me enough to figure that out," I said.

"That's great, Jared, really," Tyler responded. "I miss when you were with Janelle, and you could only flirt, not touch. This version of you is insufferable."

"For real," Drew agreed. "I thought you were bad then. I didn't realize how much worse it could be."

I stopped walking right as we got to the stairs and turned to them. My gaze hardened.

"When did this become shit on Jared night?" I questioned. "Lay off, and let's go make a halfway decent impression."

Drew and Tyler muttered a halfhearted apology as we ascended the steps to the balcony.

"Hey man," Dean said as we approached. "Great show tonight."

Al nodded in agreement. "You guys seriously get better every time."

"Thanks for coming." I glanced at Dean. While he was already my biggest supporter, I appreciated him being here even more now that Janelle and I had broken up. She had seemed supportive at first. When we were in the honeymoon phase of our relationship, she had come to any show we played that wasn't a wedding. But as our gigs increased, her interest declined.

"We're going to head out," Dean interrupted my

thoughts. "I've got to get to the restaurant early tomorrow for a shipment."

"Right, right. I'll see you there tomorrow night."

Dean was the partial owner of two of the most popular restaurants in Chicago. Luna and Luna Two. When I had fallen on some hard times and couldn't get my life together a few years back, he had graciously offered me a bartending job. I still worked there all these years later.

I smacked Dean on the back and squeezed Al's shoulder as they walked past me, congratulating the rest of the band on their way out.

Cam remained seated in the booth whispering something to the girl seated beside him. While their eyes were still off me, I took a second to take her in. Her delicate milky white skin glowed under the harsh fluorescent lights. Her faded pink hair fell just past her bare shoulders. Freckles dotted her face, and her button nose scrunched in concentration as she took in whatever Cam told her.

"Hey, Cam," I said.

Cam snapped his head up and waved us over. "Sit."

"I don't think you've officially met the band, but this is Drew, Tyler, and Max. Cam is a friend. He's been to a few of our shows."

"Thanks for coming," Tyler stuck out his hand, and Drew did the same.

Max nodded his greeting. "I think I've seen you around."

"And this is my cousin, Evelyn."

She smiled at us. "Evie, actually. It's nice to meet you. Great show, by the way."

"Thanks," I said before taking the seat next to her. "We practice a lot."

Drew, Tyler, and Max sat in the booth across from us and leaned in so they could hear.

"Thanks to me," Tyler chimed in. "If it was up to you guys and your shitty scheduling, we'd practice once a month."

I shot him a warning glare, and he held up his hands before leaning back into the seat. Bickering bandmates was not the impression I wanted to leave Evie with.

"So," I continued, directing my attention back to her. "Cam mentioned you might be able to help us out."

She bit her full bottom lip, and I tried my best to keep my gaze fixed on her large blue eyes. "I think I can."

Cam used his elbow to nudge her in the ribs.

"I mean, definitely."

I glanced over at Max.

"You sure?" he asked.

"Evelyn has almost one million followers on a few different platforms."

My eyebrows shot up. "Really?"

"Doing what?" Drew asked.

"I-uh…it's just…"

"Being herself, obviously. People follow her just to see what she's up to. Whatever the case, she literally built all of her accounts from scratch, so you'd be lucky to have her."

We all looked at each other, silently conferring.

"Well, that sounds great," I finally said.

"When can you start?" Max asked.

"I-I mean pretty much immediately. I might just need to sit down with you all—or one of you—to get some information and come up with a plan."

Max pointed to me. "Jared is in charge of our social media."

"I would hardly say I'm in charge."

"That is what we agreed to," Tyler insisted.

Drew nodded.

I rolled my eyes. "I guess I'm the person you can talk to, then," I said, looking back down at Evie. "You free tomorrow?"

"Uh, tomorrow? Sh-sure." She met my gaze and smiled, but I noticed her knee bouncing furiously up and down.

"I've got work, but you can stop by the bar. It'll be busy, but we can talk whenever there's a lull."

"Perfect," she said.

The guys thanked her and discussed how awesome it would be if we could just blow up on social media. Cam interjected with a story about someone from his work who had just gone viral and got thousands of followers. As they all chatted, I leaned down to whisper into Evie's ear.

"Hey, we match."

She glanced down at her outfit and then to mine. My green crewneck was the exact same shade as her top.

Her cheeks flushed. "It's my favorite color."

"What a coincidence. It's mine too," I said, putting on my best charming smile.

"I just made this shirt. It's my first time wearing it."

"Seriously? You made that? That's amazing."

She looked down at it and beamed. "You think so? Cam was just making fun of my crocheting."

"Cam makes fun of everything."

"True."

I leaned in further to ensure the rest of the group couldn't hear me. "Is it just me, or did you sound nervous when agreeing to help us?"

"What?" She looked at me, eyes wide and mouth open. "N-no way. I'm not nervous."

I smirked down at her. "Spill."

She sighed and looked at her feet before glancing back at me. "Okay, fine. Don't tell Cam I told you, but I haven't exactly done this before."

My eyebrows knit together. "Social media?"

"No, that part is true. I do have a lot of followers. I've just never helped someone else grow their account before."

"And you don't think you can do it?"

She tilted her head. "No, I'm pretty sure I can. I've got a lot of ideas already."

"I promise you, any amount of confidence is a hell of a lot better than what we've got now."

"Really?"

"Trust me. Currently I just send off a badly edited picture into the abyss and pray for five likes."

Her soft laughter caused my lips to turn up.

"You're funny," she said. "And don't worry, everyone starts out like that. I remember when I first started posting, I would jump for joy at every individual view."

"And look where you are now."

She smiled. "Exactly, it took a lot of persistence, but it was worth it. I love it."

I decided I really liked this girl's energy. Despite her nerves, she still exuded this mix of optimism and warmth. Hopefully, with her on board, we'd be able to build a solid fan base. And hey, getting to know her better would definitely be an added bonus.

"Excuse me, I was just wondering how much longer you'd be?" I looked up to see the girl from earlier standing at our table. What was her name? Laura?

"Hey, doll. I'm just finishing up."

I looked back to Evie who smiled shyly at me. "Life of a rockstar, huh?"

I chuckled. "You could say that."

"I'll see you tomorrow?" she asked.

I nodded, standing to sling an arm over the brunette's shoulder.

"Cam can tell you where the restaurant is. Stop by at eight?"

"I'll see you there."

SIX

Evie

"You should change," said Cam as he eyed my outfit.

I looked down at the maroon crocheted cardigan I had thrown on over a plain white tank top.

"What's wrong with this?"

"It's a Friday night." He pointed out. "And do you have to wear something crocheted every day?"

I grabbed my bag off the counter, glaring at him. There were plenty of non-crocheted pieces in my wardrobe. Homemade items just happened to be my favorite.

"This is fine, Cam. Stop hovering. We're just meeting to talk about his band."

He sighed. "Fine, don't listen to me." He glanced at me and then back to the TV. "Jared is pretty cute though, right?"

"Don't start with this again."

"I'm just saying."

"Fine, he's obviously cute. So what? Did you see that girl he went home with last night? I would clearly never be his type. And more importantly, we're working together. What is with your obsessive need to play matchmaker?"

"Whatever," he muttered.

"And besides all that, I'm not even here for that long anyway. Why would I try to start something with a guy?"

He held up his hands. "Forget I said anything."

"Maybe you should be scrolling the dating apps instead of trying to set me up."

He groaned. "They're hopeless."

"Maybe if you had a better attitude."

"My attitude is fantastic."

"You're right. I'm sure the guys love your sunny disposition."

He leveled me with a stare.

I turned away from him and took in my appearance in the hall mirror. While I didn't want to look like I was trying too hard—*and I wasn't*—I still wanted to look nice. As I fussed with my hair, I heard Cam clear his throat.

"Um, so I just spoke to my mom this morning."

I glanced at him. "Oh? Did you tell her I said hi?"

"Of course. She wishes she could come into town for a visit, but work is hectic for her right now." He paused, and I could tell he was holding back.

I sighed. "Just tell me whatever you want to tell me, Cam."

"It's about your parents."

The hairs on the back of my neck bristled. "I figured. Just get on with it so I can go."

"My mom just mentioned they moved is all. I guess your mom called her and asked her if she wanted anything from the basement a while back."

My brow knit in confusion. Moved? That didn't sound

like them. I always figured they'd be in that ancient farmhouse the rest of their lives.

"Did she say when?" I asked. "Or where?" I hated that I was curious, but I couldn't help it.

"She said it was a while ago. Maybe eight months or so? Apparently, they're in a condo closer to town now."

My mouth hung open at this revelation.

"A *condo*?"

The thought of my recluse parents at an HOA meeting was impossible for me to imagine.

Cam shrugged. "I guess so."

"Weird," I muttered, staring blankly back at my reflection.

"Are you okay?" he asked. "I know you hate talking about them."

"I'm fine. So what if they moved? Doesn't make a difference to me."

If anything, I was glad to be even further removed from that house.

"My mom said she had the address. If you were interested."

I whipped around and glared at him. "Why would I be interested? What am I going to do, stop in for a visit? Hi Mom and Dad. Just your estranged daughter checking in. How have you been all these years?"

Cam huffed. "Jesus, don't shoot the messenger."

"Ugh, I'm sorry." I rubbed my eyes. "It's just weird for me to think about them being so close."

"I know." He got up from the couch and walked over before tentatively hugging me. "I'm here for you if you ever want to talk about it."

"Thanks," I mumbled into his shirt.

He pulled away and looked at me. "Don't you have to get going?"

"What time is it?"

He pointed to the clock on the stove. "It's already past eight."

"Ugh, why didn't you warn me." I glanced at myself in the mirror one last time before rushing out the door.

As I entered the restaurant, the sound of chatter mixed with the clinking of silverware and glasses greeted me. Every table was occupied, and groups of people stood waiting by the door. I squeezed past the patrons and stood in front of the host stand.

She greeted me. "Welcome in. Do you have a reservation?"

"Um, no." I chewed my lip and glanced at the bar, noticing one empty chair. "I'm just meeting someone here. Can I take that seat at the bar?"

"Of course."

I scanned the room on my walk to the bar. The exposed brick walls created a cozy atmosphere, and soft lighting cast a golden glow over everything. The aroma of sizzling steaks and roasted vegetables wafted through the air, making my mouth water. I arrived at the polished wood bar and grabbed the last available seat.

I leaned over and watched as Jared and Dean mixed drinks and chatted with the other patrons. Jared glanced my way and grinned as soon as he saw me. He held up a finger, signaling he'd be over to talk to me in a minute.

Grabbing a drink menu, I scanned it to kill time.

"There you are. I was worried you forgot." Jared stood in front of me.

"Sorry." I gave him an apologetic smile. "I lost track of time."

He waved off my excuse. "No worries, I'm just glad you made it. Can I get you anything to drink? On the house."

I squinted back at the menu.

"Anything non-alcoholic? Not really in the mood to drink tonight."

The skin around his eyes crinkled as his smile widened. "Let me make you something. I've been experimenting with a new mocktail."

"Sounds perfect."

He poured a few different bottles into a shaker and added a splash of soda water. He tossed the shaker from one hand to the other before producing a glass. A clear liquid with a slightly purple hue flowed out.

"Order up." He slid the drink my way, and I took a tentative sip.

It was citrusy, bubbly, and refreshing.

"Mmm." I took another sip. "Thank you. That's so good."

He threw the bar towel over his shoulder. "So," he started. "What's the plan to put our band on the charts?"

I snorted, setting my drink down. "Let's not get ahead of ourselves, but I do think I can help you guys."

Jared leaned forward, resting his elbows on the bar. "Yeah? That would be amazing. Between the four of us, we're hopeless when it comes to that stuff."

"That's good news for me. You wouldn't need me if you were any good at it."

He smirked. "What did you think of our band last night? Be honest."

"I think you guys are really talented. The crowd was so into the performance." I took a deep breath. "But if I'm being honest, your online presence sucks. I couldn't even find your page after the show. It's like you're non-existent online."

"I know." He hung his head. "None of us have put in the effort. I think we all thought this band wasn't going anywhere. But then we kept booking more and more gigs. Now it's bringing in more money than a part-time job. I know that might not seem like a success story, but to be making money off of music feels incredible."

"You don't need to tell me. When I first started my channel, no one watched my videos. When I made my first fifty dollars from an ad, I nearly lost my mind with excitement."

"What kind of videos?" He tilted his head.

Heat rushed to my cheeks. I might as well tell him. I opened my mouth to answer, but thankfully, someone waved from the other end of the bar.

"Hey, I'll be right back. I need to check on those people."

As he sauntered away, I rested my elbow on the table and cradled my chin in my hands. I watched him as he effortlessly charmed the older couple seated at the end of the bar. He certainly had a confident aura about him. He seamlessly combined ingredients for a new cocktail while placing glasses on the bar. My eyes moved down to his tattooed arms that were poking out of his rolled-up sleeves. The muscles in his forearms flexed while he held the shaker in front of his chest.

He looks nice in that shirt.

"Hey, Evie."

I jumped, tearing my gaze away.

Dean had appeared in front of me. Hopefully, he hadn't noticed me staring.

His smirk told me that he probably had.

"Hey, Dean." I shook off the guilty feeling of being caught. "This place is amazing."

"Thanks." He beamed, looking around the packed restaurant. "Cam will have to take you to our other location at some point."

"I'm sure it's on the list. He's got like a million things he's dying to show me."

"He's pumped you're here."

"I'm pumped to be here. We haven't been in the same city in years."

"That's cool you guys are so close," he said, grabbing two beers for the people sitting to my right.

"Same with you and Jared." I gestured to him. "Al said you two grew up together. Not many people can keep a friendship going for that long."

"Well, he got me through some rough years."

"Yeah?" I asked, my interest officially piqued.

"I don't want to get into it, but we didn't grow up in the best neighborhood. I'm glad we both got out of there."

I nodded, easily relating to the desperate need to get out of the place I grew up.

I glanced back at Jared as he continued to captivate the customers. To my surprise, I felt a slight pang of jealousy. He had grown up in a lousy neighborhood, yet here he was. Confident, cool, and collected. He could fit in wherever he chose to go. I wished I could be more like that.

Despite always moving, I did more blending in than fitting in.

"It seems like you both made something of yourself," I finally said.

Jared walked back over to us and patted Dean on the back. "Did you hear? Evie is going to make me a star."

I laughed. "Hey, no promises." Al wasn't kidding when she compared Jared to a golden retriever. He walked around with endless energy, and a smile hardly left his face.

"I better leave you two to it." Dean waved and went back to talk to a few new customers.

Jared leaned against the bar, and I pulled out my phone.

"So, let's get into it. What's the name of your band's profile?"

He winced and looked at the floor.

"What?" I asked.

"It's just" His voice trailed off, and he looked pained. "We don't exactly have a name."

I scoffed. "Isn't that like the first thing you're supposed to decide on when you start a band?"

"I know, I know. Trust me. We've had this argument a thousand times. We just can't agree on anything."

"We need to change that. If your profile isn't your band name, then what is it?"

He scrunched his nose and looked back at the restaurant entrance, clearly not wanting to tell me.

"Come on, Jared. I'm here to help. What is it?"

He muttered something so quietly I didn't even hear him.

"Sorry I didn't catch that," I said, leaning closer.

He sighed. "The Wedding Band."

"That's your profile?"

He nodded.

"Why?" I asked, already plugging the words into my search bar.

"At first, we mostly played weddings—we still play them occasionally. At the time, it just seemed like an easy way for people to find us. We've gotten a lot of inquiries just from people searching that phrase."

I bit my lip and tilted my head, assessing their profile.

"You know, that isn't the worst idea. Search engine optimization is huge." I scrolled to a picture of the band they posted a few days ago and held it up. "These guys don't look like a wedding band to me, though. Is that your goal?"

"Hell no." His floppy hair bounced as he shook his head. "It's been fun, and a great way to make money, but we want to play music we love—music we wrote."

I nodded. "Then your profile and your name have to reflect that. Thankfully you don't have a huge following yet, so it won't be too confusing when we change your name."

"Do you think you could help us?" he asked.

I hesitated. Getting involved in band decisions seemed too complicated for my liking.

"How about I help facilitate a discussion?"

"That would be good. We always get irritated with each other and end up putting off the topic."

"Can I have the password to this account so I can start posting?"

"Sure, just nothing embarrassing." He winked at me, and heat rushed to my cheeks.

I fought to keep my composure. "I wouldn't dream of it."

Jared sighed. "I'm so glad you're here. This whole thing was majorly stressing me out."

"I got you." Hopefully, that was the truth.

He relayed the account information to me. Once signed in, I went to create a new post.

Jared leaned over the bar. "What are you doing?"

"Posting a video I took at your show last night. I captioned the video with a bunch of hashtags and tagged the bar's location before posting it. Tagging the bar will help you show up in more search results."

"Nice." He looked impressed. "You were saying earlier that you make videos?"

"Right."

He raised his eyebrows when I didn't say more. "Care to elaborate?"

"Um-they're silly. Have you heard of LifeCraft? It's a game—"

"I used to love LifeCraft."

His revelation eased the tension in my shoulders. I wasn't embarrassed by what I did, but for some reason, I wanted Jared to think I was cool—someone he could see himself hanging out with.

"I record videos of myself playing. Usually, I just build these extravagant houses and do walkthroughs and tutorials."

"Seriously? That's really cool. Can I see one?"

"Um, sure. I'll send you my profile."

"You're an interesting one, you know that?"

"That's what I've been told," I muttered.

His eyebrows knit together. "I hope you know I meant that as a compliment. I just met you, and I'm already dying to know more."

My eyes went wide as he regarded me. I hadn't spent much time around guys as forward as Jared. I doubted I had ever met anyone quite like him. He claimed I was the interesting one, but everything about him drew me in.

I scanned my brain, trying to think of a coherent thing to say.

"Did Cam mention my trip?" I blurted out.

He scratched the back of his head. "What trip?"

I looked at him apologetically. "I won't be in Chicago long. I'm leaving in a couple months for this big bucket list trip around the world."

"See." He motioned to me. "Fucking fascinating. Where are you off to?"

I laughed and told him about my ambitions, which included backpacking through Bali, wandering the streets of Paris, and maybe even taking in the views of Patagonia. I hadn't thought any of it through, but that was half the fun.

He whistled as I wrapped up. "You're awfully adventurous, aren't you?"

I shrugged. "I try."

"Well, the band is happy to have you help out for as long as you're here."

"I think I can get a lot done in that time. And even when I leave we can stay in touch. I'm happy to help where I can and answer any questions."

"That's perfect," Jared said, holding out his hand.

I tentatively reached mine out before he engulfed it with his. He shook it exuberantly, and I couldn't deny the small, electric sparks I felt at his warm touch.

"So, my leaving won't be a problem?" I confirmed.

He shook his head. "Definitely not."

SEVEN

Jared

Amps and cables littered the floor surrounding us as I sat on a stool playing around with a new guitar riff I had written. Max listened while Drew and Tyler argued about something irrelevant. I tried my best to drown them out.

"My part is fine. I'm so sick of you telling me to rewrite everything." Drew crossed his arms as he glared at his brother.

Tyler sat behind his drum kit, tapping his sticks on the snare. "I just think my ideas are better."

"You're micromanaging me," Drew said.

"I'm not micromanaging you," Tyler shot back. "What? Am I just supposed to shut up even when I'm right?"

"You're not right!" Drew shouted.

I put down my guitar and stood up. "You're giving me a headache."

They didn't even glance at me as they continued to argue, their voices rising with each passing second. Max rubbed his temple and looked at me warily. These fights needed to stop if we were ever going to make any progress.

I thought back to the conversation Max and I had yesterday when I dropped by his house to discuss Evie helping us out. Although we were a four-person band, Max and I had gotten into the habit of meeting alone occasionally. It was a hell of a lot easier to think without dumb and dumber going at it constantly.

When I told Max I thought Evie could help us out, he had said, "I sure hope so."

We weren't Max's first band. He had been at this for years. After multiple failed groups, it must be getting tiresome for him.

"We're going to be something, man," I told him. "I can just feel it."

He sighed. "I feel it too. You've got something, Jared. It's like this undeniable spark that can't be taught."

"We're all good."

"But you're what's going to set us apart."

When I left his house, I wasn't sure what to make of that. For all of my cockiness, part of me still felt like that teenager playing guitar on his beat-up twin mattress. I wanted so badly to be something. Something more than what I ever thought I could be. But as much as I tried to manifest it, deep down, I still had my doubts.

"Hey, guys," Max said, his firm voice bringing me back to the present. "Shut the hell up."

Drew and Tyler wavered and finally looked at us. Max rarely raised his voice.

"Can you just tell him that he needs to lay off? Bass is my instrument," Drew demanded.

"Tyler, just let him play his part. If we need to rewrite something, we can do it later. We're never going to get a song done if we argue over every chord," Max said.

Tyler lifted his hands in surrender. "Fine, whatever."

"Good." I picked my guitar back up. "Now, no more fighting. Evie will be here any second."

"Right," Max agreed. "We don't want her to think we're just a bunch of idiots that can't agree on anything."

"Aren't we?" Tyler muttered.

I winced. "Speaking of that. We need to pick a name."

"If we have to talk about names, then she's definitely going to think we can't agree on anything," Drew said.

"I know, I know." I ran my hands through my hair. "But she says it's vital for our social media presence. I mean, she's right. Someone can't even find us online after a show."

Tyler nodded. "We can't keep putting this off."

"Should we make a short list of ones we've talked about before she gets here?" Max asked, pulling out his phone.

"JDTM," Drew said.

I glared at him. "I'm going to walk out this door right now if our initials is the best name we can come up with."

Max dragged his hand over his face. "Glad we're off to a good start."

A soft knock sounded at the door.

"It's Evie," I whispered, getting up. I looked back and pointed at each guy. "Remember. Best behavior."

I opened the side door that led to the driveway to see a mess of pink waves and shopping bags. Evie donned bright blue overalls with a mustard sweater underneath. She didn't seem to take herself too seriously, and I found myself drawn to her quirkiness.

"I'm glad you could make it. The guys are all in here."

"Of course. This is going to be fun. I've never been to a band rehearsal before."

"Hopefully your expectations aren't high."

I swung open the door all the way and let her step in. She looked around as the rest of the band continued to debate our name.

"We are not calling ourselves The Guys. That's the dumbest name I've ever heard," Tyler insisted.

"I don't hear you coming up with any suggestions," Drew said.

"Look who's here." I kept my voice friendly, but since Evie's back was to me, I shot daggers at each of my bandmates.

"Hey, Evie. Thanks for coming," Max greeted her.

"Not any further along on the name, huh?" she asked, settling into an armchair in the corner.

"For a band, we're not very creative." I said, trying to keep the mood light.

"Maybe I can help. What are some words that describe you as a band?" She pulled out her phone to take notes.

"There are four of us," Tyler offered.

"No shit, Sherlock." Drew rolled his eyes.

Evie held up her hand to quell the bickering. "Hey, everything is helpful here. What else?"

"Our initials are J. M—"

"Shut up about our initials!" Tyler shouted before he and Drew started to argue again.

Max looked apologetically at Evie. "Sorry about them. We probably should have thought harder before we let two brothers into the band."

She sighed. "It's alright. Maybe we can come back to this."

I caught her eye and gave her a half smile which she returned. The defeated look left her eyes quickly, and she sprang up from the chair.

"Alright, let's move on to other things." She clasped her hands together and started pacing. "I'm thinking daily posts. I'll make sure to get more footage at your next show. The video I posted last night did alright, but I think if I get different angles, it'll do even better. Also, we need to spotlight your original songs more. Artists go viral all the time just teasing parts of their songs. I can record you guys at practice and post tidbits of anything that's a work in progress." She continued to rattle off strategy after strategy as I stared on in awe.

This kind of no-nonsense, actionable plan was exactly what our band needed. Our ambition lacked vision, something Evie obviously had an abundance of.

"How does that sound?" she asked. "Any input?"

"Just that you're an angel that was sent to Earth specifically to help us," I said, grinning from ear to ear. "That all sounds amazing."

The rest of the band echoed their agreement.

"Perfect, let's get started then. Would you mind if I recorded a quick video of the chorus of the last song you played at your show?"

My chest puffed with pride that she thought one of my songs was worth showcasing. "Definitely," I said, grabbing my guitar.

The rest of the band got into place, and I strummed the opening chords to the chorus. Evie attached a ring light to her phone and recorded us, slowly panning over us to get every angle. Her nose scrunched in concentration as she carefully focused on each band member before returning the camera to me.

After a few more takes, she signaled for us to stop, satisfied that she had got the shot.

"These are great," she said, scrolling through the videos.

"Let me see." I stepped behind her and leaned forward so I could see her phone.

She smelled nice. Subtle—like she had just walked through a flower shop, and the remnants of the scent had clung to her skin. Realizing my proximity, I cleared my throat before taking a step back.

"Those look perfect," I said. "When we try to record ourselves, the videos always look flat."

She nodded. "I also noticed you don't have many pictures of the band."

I shrugged. I hadn't thought about it before.

"How do you guys feel about a photo shoot?"

EIGHT

Evie

"I can't believe I let you talk me into this," Cam whined from the seat next to me on the train. "This is ungodly early."

"Remember when we took that train ride to Chicago with your mom," I whispered.

A smile played on Cam's lips. "How could I forget? High tea with dolls? What a dream for us at twelve."

"And she let us order whatever we wanted off the menu."

Cam chuckled. "That was such an amazing day."

My mind flashed back to that day. My parents were out of town to visit my ailing grandfather, whom I had never met. They let me stay with Cam and his mom. It was one of the few times I recall ever sleeping somewhere other than my home.

Renee woke us up early on Saturday and asked if we wanted to go on an adventure. My little mind had been bursting with the idea of getting on a train. Leaving our tiny town felt monumental. Cam and I pointed out something every few minutes as we watched the world outside whizz by from the train car. Renee laughed and reveled in our joy.

My mother and Renee hadn't seemed so different to me when I was a young child. They both had a strict upbringing and held similar values. I think what made the most significant impact on the wedge that slowly divided them was that Cam's father passed away when he was just three. I didn't even remember him. I know from hearing stories that he was like my father.

Renee remained untethered, and as the years went by, her hair grew wilder, and her wardrobe became brighter. When I would visit, she let us have sweets and watch funny movies on TV. Eventually, it became hard to recall that similarities ever existed between her and my mother.

We still saw them, but the relationship became progressively strained.

I remember thinking that the day she took us to Chicago was the best day of my entire life. Nothing would ever top it. We wandered the busy streets and looked up at the high rises. When Cam and I had spotted the Ferris wheel in the distance, we begged to ride it. Renee laughed and agreed, assuring us we would go before we left.

Everything changed around dinnertime. My mother called her. I could hear her yelling on the other end of the brick-like cell phone Renee carried. Renee assured her everything was fine, but her eyes were panicked. After she hung up, she said we had to leave right away. She tugged on our hands, and I turned around one last time to see the pier in the distance.

I somehow knew I wouldn't be going on any more adventures.

I leaned my head against the window as the train emerged from underground. The darkness still encased the city this early.

"I don't think we saw you and your mom much after that day," I said.

Cam reached over and squeezed my hand. "Only on some holidays."

A few commuters were scattered around our train car. Being awake before most of the city stirred felt special, as if I were a part of some behind-the-scenes experience.

"I remember thinking how beautiful Chicago was," I murmured. "It feels strange to be back now."

"It's even more beautiful when the sun is out."

I gave him a pointed look as we let the bittersweet memory pass.

"It's kind of hard to do a sunrise photoshoot if the sun is already out."

"What kind of masochist wants to do a sunrise photoshoot?"

"The kind that understands how beautiful the lighting can be and how perfect the background is when it's free of people."

"It's only free of people because we're the only ones insane enough to be up at this hour."

"Can you stop being dramatic and enjoy the moment?"

He glared at me. "I'm only doing this because it's right by my office."

"Fine, fine. Just rest your head on my shoulder and shut your mouth. We're almost there, cranky pants."

Cam finally stopped talking, and I resumed gazing out the window. I had only been in Chicago for a short time, but I couldn't deny that the city had already won me over. It had this incredible energy, and the people here were so friendly. Plus, despite Cam's current grumbling, having him here to show me around was a refreshing change. Usually, when I moved to a new city, I knew no one. So having a close family member—a friend—here with me felt amazing.

I jostled Cam awake as we approached our stop.

"We're here, sleeping beauty."

"Fantastic," he said. "We need to stop for coffee, or I'm going to be grumpy."

"If this is you not grumpy, I would hate to subject the guys to what you would be like without coffee," I said as we rose from our seats and departed the train.

"It wouldn't be pretty."

We stopped at a nearby chain coffee store before walking to the lake. Jared and the rest of the band were supposed to meet us there. Like Cam, they hadn't been pleased about the idea of a sunrise photoshoot, but I managed to persuade them. They didn't have much content for me to post, and I needed something that looked professional.

Sipping our coffees, we made our way through a nearby park. A faint glow emerged on the horizon. Our timing couldn't have been better. I glanced at my phone to confirm that the guys were on their way.

> Evie: Hey! Just want to make sure you're awake and almost here.

> Jared: I have collected all three cranky bandmates, and we just parked. I did not trust them to get here on their own.

I laughed at his message.

"What could possibly be funny at this hour?"

I showed him Jared's text.

He smirked and eyed me. "You two are texting now?"

I jerked my phone away. "Only because I'm helping the band. You're so annoying. I swear you'd try to set me up with your dentist if you thought I'd bite."

"I have ulterior motives. Maybe if you met a guy you like, you'd stick around for longer than two months."

"That's not going to happen, Cam. I'm going on this trip. Besides, if you can't make me stick around, no one can." I threaded my arm through his. "Let's just have fun while I'm here. And who knows? Maybe I can convince you to drop everything and travel with me."

"Hah," he exclaimed. "Fat chance of that. I love it here. And I'm not exactly the backpacking type. I much prefer a luxury hotel."

The deep blue water of Lake Michigan loomed in front of us as we crossed a bridge over Lakeshore Drive.

"There they are." I waved to four figures standing just ahead.

Jared's bright smile shone even in the dim light as we approached.

"Morning Evie." He extended his arms and gave me a quick hug. He held out his fist to Cam, who eyed it before high-fiving it. "Surprised to see you here, Cam. You don't strike me as a morning person."

"Me? I love it. Can't get enough of these sunrises."

"Sounds like your company is just as cranky as mine." He gestured to his bandmates behind him. "I practically had to go inside and drag Drew out of his bed for this."

"He's lying," Drew called from behind him.

"We should get moving. The sun is almost up now, and

I want to get as much time with this lighting as possible."

We trudged closer to the water. When I was happy with the spot, I set down my camera bag and unzipped it. I placed the strap around my neck and assessed the guys. Thankfully, they had all worn casual outfits that complemented each other like I had asked. They looked like a real band.

"Okay, why don't we start with the four of you standing here. Jared and Max take two steps forward, so there's a little dimension to the pose."

They followed my instructions as I continued to pose them and snap pictures. By no means would I consider myself a professional photographer, but I had gotten pretty decent with a camera over the years. Besides, it wouldn't be that hard to improve upon the phone selfies currently posted to their account.

"These look great, guys. Cam, can you grab my other lens?"

Cam grumbled something inaudible but handed me what I needed. I knew, despite his attitude, that he wanted to be here. When I told him about the photo shoot, he immediately volunteered to help. To be fair, this was before I told him what time it was. But still, even when he found out, he didn't bail.

"Can I see?" Jared asked while I switched my lens.

I walked over to them and turned my camera around so they could see the small screen.

"These look professional," Max said, his tired eyes finally fully open.

Tyler nodded. "If people see these, they'll think we're a real band."

"We are a real band, dipshit," Drew said.

Jared shook his head. "I swear to god, if you guys start arguing, I'm throwing someone's ass into the lake. It's too early for this shit."

Drew lazily saluted him. "Got it, boss."

We resumed taking pictures for the next forty-five minutes. Everyone had brought extra shirts, so I had them change before repositioning them in front of the sprawling city view. Now I would have a mix of pictures to choose from when posting so it didn't all look like the same day.

"Alright, guys. I think that's a wrap." I clapped my hands. "I can't wait to get these on a computer to see them up close."

"Thanks, Evie," Max said.

"Yeah, these are going to look sick." I tentatively met Drew's raised hand for a high five.

My stomach rumbled as we walked back to the van, reminding me that I hadn't had time to eat anything yet today.

"Anyone want to grab breakfast?" I asked.

"I have to get to work," Cam replied.

"Me too," Max said.

Drew and Tyler also echoed the sentiment.

"Oh, bummer," I said, feeling deflated. I loved my job's flexibility, but sometimes I wished I had more people to hang out with during typical working hours.

"I'm off today," Jared offered. "Let's do it."

My eyebrows shot up. "Really? You sure?" I hadn't anticipated eating alone with Jared when I had thrown the idea out there. Suddenly my stomach twisted into knots.

"Definitely. I know a great diner around here." He threw the keys to his van at Max. "Mind driving the van home? I can come grab it later."

"Sure, man. I'll see you later."

I wrung my hands together as I watched the band pile into the van. Max backed it out of the parking lot as Cam walked toward the direction of his office.

"Bye, you two. Have fun." He winked at me, and I prayed that Jared hadn't noticed.

I balled my clammy hands into fists and tried not to think too hard about the fact that it was now just the two of us.

What would we talk about? Would we run out of things to say? When I met him at work the other day, there were plenty of distractions.

Now it would be just us two.

Making conversation.

For an entire meal.

I hated that he made me nervous, but his forwardness and easy-going attitude mixed with a face like that made it impossible for me to feel calm around him.

"Ready?" Jared pointed down the street. "It's that way."

"Let's go," I said, hoping my voice sounded more confident than I felt.

"How do you think the photoshoot went?" he asked. He kept his long strides slow so that I could keep up.

"I think I got some really good shots."

"Anything is an improvement over what we have now."

"You can say that again."

"Ouch." He clutched his chest. "You could at least pretend it isn't that bad."

I ducked my chin, cursing my fair skin for always betraying me when I blushed. "Did you hire me to be nice or to market your band?"

"Both?" He raised his eyebrows and smirked at me.

"I'll try to preserve your ego from now on. How does that sound?"

"Sounds perfect. Sorry again about Drew and Tyler. Those two drive me nuts."

I shrugged. "I'm sure all bands have disagreements. At least their arguments seem pretty surface-level."

"I guess." He came to a stop and opened the door to an unassuming diner.

Inside, plush red booths lined both walls. Only a few tables were taken. We walked past the "Seat Yourself" sign and took an empty booth in the back.

I slid into one side. "I love diners early in the morning."

Jared looked around. "Me too. I love how quiet it is on a weekday."

"Being up and doing something while most of the city is still sleeping is my favorite thing."

"I never thought about it that much, but it is great. Some people might shit on me for being a bartender, but I love my schedule. I don't think I could sit behind a computer all day." He turned up his nose at the thought.

"Ew. Anyone that shits on you for being a bartender is disgusting. I would *love* to learn how to bartend. The way you poured drinks the other night was practically an art."

He chuckled and looked at me over his menu.

"What's so funny?" I asked.

"It's just funny you said that." His eyes twinkled as he regarded me. "My ex used to give me a hard time for being a bartender. She wanted me to quit that and the band and get a real job."

"Sounds like she's an ex for a reason." I shuddered at how judgmental she sounded. Having an unconventional job myself, I had some experience with people turning up their noses when I described what I did. "How is being a bartender not a real job anyway? Just because you aren't plugging away for fifty hours a week at a corporation? I'd take what you're doing over that any day."

His eyes lit up. "Me too."

As he went back to assessing the menu, I couldn't help but sneak glances at him. Everything about his appearance intimidated me, from his ridiculously good looks to his many tattoos. But strangely enough, he also managed to make me feel more comfortable than any stranger had in recent memory. His genuine warmth and friendly demeanor were contagious.

"What are you going to get?" he asked.

"Oh-uh, pancakes, maybe?"

He nodded. "If I get the scramble, do you want to split?"

My eyebrows knit together. "Seriously? Isn't splitting meals reserved for old married couples?"

"Is it? I just want something sweet and savory."

"I mean, I guess I want that too."

"Great. We'll split it then." He grabbed my menu and flagged down the waiter before giving me a chance to change my mind.

After the waiter took our order, I put one elbow on the table and placed my chin in the palm of my hand. "You're a unique guy, Jared."

He winked at me as the server came back with our coffees.

"I'm only half as unique as you, Evie." He took a slow sip from his mug. "Speaking of you—"

"I don't think we were speaking of me."

"Well, now we are."

I bit my lip and fiddled with the handle of my mug. "What about me?"

"Tell me about yourself. Why do you move around so much? Where did you grow up? What's your family like?" He rattled off rapid-fire questions as he threw a finger up for each one.

My hands started to shake. I set my coffee down to avoid spilling it. "Okay, okay. Slow down. Um-my family—how I grew up—it was…interesting."

"Interesting, huh?"

My hands tugged at the frayed corner of my T-shirt. I hated talking about my past.

"Hey, sorry. I didn't mean to be pushy." I glanced up to see Jared's sincere eyes staring back at me. "You don't have to tell me anything."

"No, it's okay," I said. "My childhood…it-it was…sheltered is all. Strict parents, you know?"

"I don't actually know." His tone told me he could tell I was holding back, but he didn't press.

"It was just a bit suffocating."

"That sounds tough, Evie."

I looked up to see concern in his eyes but no pity.

"I wouldn't say tough."

"What would you say?"

I thought about all those years feeling stifled, dying to get out and have a new experience. I thought about the day I finally left and how it felt a little bit too much like escaping. I thought about the resentment I had felt about all of the missed opportunities in my childhood.

"I would say it was complicated."

"Fair enough."

"Anyway, I guess I can thank that life for making me

who I am now. The whole reason I love to move around is because I hardly saw more than a fifty-mile radius my whole childhood."

"Where have you lived?" he asked.

I rattled off city after city as he stared at me in awe.

"Damn. That's impressive, Evie. To not only go off on your own like that but to also try all those new places? Takes some major guts. I've hardly left the Midwest."

My cheeks reddened at his praise. "Well, if you're going to stay in one spot Chicago seems like a good option."

"It is a great city."

"Did you grow up here?" I asked, desperate to move the topic of conversation to him.

The waiter stopped by our table and set down our orders. Jared went to work, cutting the portions in half and splitting them between the two plates.

"Um, close by. Dean and I grew up in a shitty town a few hours away." He handed me my plate.

I took a bite. "What was so bad about it?"

He shrugged. "Not a lot of money but an abundance of drugs and alcohol. I fell in with some bad guys after high school."

I winced. "I guess it's good you got away, then."

"Definitely. Dean saved me. He bailed me out—literally—and took me with him to Chicago. He got me a job and basically forced me to get my act together."

I mentally noted the whole "literally" getting bailed out reference.

"Sounds like Dean is a pretty great friend."

"He's like my brother. You got any friends like that?"

I scrunched my nose and thought about it. "Not really. Cam is probably my closest friend. He let me stay with him after I moved out, and he's been there for me ever since. I like meeting people in new cities, but it never amounts to more than someone I catch up with occasionally through social media."

"At least you have Cam. He seems like a good guy, despite his...dryness."

I laughed. "Oh, he is. I promise you half of what he shows everyone else is a front. He's just a big softie underneath it all."

"What has he shown you of Chicago so far?"

"Mostly restaurants and bars," I said, in between bites of eggs and pancakes. Jared was right—you did need savory and sweet together.

"Anything you've been dying to do?"

I hesitated, thinking again about my trip here over a decade ago. "I really want to go to Navy Pier."

He groaned. "That's such a tourist trap."

"I know, I know. That's what Cam said. But I *am* a tourist."

He pushed away his empty plate and considered this. "Maybe we should have a touristy day then."

"You'd be willing to sacrifice a whole day to do touristy things with me?"

"Why not? Sounds like fun."

I tried not to look shocked at his offer to spend all day with me doing things other people would probably cringe at. He hardly even knew me, after all.

But I realized something as I took in his sincere, excited expression.

Jared wasn't like most people.

"What did you have in mind?" I asked.

NINE

Jared

"Here it is." I motioned in front of me as if unveiling a never-before-seen masterpiece. "The first stop."

"Cool," she stated simply.

"*Cool?*" I pretended to mock her apathetic reaction. "*The Bean* is the top tourist attraction in the city of Chicago. Show some respect."

She smirked and circled the giant reflective sculpture. "I guess it *is* impressive."

"Don't placate it now. It's already offended."

"I read its real name is *Cloud Gate*."

"No one calls it that." I waved my hands and shook my head as if she had just said the most ridiculous thing I had ever heard.

Since it was still early on a weekday, there weren't many people here besides us—a welcome change to the crowds that usually swarmed this place. I wouldn't be caught dead here on a weekend.

"Come here." Evie grinned and held her phone in front

of her, positioned at the sculpture. "Take a picture with me."

Without hesitation, I walked up behind her and leaned down so that my face was level with hers. I put on my biggest, cheesiest grin. She laughed at my exaggerated expression and snapped a few pictures.

"It is kind of beautiful," she said, still staring at the enormous stainless surface. "The way you can see the whole city in its reflection."

She walked underneath it and turned around a few times. It looked like she was genuinely in awe. I stood next to her and found myself stealing glances at her while she examined the blurred details of the city.

After our conversation over breakfast, I found myself captivated by my newfound perspective of her. She clearly had been impacted by a heavily sheltered upbringing. Her reluctance to tell me her whole story only fueled my desire to unearth every detail about her. What happened to transform her into the girl that stood before me today? The one that had the desire to roam around a new city and drink up every experience.

She was fucking refreshing.

Evie turned around at that moment, and I cleared my throat, tearing my gaze away from her. When I looked back, her raised eyebrows told me she had most likely caught me staring.

"So," she said. "What's next?"

"A BOAT?" SHE EYED ME WARILY AS I LED HER DOWN STONE steps toward the river.

"Come on." I grabbed her hand and pulled her forward. "It's fun."

"Isn't it kind of chilly?"

"Didn't you move here from Seattle? Aren't rain and boat ferries a thing there?"

"Fine, fine. You're right."

We continued down the steps and purchased our tickets before waiting in line to board. There were only about thirty other people here. The cloudy weather was probably a contributing factor.

"What is this anyway?" she asked.

"It's an architecture tour. They drive us around the river and talk about the buildings."

She tilted her head. "I guess that does sound interesting."

"I've heard it's great. I've always wanted to try it."

She eyed me. "You've never done this before?"

I smiled sheepishly. "It always seemed like a silly tourist trap."

"It's a good thing you've got yourself a silly tourist to spend the day with."

"It's the perfect excuse," I agreed.

They ushered us onto the boat, and we handed our tickets to the tour guide.

"Welcome aboard," the guide said. "There is a bar below deck. You have a few minutes to get a drink before the tour starts."

"Want to get a drink?" She moved toward the bar.

"Um," I scratched the back of my neck. "I don't drink."

"I just meant a coffee or a hot chocolate."

"Oh, right yeah, for sure."

"I'll get them," she offered, turning to the bartender and placing an order.

She handed me a Styrofoam cup, and my chest swelled with appreciation at her lack of follow-up questions.

Janelle loved to poke fun at me in front of her friends. "Who ever heard of a bartender that doesn't drink," she'd say. Never mind that I was mentally and physically the healthiest I had ever been. I shook my head and assessed the rows of seats.

"Where should we sit?" I asked.

"Up front, for sure. I can't miss a second of this!" Evie exclaimed.

She led the way and took the seats directly in front of the tour guide. Her pink hair whipped back and forth as she looked up and down the river. I bit back a smile. Her giddiness reminded me of a little kid. I hated that my mind wandered once again to my ex, but the difference between them was staggering. Janelle wouldn't have been caught dead doing something like this. Image was everything to her, and she only liked to do things others deemed trendy.

Looking back, I found it impossible to remember why I had ever thought we fit together.

As we settled into our seats, my arm inadvertently pressed into Evie's. I liked how her warm skin felt against mine, so I didn't pull away.

She didn't move either, probably grateful for the warmth it provided.

The tour guide grabbed a microphone and welcomed us.

"Where are you all from," he asked the crowd.

A moment of silence ensued before Evie shouted, "Seattle."

I looked down at her with raised eyebrows. She smiled and shrugged at me.

"It's fun to be cringey," she whispered.

We spent the rest of the tour craning our necks to see the buildings the guide pointed out as he rattled off their history. Skyscrapers soared around us as we drifted on the river between them. A few small raindrops fell from the moody sky, but it wasn't enough to drive us inside. I found myself repeatedly glancing over at Evie as she soaked in the sights.

Eventually, we were at the connection point to Lake Michigan, Navy Pier visible in the background.

"There it is!" Evie exclaimed. "You have to ride the Ferris wheel with me later."

I chuckled at her excitement. "If you insist."

"We need another picture." She gestured for me to lean into her as she held out her phone. We both put on our best cheesy smiles, and she snapped a few with the river in the background.

"Beautiful," I said, looking at one where my cheek was pressed against the top of her head. "That should go on the band's profile."

She shook her head. "No way. An attractive lead singer that's single is half the appeal of a band."

"So, you're calling me attractive?" I winked at her.

She rolled her eyes and smacked my chest. "Please, you *know* you're attractive. In fact, I don't think I've ever met someone so aware of how attractive they are."

"Ouch." I winced. "Are you saying I'm cocky?"

"In an adorable way."

I wrapped my arm around her shoulders. The gesture came easily.

"Wow, attractive *and* adorable? Watch out, or you might just fall in love with me."

"Not likely," she said, laughing.

My chest warmed at the sound. She continued to take pictures while fully engrossed in listening to the guide for the second half of the tour. It was so damn adorable how invested she was in all of this. It served as a great reminder not to take life too seriously. I might give off an air of confidence, but deep down, I cared quite a bit about what people thought of me. Sometimes being myself came effortlessly. Other times it felt like I was trying painfully hard to achieve this effortless rockstar persona—desperate to ensure I had scrubbed myself clean of every residual attribute of who I used to be.

I tugged her hair lightly to get her attention. "I like you," I said.

Her cheeks went pink. I had only known her for a short time, but I already liked that about her. She couldn't hide her emotions.

"What are we, in fourth grade?" she asked.

I couldn't stop staring at her. "I just feel like we click."

She scrunched her nose in that cute way I was already addicted to.

"I like you too, Jared. It's not every guy that will spend a whole day just wandering the city with me."

"It's my new favorite activity," I said as the boat pulled into the dock.

TEN

Evie

"I don't know about this one." I eyed the food in front of me. I wasn't a big meat eater to begin with, and this bun was loaded with things I had never seen on a hot dog before. "Pickles? Tomatoes?"

"Just trust me." He leaned across the table and pushed the plate closer to me.

"You promise you won't be mad if I don't like it?"

"I promise." He stared at me expectantly. "I just might never talk to you again."

"Glad the stakes are so low."

He chuckled. The delicate skin around his eyes creased as his smile widened. After looking at them so much today, I realized his eyes were more hazel than brown like I had initially thought. They almost looked gold when the light hit them just right. I tore my gaze away from Jared's and returned it to the Chicago dog in front of me.

"Okay, I'm doing it." I picked it up and took the biggest bite I could manage, ensuring I got every topping into my mouth.

It was fine. I didn't like hot dogs enough to have much of an opinion.

"Well?" Jared demanded.

I had to chew for a few seconds before swallowing.

"It's good," I finally said, covering my mouth with my napkin.

"Just good? Not the best hot dog you've ever had?"

"It's the best hot dog I've ever had."

"Don't appease me, Eves," he said, grabbing the remainder off my plate and taking down half of it with one bite.

"Hey," I protested. "What if I wanted that."

He shook his head. "Got to save room."

Two blocks and thirty minutes later, we stood outside with a small box that smelled incredible.

"Okay, maybe the hot dog wasn't your thing, but there's no way you won't like this," he said, lifting the box to reveal the thickest personal-sized pizza I had ever seen.

"Is that a pie or a pizza?" I asked.

"Just shut it and try a slice."

I snatched a piece. The cheese melted off the side, and the sauce pooled on top. It looked messy, but I didn't care.

I took a bite and moaned. "This is amazing."

He looked pleased as he grabbed a slice and started devouring it. We were both silent as we inhaled the pizza in record time.

"I'm so full." I clutched my stomach. "No more food stops."

He held out his arm for me to grab onto. "Time to walk it off."

Multilevel stores surrounded us as we walked the busy streets. The crowds had started to pick up now that it was mid-afternoon. Tourists and locals bustled in and out of shops and restaurants.

"Oh, look at this," I ran to a window display before seeing something else that caught my eye. "Jared, over here."

We continued like this for a while. I dragged Jared into whatever store caught my eye. We even stopped to admire some of the extravagant window displays in the designer stores we could never afford.

While we stood waiting to cross the next block, I noticed two older women staring openly at Jared. I wondered whether it was his tattoos or his good looks that caught their attention. The fact that I had once found him intimidating now seemed laughable. He was probably one of the warmest, down-to-earth humans I had ever met. Being around him felt easy in a way that I couldn't quite put my finger on.

Moving around so often gave me an easy excuse to keep everyone at a healthy distance. I had grown up without any close friends, so it didn't seem that strange to me not to have any in adulthood. Surface level was all I tended to do.

Plus, why would I allow myself to get tethered down somewhere? If I made too many close friends in one city, I might feel inclined to stay. Then I would eventually end up feeling suffocated all over again. I couldn't let that happen.

But as I followed Jared around, those fears of letting someone get close weren't as present as they usually were. Maybe it was his openness. Or maybe it was just because I knew I was leaving for my trip soon, and nothing would change that. Whatever it was, I found myself relishing this newfound comradery between us. Running around a new city like this with a guy I was just getting to know invigorated me. We had been at it for so many hours that the sun had begun its descent, casting a soft glow as dusk gradually enveloped the streets.

We passed a six-story discount store, and I pulled Jared inside.

"You never get tired, do you?" he asked as we rode the escalator up a level.

"I like to keep busy," I admitted.

"Why is that?"

"I get a bit restless if I sit still for too long."

Jared tilted his head and shifted his eyes to the ceiling. "Yeah, I know what you mean."

"You do?" I asked, hopeful. Cam made fun of my crocheting, but if I didn't have some sort of hobby to busy my hands with I would never be able to sit still.

"I always need to be playing guitar or at work. If I do ever find myself with some downtime, I almost always go over to Dean's place." We exited the escalator. "I guess I don't like being alone with my thoughts too much." He smiled, trying to hide the heaviness of his words.

I stared ahead as we walked through the displays of clothes. Was that what it was for me too? Could I not stand to be inside my own head?

"Do you know what I mean?" Jared asked when I didn't respond.

"Kind of," I mumbled, distracting myself by sliding hangers along a clothing rack. I searched the selection instead of looking at Jared. He seemed to sense my reluctance to say more because he started browsing next to me.

"Are you getting something?" He asked.

We had been window-shopping all day, but this was the first time I had actually stopped to look at clothes.

"It's getting chilly out there. I want something warmer." I gestured to the thin T-shirt I had put on this morning, not realizing I would be out until sunset at the time.

"Good idea," he said.

He pulled out a plain black hoodie while I produced a bright yellow one with a pink and green design.

He raised his eyebrows at my choice. "You don't like to play it safe, do ya, Eves?"

My stomach fluttered at his new nickname for me.

"Where's the fun in that?" I said, gesturing to his plain black hoodie.

"I already stand out in other ways." He waved to his facial piercings and neck tattoos.

I grabbed the sweatshirt from his hands as we walked over to the front of the store. "You know, you almost make me want to get an eyebrow piercing."

He wiggled his and grinned down at me. "That can be next on our agenda."

"I said *almost*."

I set the hoodies down at the register and fished around my bag for my wallet.

"Hey, let me at least get mine," Jared protested.

"No way. This is payment for being my tour guide today. Besides, you already bought me food."

"Well, I'm getting your Ferris wheel ticket," he insisted as I grabbed the bag, and we returned to the escalator. "Ready to head there now?"

My heart raced with anticipation. It felt silly, but something about going there felt like a milestone. It felt like I was doing it for twelve-year-old me.

We stepped out of the store, and I put my new hoodie on, snuggling into the soft fleece.

Jared pulled his over his head and shook out his messy hair. Somehow the imperfect bleached tips suited him perfectly. He fell into step next to me and slung his arm across my shoulders carelessly—as if he had done it a hundred times before.

"Thanks for today. I can't remember the last time I had this much fun," he said.

Jared had this way about him. When he gave me his attention, I felt like the only person in the world that mattered. It felt like I had known him much longer than a week.

"This has been my favorite day in Chicago so far," I responded.

He chuckled. "I think this has been *my* favorite day in Chicago so far."

"Tourist traps not so bad after all, huh?"

"It's just you that makes everything fun."

"You do too." I tucked my chin down, not wanting him to see the blush that crept across my cheeks. "Moving so much makes it easy to meet people but hard to make friends." I glanced up at him, suddenly feeling awkward. "Not that we're friends yet. I just meant—"

"Relax," he said, chuckling. "We're definitely friends."

We walked a few more paces before he looked down at me.

"What's the difference anyway?" he asked.

"Between what?" I had been mentally cursing my forwardness and had already forgotten the rest of what I said.

"Between meeting people and making friends."

"Seriously? There's a huge difference. Meeting new people can be fun, but it's exhausting. You always have to make small talk and get to know them before deciding if you like each other. When you meet someone that you click with right away, it's totally different. You can tell because being around them gives you energy instead of taking it away."

"Then I guess my bandmates aren't my friends because they constantly drain my energy," he joked, removing his arm from around my shoulders and stuffing his hands in his pocket.

"That's different. You guys are trying to work together to build something. That's going to be just as draining as it is energizing."

He nodded. "It's definitely both."

"How did you get into music anyway?"

"My mom." He scratched the back of his head. "We didn't have a lot, but she made sure the house was always full of music. When I was thirteen, I taught myself how to play the guitar."

"That's impressive." I nudged his arm. "What's she like? Your mom."

"Strong as hell. She raised me by herself. Never had a dad and never needed one. Not even sure who the guy is. But she worked her ass off to make sure we were always okay. Even though our house was falling apart and our neighborhood wasn't the best, she always made the most of it. Filling the kitchen with fresh flowers. Finding furniture someone else was throwing out and fixing it up to be some new treasure. She never made me feel like I couldn't do anything or couldn't be anything that I wanted to be."

My vision blurred, so I blinked a few times. "She sounds amazing," I murmured.

"She is," he said. "What about your parents?"

I froze. "They're fine. You know—strict, but fine."

Jared's golden eyes peered down at me. I looked away—my face hot from the lie.

The sky darkened as the sun dipped lower in the sky behind us. The lights of the rides illuminated the brisk evening.

ELEVEN

Jared
———

WE SETTLED INTO OUR SEATS, AND THE DOOR TO OUR compartment sealed shut. Evie had been quiet since I mentioned her parents, and I cursed myself again for bringing it up. I could tell back at the diner that it was a sore subject, but I couldn't help myself. I wanted to know more about her. Hell, I wanted to know everything about her.

Still, even her stiff demeanor couldn't hide how her eyes lit up as the ride moved, slowly bringing us into the sky. Even with the entire city as our backdrop, I couldn't tear my gaze away from her as she looked out the window with childlike wonder—her skin only inches from the glass.

As we soared higher, the twinkling lights of the buildings came to our eye level. They contrasted against the sky that had been painted in hues of pink and orange by the setting sun. I leaned back in my seat as the last remnants of daylight slipped away.

Evie snuck her phone out of her pocket to take a few pictures.

Desperate for our silence to end, I said, "I don't think I've had this much fun with someone in a while. Thanks again for today, Eves."

Her eyes shifted to me, and my heart pounded against my chest. "Stop thanking me. You're the fun one."

I scoffed. "Some people don't think so."

"Like who? Need me to beat someone up for you?" She nudged my knee with hers, and I laughed, grateful the tension between us had passed.

"This is going to sound like such a cliche, but I feel like the whole time I dated my ex I kind of lost myself a little bit."

"What do you mean?"

I felt guilty for dumping these thoughts on her, but at the same time, I also hoped that if I shared more about myself, she would be comfortable doing the same. "She always wanted me to be a certain way. She hated that I was in a band. Even though we *met* at a wedding my band was playing at." I shook my head. "She wanted me to be just like her friends. Get an office job, go to happy hour, wear a collared shirt to cover up my tattoos."

Evie made a disgruntled sound, and I looked up to see her brows knit. "That's awful. If she loved you, then she would have never tried to change you."

"I know that now. I just wish I realized it a year ago." I stared out the window, my jaw tense.

"Do you miss her?" Evie's soft voice barely carried over the sound of the ride.

"Not really. She was my first serious girlfriend. At the time, I thought that meant we were supposed to be together."

"Doesn't sound like it. I'm glad you got out of there intact."

I winced. "She broke up with me."

"So what? She did you a favor, then. You would have realized she was holding you back eventually."

"That's the thing," I said. "I'm kind of worried that I wouldn't have."

She shook her head. "You shouldn't waste any time worrying about what could have been. The point is you're happier now."

I gave her a small half smile that she returned.

"Have you ever been in a serious relationship?" I asked her, trying to hide my curiosity.

"Eh, not exactly."

"Elaborate."

"I mean, growing up, dating was not an option. Since I've been on my own I've gone on dates, but it's hard to have anything serious when I move around so much."

"Ever think someone might come along and make you think about staying?"

"You sound like Cam." She sighed. "I don't know. I guess I should never say never. I just can't imagine staying in one place again."

"You want to be free?" I guessed.

"I just want to be able to do whatever I want to do with my life." She bit her lip and glanced at the floor. "I'm sorry I clammed up earlier when you asked about my parents. It's just not my favorite subject."

I shook my head. "You don't have to tell me anything you aren't comfortable telling me."

"That's the thing, though." She resumed staring outside. "I am comfortable with you."

I ignored the little flip I felt deep in my gut.

"To answer your question from earlier...my parents aren't fine, at least not with me. My whole childhood was spent under their microscope. I couldn't do anything they deemed inappropriate, which was pretty much everything. I was homeschooled, couldn't play any sports, and didn't have friends. My whole life was pretty much whatever they decided it should be. I felt smothered every single day. As soon as I got out of there, I've never looked back."

My jaw clenched at the pain in her voice. Thinking about Evie and all her vibrancy being stifled angered me.

"Do you still talk to them?" I asked because I didn't know what else to say.

She shook her head. "Not really. I tried calling them a few times over the years, but the conversations never went well. They usually just get defensive and act like they're victims or something because I up and left. The conversations don't last long, and I haven't seen them in person since the day I moved out."

I reached across our compartment and grabbed her hand, squeezing it tight. She looked up at me with glassy eyes.

"Well, it's their loss," I said.

She sniffed and smiled at me.

"So now you can see why I'm always on the go. Cam used to bug me about staying in one place and settling down. But why? Why should I settle down and dictate my life around what someone else thinks I should want? I spent my whole childhood doing that, and it was miserable."

I nodded intently. "You shouldn't have to settle for anyone. Janelle was always telling me to settle down. Like, what the hell does that even mean, and why is that the end goal?"

"Right? 'Settling down' sounds more like accepting defeat than some sort of life victory." She bit her lip. "We should settle up instead."

I chuckled. "That sounds like we're getting ready to pay off our debts."

"Except the only debt we have is to ourselves and paying it off means never having any regrets."

"You're right," I said, staring at this person I hardly knew yet felt like I'd known my entire life. "I'm so fucking glad I met you."

"Ditto." She grinned.

The ride halted. Our conversation had completely captured my attention, and I hadn't even realized it was almost over.

Hopping out of the cart, I turned around to offer Evie my hand.

"Such a gentleman." She took my hand and gingerly stepped down. "Want to walk down the rest of the pier?"

"Let's do it." My phone buzzed in my pocket, and I signaled Evie to wait as I pulled it out. "Sorry, let me just check this."

> Dean: Hey, man. Sorry to ask you, but can you come in tonight? A couple of people called in sick.

I sighed and typed my response. As much as I looked forward to my nights off, I would always drop everything to help Dean.

> Jared: Be there in thirty.

My heart sank when I looked up to see Evie still waiting expectantly.

"Ready?" she asked.

"Ehh." I scratched the back of my neck and looked down at her. "Would you kill me if we called it a night?"

"Oh, you have plans?" Her face fell ever so slightly.

I felt a pang in my chest knowing I had caused her even the slightest amount of disappointment.

"It's just Dean asked if I could come in. They're short-staffed."

"Say no more." Her bright smile returned as if it had never left. "I totally get it."

"Are you sure?" Unfamiliar guilt coursed through me. Suddenly I felt like I would stay if she just asked me to.

"Definitely. I'm getting tired anyway."

"Are you sure? Want me to walk you somewhere?"

She shook her head. "Stop asking me if I'm sure and go. I'll be fine."

I nodded, still unconvinced.

"Bye, Eves." My entire body strained as I turned away from her, and my feet felt heavy as I walked in the opposite direction.

"Thanks again for today!" she called.

I turned back to see her beaming face and gave one last wave.

As I walked to the train, all I could think about was Evie as today's events ran through my mind like a highlight reel. It had simultaneously flown by and felt like the longest day I had ever experienced. We had already had more in-depth conversations than I had with Janelle months into our relationship. Hell, maybe ever.

What was I doing?

Just making a new friend. That was all this was. Evie was cool and easy to talk to. Why wouldn't we be friends? I obviously didn't want another relationship, and Evie wasn't sticking around long anyway.

Even as I thought this, my mind shifted to her adorable scrunched-up nose and how easy it felt to reach out and touch her.

TWELVE

Evie
―――――

As Jared's figure faded into the city scene, I sucked in a breath and looked up into the dark sky. The cool air felt refreshing as it tingled my nose. Today had been unreal. Everything had been unexpected.

Fatigue hit me like a brick wall. I glanced back at the pier one last time before making the short journey to Cam's apartment. Coming here had been like fulfilling some sort of obligation to my younger self. But standing here now I felt light years away from that moment all those years ago. I felt so at peace now that I was headed to a cozy apartment where I could curl up on the couch and rehash the day with someone who genuinely cared about me. I felt sorry for that poor, scared girl who felt all alone in the world.

That day, after my mother had called, Renee scooped us up and put us on a train home. I could still recall how hopeless I felt as the same scenery I had marveled at just earlier that day whizzed by the window. How empty I felt when I walked into my home. My father and mother demanded I go to my room as soon as I crossed the threshold. I held a pillow over my head to muffle the sounds of them yelling at Renee. They had managed to turn the best day of my life into the worst.

After that, they kept a close eye on me. My life consisted of household chores, home school, and learning skills like cooking and crocheting. I guess I could thank that time for my obsessive hobby. It was my only form of entertainment. I didn't go anywhere without them for a long time. Going to the small store in town with my mother became my new weekly highlight.

It still amazed me that they were shocked when I finally left years later. How was anyone supposed to live like that? With their light constantly being dimmed until it eventually flickered out.

It was no wonder I had become so restless.

I walked in the door to find Cam on the couch with two other people.

"Yay, you're home. I was just going to call you," Cam said. He lifted the blanket on his lap and patted the seat on the couch next to him. "Come sit and meet my friends Nora and Sean. They used to live in that house with me and Al."

Settling in next to him, I greeted the guy with short hair and glasses and the girl with midnight blue hair and a warm smile.

"It's nice to finally meet you," said Nora. "Cam has been talking about you nonstop."

"She's exaggerating," Cam said.

"No, she's not," added Sean.

I smiled and nudged him. "Don't be embarrassed. It's okay to be obsessed with me."

"Where have you been anyway?" Cam asked before

glancing at my new sweatshirt. "And what the hell are you wearing?"

I shrugged. "I've been all over."

He rolled his eyes. "Thanks for the cryptic answer."

"After Jared and I got breakfast, we decided to—"

"Hold up," Cam leaned forward, eyes wide. "You've been with Jared *all day?*"

My red cheeks told him everything he needed to know. "So what?" I asked, feeling defensive for some reason.

"I can't believe you've been hanging out with him for"—he checked his phone—"almost *twelve* hours."

"Wait, Dean's Jared?" Nora asked, looking intrigued.

"Yes," I told her. "I just started managing his band's social media. We did a little photo—"

"What could you have possibly been doing all this time?" Cam interrupted.

My eyes flickered to both of their expectant faces. Even Sean looked like his interest had been piqued.

I cleared my throat and started playing with the tassel on the blanket while I rattled off everything we had done that day. When I finished, Cam's face scrunched up, and his eyes narrowed.

"Why are you looking at me like that?" I asked. "He's a cool guy. We're friends."

"Oh, you two are friends now, are you? Pretty sure earlier today you were basically strangers, and you insisted you were just helping him with band stuff."

"Lay off, Cam," Nora said. "You can be so intrusive sometimes."

Cam's mouth hung open as he feigned offense. "Me?"

I hit him with the pillow next to me, and we all cracked up.

"Yes, *you*," Nora continued. "When Sean and I got together, you were always asking leading questions and sticking your nose into our business."

"And look where you are now? In love and thriving. I don't see the problem."

Nora rolled her eyes. "Like that had anything to do with you."

"Prove it didn't."

I laughed as they went back and forth for a few more minutes. I had to admit I envied this easy banter Cam, Nora, and Sean had. It was clear they were close in a way I had never been with anyone. The way that allowed them to come over just to sit around and catch up on life.

In all my effort to soothe my endlessly restless mind, I hadn't placed any priority on relationships. Now, as I sat here amongst close friends and observed their familiarity, I felt a pang of regret.

"Evie, what do you do again? I think Cam mentioned something about videos," asked Sean, tearing me from my thoughts.

"Oh my gosh, yes. He's always bragging about you. Tell us more."

"Am not," Cam muttered.

I ignored him as I told Sean and Nora all about my LifeCraft videos. They nodded and asked questions with genuine interest, and my heart swelled with pride.

"That's seriously so cool," Nora said.

I asked what they did. Funnily enough, Sean was in finance, and Nora was an artist. Their opposites-attract vibe wasn't just physical.

"Are you good with digital art?" I asked.

Nora nodded. "It's my specialty."

"Any chance you'd be interested in designing a T-shirt for Jared's band? I haven't brought it up yet, but I think it'll be a good idea, and I definitely don't have those skills."

"Oh my gosh, how fun!" she exclaimed. "I'd love to help."

"Alright, enough of this love fest," Cam said. "Let's pick that movie, or we'll be up all night deciding."

As Cam and Sean argued about what to watch, I pulled out my phone, which I had felt go off a few times. My cheeks flushed when I saw Jared's name. I snuck a peek at Cam to ensure he wasn't paying attention to me and opened the messages.

> Jared: Work is boring. I should have never left you.
>
> Jared: Having fun without me?

I smirked.

> Evie: Nothing could beat eating pizza on the street corner and riding Ferris wheels with you.
>
> Jared: Thank god! I was worried.

I set my phone down, only for it to vibrate again.

> Jared: Sorry again about bailing. I wish I could have stayed. Would have had a way better night with you.

Biting my lip to suppress my smile, I put my phone away as the opening credits of whatever movie Cam selected played.

I leaned my head against his shoulder and nestled into the fleece blanket. I spent more time laughing at everyone's commentary than I did at the bad puns of the comedy. As the movie played in the background, I fought my eyelids to stay awake. But the couch enveloping me wasn't doing me any favors.

As I glanced around the room, I realized something.

I wasn't sure I had ever felt more at home than at this moment.

THIRTEEN

Jared

"Can you get off your phone and start playing?"

I looked up to see Drew glaring at me.

"Oh, are you and Tyler done fighting about who loads the dishwasher more often?"

"Whatever," Tyler muttered. "You've been on your phone the whole night."

"I'm texting Evie," I said, holding my phone out as if they'd want to examine it for proof. "She had a question about our next show before she posted about it."

"Is she going to come record more footage for us?" Max asked. His voice sounded exhausted.

I looked at my only ally in this band. His normally neat hair was disheveled, and he looked stressed.

"She is." I slung my guitar strap over my shoulder and eyed his ragged appearance up and down. "Everything okay with you, man? Does work have you doing overtime again?"

He shook his head. "Nah, it's more…personal."

Drew snapped his head up. "Does Max have girl problems?"

"No." His glare gave everything away, and we all laughed. "I don't want to talk about it."

I chuckled, grateful it wasn't me that looked that strung out over a woman. When Janelle and I were still together, I frequently showed up to band practice with tired eyes and low patience. Her presence in my life did not allow my creative energy to flourish.

I smirked down at Evie's last text and thought about how she had the exact opposite effect on me. She made me feel like a kid again. Everything felt new and exciting with her. Since last week's tourist day, we had gone to breakfast together twice—slowly trying all of the divey diners Chicago had to offer. We always split so we could try more things off the menu.

"Evie brought up the band name again. We need to figure that shit out." I plugged my guitar into the amp.

"Seems like you care an awful lot about what Evie thinks." I looked up to see Drew wiggling his eyebrows obnoxiously at me.

"No, dickhead. I just think having a band with a name is pretty important."

Max sighed. "You're right. You're right. Should we revisit The Core Four?"

"I'm going to smash my bass over my head." Drew groaned.

"We could try one of those online generators," Tyler suggested.

"That's even worse." Drew held up his bass and pretended like he was going to swing it over his head.

"Well, I don't hear you coming up with any ideas, genius."

"Shut up, Tyler."

Max looked at me tiredly as they once again began to argue. If this is how they were as adults, I couldn't imagine what they were like growing up. Their mother must be a saint.

"Are there any bands out there with just guitarists?" I mumbled.

Max tilted his head as if considering the suggestion. "We might sound a little flat, unfortunately."

"Might be worth it."

"I can't believe our account has already doubled in followers," Max said. "We should have put effort into this a long time ago."

"I think Evie being involved is the key. Us putting in effort would have garnered us a few likes at best."

Max nodded. "We do suck at it."

"Hopefully we can get a good amount of growth in before she leaves."

"Right. You mentioned she was going on a trip. How long do we have her for?"

"Just until the end of next month." I tried to ignore the unwelcome pang in my chest as I said this.

"That gives us some time. We need to line up more shows."

"We will, man," I said. "We're so close to something. I can feel it."

"Your eternal optimism and confidence have gotten us this far. I'm sure it'll take us all the way." Max winced as Tyler started banging on his drums to drown out whatever

Drew was trying to say. "That is if those two don't end up killing each other first."

I ran my hands over my face before walking between my other two bandmates.

"Alright, that's enough!" I yelled. Tyler stopped banging, and Drew folded his arms across his chest. "We need to move on. We've got to tighten up that new song if we're going to close with it."

Max nodded. "Two original songs in our set is pretty good."

"It's fine, but we need more," Drew said.

I scratched the back of my neck, thinking about the song I wrote that I hadn't shown the group yet. I wanted to perfect it before I shared it with anyone.

"How's writing coming?" Tyler asked me.

"It's coming. I'm almost ready to show you guys something."

"Good," Drew said. "And while you're at it, if you're so creative, can you please come up with a new band name that doesn't suck?"

"Can we please watch anything else?" I whined as I tried to steal the remote from Al.

Maybe I should spend less time at Dean's place now that he had a live-in girlfriend, but old habits die hard.

She huffed and held it out of my reach. "I've been waiting to watch this show all week."

The show in question was one of her trashy reality TV shows that she guiltlessly enjoyed.

"You're rotting your brain with this stuff," I insisted.

"What are you going to put on? Football? A movie with half-naked girls and car chases? Sounds really intellectually stimulating."

I held up my hands in surrender and pretended to sit back and watch. As soon as she took her eyes off me, I sprung, reaching for the remote.

She screamed and tried to snatch it away from me, but we both had a hand on it. I tried to wrench it from her grip, but she was surprisingly strong.

"What the hell are you two doing?" Dean emerged from the bedroom where he had been changing after getting home from work.

Al and I froze, and she took the opportunity to yank the remote from my hand.

"Ah hah!" she cried victoriously.

Dean shook his head. "I swear you two act like siblings sometimes."

"She won't let me watch TV." I pretended to pout.

"You know where you could watch TV?" She stroked her chin, pretending to mull it over in her head. "Your own house."

"Ha. Ha," I replied dryly.

"Want to hang out outside?" Dean suggested.

"He'd love to," Al responded before I had the chance to say anything.

"Fine," I grumbled and pushed myself off the couch, ruffling Al's hair on my way out.

"Hey," she protested.

I turned around and winked at her before following Dean out to his deck. He had a spacious one for Chicago. It overlooked the small courtyard of his building, and you could just make out the taller skyscrapers over the rooftop.

Dean opened a cooler and cracked open a beer before tossing me a soda water.

"Thanks," I muttered, sitting on one of the chairs.

"How's the band?" he asked.

"Great. Evie has been killing it. She's already doubled our followers, and it's only been a couple of weeks."

His eyebrows shot up. "That's pretty good," he said. "She seems cool."

"She is."

"I noticed you've been spending a lot of time with her." I glanced up to see Dean staring out at the view. I could sense his interest despite the nonchalance of his tone.

When Dean and I were working at Luna Two last night, Evie stopped by before closing. I thought back to his surprised face when he found out the two of us were hanging out.

"Nice of you to stop by," Dean had said while cleaning off the bar.

"This spot is great," she said, admiring the décor. "I love the subtle differences between the two restaurants. Let me know if you ever want to spruce your social media up. I'd be happy to take a look."

"Thanks. I might take you up on that offer."

"She's great at it," I told him.

"What brings you in any way?" he asked her. "We're just about to close."

"Oh, um, right. Jared said just to meet him here."

Dean had glanced at me with raised eyebrows.

"We're going to see a movie."

We were going to a late-night showing of a new horror movie after discovering that movie theater popcorn topped both of our favorite foods lists.

Dean had seemed thrown off hearing about our plans. I knew what he was thinking. Why hadn't I invited him? Something I would typically do. But I couldn't even explain it to myself.

Evie was a friend.

Who I liked spending all my free time with.

Alone.

But nothing more than that.

I shook the thoughts from my head and stared out at Dean's courtyard. I needed to respond to his statement carefully. "She's my friend, and she's helping the band. Of course, I'm spending time with her."

Dean glanced at me. "I've known you basically your whole life. I've never seen you have a female friend before."

I scoffed. "That's ridiculous."

"Name one, then."

"Al," I said confidently.

He rolled his eyes. "My girlfriend doesn't count."

"Why not?"

"Because number one, you're forced to hang out with her, and number two, if you ever looked at her as anything else, I would murder you."

My head sank back into the plush cushion. "Don't get all macho on me. I would never do that."

"I know that, obviously. I'm just making my point that Al doesn't count."

"So, maybe I haven't had a female friend before. That doesn't matter. Evie is different. She's like…refreshing. She's always down for whatever."

"It seems like you like her."

"I do like her."

"You know what I mean," Dean insisted.

"Come on, D. It's not like that at all. I just like hanging out with her. She's fun."

"That sounds like the beginning of a relationship to me."

"It's *nothing* like a relationship."

"What do you think a relationship is, dude?"

I pretended to look thoughtful. "Suffocating?"

Dean winced. "I guess you haven't had the best experience."

"Says the guy outside because his girlfriend has commandeered the TV."

"Hey, I love watching those shows with her," Dean warned. "I'm only out here because my best friend doesn't know what the word 'boundary' means."

"Fair enough," I said.

This conversation had my mind wandering to Evie. Maybe she was free tonight. I should text her—

"Are you thinking about Evie?"

"No," I replied, too quickly.

Dean smirked.

"Shit, alright, maybe I was. But only because I was thinking about asking her to hang out after this."

"Asking her to hang out because you like her."

"I miss the days when you were the cynical one, and I was on your ass to get your act together."

Dean glanced back through the window at Al. "I don't miss those days at all."

"Jesus, you're so in love it's disgusting." I pretended to gag. "Me wanting to hang out with Evie only proves that I like her as a friend. There's no way in hell I'm jumping into another relationship. Besides, she's leaving soon anyways."

Dean nodded. "Right, because it's totally human nature to ignore feelings because the timing isn't convenient."

I stood up and smacked him on the shoulder.

"Ouch. What the hell was that for?" He glared at me.

"For being so goddamn nosy. I'm not ignoring feelings."

"Whatever you say," he muttered.

I pulled out my phone to text Evie. Dean was so obviously wrong about us.

We were just friends.

FOURTEEN

Evie

"Should I make popcorn," I asked as Al and Cam settled onto the couch.

"Do you even need to ask?" Cam said.

"Thank you!" Al called.

I added oil and salt to a pot and poured the kernels in before shaking it around on top of the stove. The oil made a soft sizzling sound as it heated up. After a minute, kernels danced around against the lid. I retrieved bowls from an upper cabinet and portioned out the snack.

"I love that you two love trashy TV as much as I do," I said, walking into the living room and handing them each a bowl.

"I miss when we lived together and watched it every night," Cam reminisced.

"Agreed," said Al. "I love Dean, but his commentary just isn't as good.

"It's an art," Cam replied.

The buzzer rang, signaling someone in the lobby calling the apartment.

Cam leaned forward on the couch. "Did we order food?"

"No, it's just Jared." I jumped up to buzz him in and unlocked the door.

Al shot Cam a questioning look as I returned to the couch.

"Is he stopping by to get something?" she asked.

"When I told him we were watching TV, he asked if he could come over."

"Did you tell him what we were watching?"

"Yep. He said he liked this show."

Al raised her eyebrows and gave Cam another look.

He shrugged. "Evie and Jared are apparently *very* good friends that like to do *everything* together nowadays."

I rolled my eyes. "We don't even hang out that much." I hoped Cam didn't call me out on my lie. In the past week, we had seen each other nearly every day.

"What happened to 'I'm just helping with the band?'" Cam questioned.

"I have been." I tossed a pillow at him. "I post every day for them, and I'm going to their next show. Now shut it before he gets up here."

At that moment, Jared waltzed into the apartment wearing faded black sweats. He whistled as he looked around, taking in the high ceilings and massive windows.

"Nice place, Cam."

"Thank you." Cam smirked at me.

I shoved him in the leg and mouthed, *Stop it*.

Jared sauntered over to the couch. His smile faded when he noticed Al. He hardly faltered before plopping down next to me on the end of the couch.

"Hey Al, fancy seeing you here."

"I just can't seem to get away from you," she said.

Jared laughed and grabbed a handful of popcorn from the bowl balanced in my lap.

Cam pointed the remote at the TV. "Is everyone settled? Can I finally start this?"

Al ignored him and turned back to Jared. "It's funny. I could have sworn a few days ago you called this a trashy reality show and begged me to change the channel."

I tilted my head to look at Jared. I noticed a barely perceptible wince that he quickly covered up.

"I was just giving you a hard time. These shows are fun."

Cam and Al both raised their eyebrows but said nothing.

Jared ignored them and slung an arm over the couch near where my shoulders rested. Cam side-eyed us, but I had grown used to Jared's touchy demeanor. It was just part of his personality.

The show opened with a huge fight. One of the men had been caught with another girl that he wasn't coupled up with last night. The two women screamed at each other, and Jared leaned in with his eyes locked on the screen.

He seemed interested enough in this show to me.

"Damn, this guy is in some shit." Jared laughed as the two girls turned their anger onto him.

"He's the worst," Cam said through a mouthful of popcorn. "You should have seen what he did the first week."

"What did he do?" Jared asked.

During the next commercial break, Cam explained while Jared listened intently.

"Anyone want anything to drink? Water? Soda?" I got up and moved to the kitchen.

"Yes, please." Cam and Jared replied simultaneously.

"I'll help," Al offered as she followed me to the kitchen.

I opened the cupboard and grabbed a few glasses to hand to her. She opened her mouth and then bit her lip.

"What?" I asked.

She glanced over at the living room to ensure the boys were still deep in conversation.

"Jared *definitely* hates this show," she whispered.

At that moment, Jared said, "No way." In a heated tone to the summary Cam gave him.

I shrugged. "Seems like he's into it."

"It does, but that's only because he's giving it a chance. Whenever he's over at our place, he's such a brat about me watching this. He literally hides the remote from me."

"Maybe he had a change of heart."

"Maybe you gave him a change of heart," she muttered.

"What are you saying?"

She sighed. "When Dean and I first got together, he helped me move."

I stared at her, confused. "That was nice of him," I finally said.

"Too nice," she insisted. "We had just met. Everyone told me that guys don't help strangers move out of the kindness of their hearts."

Gears shifted in my brain as I understood her implication.

"Helping you move is hardly the same as Jared wanting to watch a dumb show with me."

"He came all the way downtown—the opposite direction of his apartment— after his shift to watch a show he hates? No way. Guess how often he used to go to his ex-girlfriend's apartment after work?"

"Not a lot?" I guessed based on her tone.

"Never. He would always say he's too tired, and she would get pissed about it."

"Any day on those drinks. We're parched over here," Cam called.

"Coming," I said.

"I'm just saying I've gotten to know Jared pretty well, and this isn't like him," she whispered as we re-entered the living room.

I tried to ignore her words as I handed Jared a glass. He smiled at me with his hundred-watt grin. The one that caused the corners of his lips to curl up.

I froze. Noticing his smile probably wasn't a very *friendly* thing for me to do.

The show played in the background, but I found it difficult to focus. Jared's knee pressed into mine, and my whole body heated as a result.

I didn't want to have a crush on Jared. That would just complicate everything.

It was strange even to think that I could have a crush on him since he wasn't anything like the guys I had dated in the past. The last guy I had seen in Seattle was quiet, bookish, and loved board games.

Jared didn't have much in common with me on the surface, but somehow our energies complemented each other perfectly. He was addicting to be around, and—let's face it—I found him attractive. Who wouldn't? I mean, what am I, blind? The guy practically radiated charisma and looked like he was plucked out of a magazine.

Ugh. I hated that Cam was right.

Jared moved his arm down from the couch and onto my shoulders before shaking me gently. He leaned down, and I could feel his hot breath on my ear.

"What are you thinking about?" he whispered. "You aren't even watching the show."

My spine stiffened as my whole body broke out in goosebumps. I shivered and hoped he didn't notice.

"Just your band," I lied, turning to him. Our faces were only inches apart, and heat pooled in my stomach. I crossed my legs to try to ignore the sensation building there.

"My band?" He raised his eyebrows.

"I-I just need more content. Your page needs more videos."

He bit his full bottom lip, and I inadvertently stared at his mouth.

"I might have something for you."

"Really?"

"I'll tell you about it later."

The show continued to play as Cam and Al gave colorful commentary. Their discussion became enough of a distraction that I eventually got my mind back on the show. Another fight brewed right as the credits rolled.

Jared sprang forward and looked at us, eyebrows knit. "They're going to leave it on a cliffhanger like that?"

"That's how they get you to keep watching," Cam said.

"Does this mean you'll finally stop trying to switch the channel on me every time you're over?" Al asked.

"I don't know what you're talking about." Jared smirked and winked at her.

She laughed and got up. "Whatever, I should probably get going. I've got an early day tomorrow."

Cam stood and stretched. "Same. I might just go to bed."

Jared's gaze flickered over to me. "Are you going to bed too?"

Al and Cam stared at me wide-eyed from behind Jared.

"I have some editing I need to do."

"Mind if I stay and hang out a little?"

Al and Cam were pointing to Jared and mouthing something at me. I ignored them, but a lump had formed in my throat.

"Sure."

Fifteen minutes later, Jared and I were alone on the couch. My legs were curled underneath me with my laptop balanced in my lap. Jared had his elbow on the back of the couch as he rested his head on his hand, looking over my shoulder.

"You never did send me your videos," he said.

"I wasn't sure if you actually wanted to watch them. Sometimes people just say that to be nice."

He narrowed his eyes. "It's really cool what you do, Eves. I mean, look at this house. It's so detailed. I had no idea you could create something like this in a game."

"It took a lot of time to figure out. I don't even want to admit how many hours of my life I've spent playing this game. It's embarrassing."

"No, it's not. It's impressive."

I laughed awkwardly to deflect the compliment. "Not really."

He nudged my knee with his. "Yes, it is."

I bit back my smile and tried to focus on editing.

"Can we watch one of your finished videos?"

I felt self-conscious as I looked over into his golden eyes. "If you want to."

He nodded and scooched in even closer.

I closed my editing software and brought up my channel before selecting my most viewed video. I let it play in the background as I shifted my gaze from my laptop to the floor. I hated watching my videos back, especially in front of someone else.

"Damn, that house is huge," Jared exclaimed. "Ten million views on this? That's unreal."

After a few more minutes, he looked over at me again.

"How'd you get into all this anyway?"

I heard the unasked portion of his question in his tone.

How did you get into all this if your parents were so strict?

"When I turned fourteen, my parents let me volunteer at the library. I started off just reading books to kids and stuff like that. Then I discovered their free computers. They had games to rent, and that's when I discovered LifeCraft. It was the perfect game for me. I could create a fake identity, live in a virtual city—have this whole life outside my house. Looking back, it's no wonder I was drawn to the game."

Jared squeezed my shoulder as I continued.

"That was when I first started lying to my parents. I would tell them I picked up extra shifts volunteering, but really, I would just sneak off to the library and spend hours playing the game. After about a year I discovered online forums. I started posting tips and tricks on a forum account before transitioning to videos. A few months after I turned eighteen, I got my first offer to make money on advertising. My parents only found out what I was doing because I had to open a bank account. When the first statement came in the mail, they screamed at me. I didn't last in that house much longer after that."

"Wow, Eves," Jared whispered. "What a rebel. Sneaking off to the library like that."

I laughed despite the bad memories. Jared reached his arm around me in a side embrace.

"All jokes aside, though, that's shit what your parents did. I'm glad you found an outlet for all those years you felt stuck."

"Me too," I murmured.

"And to figure it all out on your own like that? It *is* impressive."

I shrugged. "No more impressive than you teaching yourself to play the guitar."

His brow furrowed as he stared at me. "It is, though. I had a support system. My mom was always there for me, telling me I could be whoever I wanted to be. Hell, she even saved for months to buy me a used guitar. You did it all on your own."

"I didn't have much of a choice." I ducked my head, feeling raw and vulnerable.

He placed his finger underneath my chin and gently tilted it back up so I was forced to look at him. "You'll never have to feel alone like that again," he said.

My breath caught in my throat at his intensity. We had only just met, and this was such a grand promise that I should have laughed. How could he possibly know or say that? Yet something in his eyes told me he meant it.

"Thanks," I whispered. "It's always been hard for me to talk about my past, but you make it kind of easy."

He backed up a little. The space allowed me to breathe, but I felt a bit of emptiness at his distance.

"I'm self-conscious about my past, too," he said.

"You? Self-conscious? That's hard to imagine."

He chuckled. "Well, I hide it well. Having a band is something I always dreamed about, but I was too afraid of failing to ever go after it when I was younger."

"And now you're crushing it," I said.

He smiled and shook his head. "I love how supportive you are, and you hardly know me."

I ducked my chin again at his compliment. My cheeks must have been redder than a sunburn.

"And I'm sorry you didn't have that support growing up," he said as he tucked a piece of hair behind my ear. "You're inspiring, though."

I still couldn't bring myself to meet his gaze. "No, I'm not."

He leaned closer to me. "Yes, you are. You created all this on your own. It's amazing what you've accomplished."

When I finally looked up, we were only inches apart. I shook my head, effectively breaking the trance we were both under.

"Enough about me," I said, moving away on the couch. "Weren't you saying something earlier about new content for your band?"

FIFTEEN

Jared

I opened the blinds to my modest studio apartment and assessed the room. The sun crept in through the west-facing window and drenched the warm wood floors in light.

Vacuum. I should vacuum.

I pulled out an ancient red machine from my hall closet and plugged it into an outlet. The antique roared to life. I pushed it along the floor, ensuring I captured every dust bunny.

Once I was satisfied with the floor, the open bathroom door caught my eye. I went inside the tiled room and evaluated it. It was relatively clean, but I should disinfect everything just to be safe. Opening a drawer, I dumped in my toothpaste and spare toiletries that littered the countertop before grabbing a cleaning solution and getting to work.

After I had wiped every surface, I surveyed the space one last time.

Evie would be here any minute.

I chewed the inside of my cheek. For some reason that I couldn't put my finger on, I felt anxious for her to see my small apartment. I had women over here all the time, but this felt different.

Would she think it was cramped?

Did it smell a little weird?

Would she think all of the posters I had lining the walls were dumb?

Before I could second guess anything else, a knock sounded at the door. I blew out a breath and checked my appearance in the large oval mirror I had hanging by the door. I flattened down a piece of hair that stuck up haphazardly and opened the door.

"Hey." Evie greeted me with a bright smile and an even brighter outfit. She wore a lavender cardigan with flowers every color of the rainbow crocheted onto it.

"Come on in." My nerves eased the moment I saw her. "Sorry, you had to come so far north for this."

She brushed off my comment and stepped inside. "Don't be ridiculous. I got here a little early and stopped in the coffee shop a few blocks over. I haven't gotten a chance to explore up here yet."

"That spot is my favorite. Sometimes I go there to write." I loved that she had found her way there without me even mentioning it.

"What a great apartment," she gushed.

My lips tugged up at her approval. There wasn't a judgmental bone in Evie's body. I should have known she wouldn't have a mean thing to say about my apartment.

"You think so? I've lived here a couple of years now. I know it's small, but…."

"It's perfect," she insisted, walking around the room and taking in my music and movie posters.

The space was a large rectangle with the kitchen and

bedroom branching off on opposite sides. It was a studio, but I had put up a folding divider to give the bed area more privacy. A worn couch sat in the center of the room with a TV in front of it and a small table behind it.

"It's so homey," she said, flopping onto the couch. "I wish I had a space like this. I try to inject some style whenever I move, but it never feels very me."

"It's hard to imagine you not in a bright space." I sat down next to her.

"Well, this space screams 'Jared.'"

"It does?" I asked, raising my eyebrows. Janelle had always begged me to let her decorate and throw out half my stuff.

"Definitely," Evie continued. "The furniture is perfectly mismatched, and I love that posters cover every inch of these white walls."

"I hated the white walls."

"You are *so* not a white wall kind of guy."

The smile refused to leave my face as I looked down at Evie, admiring my apartment. It felt great to have her settling into my couch—my space.

"So, are you ready to show me?" she asked.

"Oh." My smile faltered. "I guess so."

"You don't have to if you changed your mind," she added quickly.

"I'm a little nervous. I've never played something like this for someone before. Usually, I'm just showing the band."

"Well, I'm honored that you're willing to play me your new song."

"Don't go getting your expectations too high. It isn't all that exciting."

She nudged my shoulder. "Where's the adorably cocky guy I've grown to know and love."

My chest tightened at her words. I knew she just meant them in a friendly way, but I couldn't ignore the effect they had on me.

Cool it, I thought to myself. I didn't see Evie like that. Just because she was intelligent, quirky, fun, and easy to talk to didn't mean something had to happen between the two of us.

I stood from the couch and grabbed my acoustic guitar off the wall.

Evie curled her legs underneath her and waited for me to start.

"I can't play if you're going to look at me like that," I said.

"Like what?" she asked, looking down at herself as if she could see the way she was looking at me.

"Like you're anticipating something amazing. It's making me even more nervous."

She rolled her eyes but turned away. A smile still played on her rosy lips.

I sighed and grabbed the pick I had intertwined in the strings. Hesitantly, I struck the first chord and started to sing. My voice floated softly over the melody of the chorus.

Just too dumb to get it right
Too young to realize
It was never worth the fight
Try as I might
You would always villainize me
I'd yell out of spite

You were never contrite
Now you can't stand the sight of me

I continued to sing a few more lines. When I glanced at Evie, I saw her slowly swaying to the melody.

After the last chord, I looked at her in anticipation.

"Well? Did it suck?"

She shook her head slowly. "That was incredible."

My stomach somersaulted, and my chest warmed at her approval.

"Really? You liked it?"

"I loved it," she insisted, her voice getting louder with excitement.

"Thank God. I was stressed all morning about playing this for you."

"Do you think I could record it?" she asked. "To post."

I raised my eyebrows. "Here? Without the band?"

She nodded. "People love casual behind-the-scenes videos like this."

I shrugged. "I guess if you think anyone will want to watch it."

"I do," she said and pulled out her phone.

She positioned me so that I sat on the couch with my posters and window behind me. Once she was happy with the lighting, she gave me a thumbs-up, and I played it for her again.

After a few more takes, I found myself completely comfortable playing my song in front of her. In fact, I couldn't even remember why I had been nervous in the first place. I glanced up at Evie as I sang. She gave me a thumbs-up like a dorky mom recording her kid's piano recital, which made me shake with held-back laughter.

Why did she have to be so fucking cute all the time?

"I think I've got it," she said after I sang the last note. "Your smile at the camera was the perfect touch."

I smirked. *I was smiling at you, dork.*

"Let me see," I said, walking behind her.

I tried to be impartial while watching, but it was always hard to hear yourself back in a video. Surprisingly, though, this didn't make me cringe.

"This is perfect." I gripped her shoulders and squeezed.

She checked the time. "I'm going to post this right now. It's a good time for engagement."

I watched as she wrote a caption. Her nose scrunched up in concentration, and I resisted the urge to trace my fingers over the fine lines that formed between her eyebrows.

She looked up and caught me staring.

"What?" she asked. "Do I have something on my face?"

I blinked a few times, unable to come up with a valid excuse. "You have a cute concentration face," I finally admitted.

Her cheeks turned pink, and her mouth hung open slightly. "I do?"

"You do."

A tension fell over us. She bit her lip and glanced around the room.

"I should probably get going. It's getting late."

I peeked at the clock above my door. "It's seven."

She laughed nervously. "I just had a few errands I wanted to run tonight."

I didn't like the thought of her leaving right now. "Can I come?"

SIXTEEN

Evie
───────

"This is your errand?" Jared asked, picking up one of the boxes and examining it.

"I didn't say it was going to be fun."

We were two blocks over from his apartment at the nearest drugstore. In truth, I hadn't actually had any errands I wanted to run today. But after Jared had played his song, I felt a moment pass between us. The same one I felt when he stayed late at Cam's the other night while I was editing. It almost felt like we might kiss or something. I knew how ridiculous that sounded. I was probably just projecting my own secret desires onto the situation.

Still, it had felt easier to put physical space between us than try and stay in that studio alone with him a second longer.

I had not anticipated him begging to come along, though. Which is how we ended up walking the aisles of the store as I placed a few odds and ends into the basket I carried. When we reached the hair care aisle, I stopped to peruse the colors. My pink dye *had* been fading, and a change sounded nice.

"Who said I'm not having fun?" Jared picked up a box depicting a woman with fire engine red hair. "What about this?"

I shook my head. "Been there, done that. Red is way too messy."

He smirked. "How many hair colors have you gone through?"

"Pretty much all of them at this point."

"What's your natural color?"

"Wouldn't you like to know?"

He moved quickly and pinched my side. I shrieked, not expecting to be tickled in the middle of the store. The outburst warranted a dirty look from the cashier at the front.

"You're going to get us in trouble," I hissed.

"Whoops," he replied, not looking the least bit apologetic.

I turned back to the boxes and grabbed one. "What about purple?"

He nodded, taking it from me. "I could see you with purple hair."

As we walked to the front of the store, Jared continued to examine the back of the box.

"Is there enough in here to do mine too?"

I raised my eyebrows and looked up at him. "You want purple hair?"

He shrugged. "Not the whole thing. Just the bottom." He tugged at one of his bleached ends that curled by his chin. "I was going to cut them off eventually. This would be fun to do in the meantime."

"What's the story with those anyway?" I asked as the cashier rang me up.

"I buzzed it awhile back, and when it started to grow in, I bleached it. You aren't the only one that likes to experiment with their hair."

"I need to see a picture of bleach blonde buzzed Jared."

He poked my side again. "Maybe I'll show you if you're lucky."

Once we were outside, I hesitated. I planned on going home, but if he was serious about dying his hair, he probably meant for us to go back to his apartment. While my original intent was escape, the fresh air and the walk had dissolved whatever tension had existed between the two of us.

"So..." I trailed off, waiting to see what he would suggest.

"Back to my place?"

As we made the short walk back, knots formed in my stomach. Admittedly I had been a little nervous to go to Jared's apartment today. I had tried on almost every piece of clothing I had before Cam caught me red-handed. I couldn't admit I was trying to look cute, so I put on a sweater I had made ages ago. I'm sure Jared did not find my colorful nursing-home style sexy.

My wandering mind hadn't even noticed we were already at Jared's apartment. He had spent the entire walk talking about their next show. Hopefully, I had smiled and nodded at all the right times.

Once inside, Jared ripped the box out of the bag and shook it. "You ready?"

"Shoot," I said, glancing down at my sweater. "I don't want to get dye on this."

"No worries." Jared walked to the other side of the room and dug through a dresser. He produced a worn-looking black T-shirt and threw it my way. "You can wear this."

"Thank—" My breath hitched as Jared stripped off his own shirt, revealing a lean, well-defined torso. His tattoos traveled all the way onto his chest on the right side of his body. I thought about how it would feel to trace the curved black lines. He glanced over at me as he pulled a different shirt down over his muscular abs. I ripped my gaze away.

"Like what you see, Eves." I could hear the smile in his voice.

"Don't flatter yourself." I pretended to keep my cool, but heat flooded my entire body. "I'm using your bathroom to change."

"Why bother?" I glanced over to see him grinning at me, and I fought desperately to calm my burning cheeks. The last thing I wanted him to think was that his shameless flirting affected me. Even though it *definitely* did.

Once inside his bathroom, I gripped the sides of the sink and turned on the faucet. Splashing cold water on my face, I assessed my appearance. Just as I feared, my face was beet red.

Crap.

I removed my sweater and replaced it with the shirt Jared had thrown me. It was soft and smelled like him. I resisted the urge to press my nose into it and inhale deeply.

Opening the door, I found Jared waiting right outside.

"This could get kind of messy," I warned.

"I like messy."

Grabbing the dye, I ripped open the box and prepared

it based on the directions. Jared sat down on the closed toilet lid and watched me.

"Did you bleach your hair yourself?" I asked.

"Um, no." He looked sheepish. "Some girl did it."

Surprisingly, I felt a small stab of jealousy in my chest.

"Wow, don't I feel special?"

"Hey, you're the first girl to color my hair. And we'll be matching."

I put gloves on before starting on the bottom section of my hair. When I finished the front, Jared stood up and moved behind me.

"Here, let me help you with the back."

"You sure you can handle this?" I eyed him through the mirror. "You better not miss a spot."

"So little faith in me," he said, grabbing the brush. "I've got this."

He carefully ran it over my hair in the back. After a minute, he stuck out his tongue slightly in concentration. I laughed.

He looked at me. "What?"

"It looks like you're concentrating so hard."

"Damn right, I am. This is going to look perfect."

When he finished, I grabbed a claw clip I had also purchased and wrapped up my dye-soaked hair.

"Your turn. Sit back down," I instructed.

Jared followed my orders.

"Last chance to back out," I warned.

"Dye me," he insisted.

I stood over him with the brush in hand, hesitating momentarily before painting the ends of his hair. I glanced down briefly to see that his eyes were on me as I worked.

"Don't look at me. I don't want to mess up."

He chuckled and continued to stare at me.

I sighed as I moved to the other side of his head. "You aren't a very good listener."

"So, I've been told."

After a few minutes, Jared's light yellow tips were covered in purple dye.

"Alright, now we wait twenty minutes before washing it out."

"Let's raid my fridge for some snacks," he said.

My stomach growled as I followed him into the living area.

"Do you want anything to drink?" he asked.

"Water is fine for me."

I took a seat at the table behind the couch and waited for him to join me. He grabbed two glasses and filled them before handing me one. He placed a bag of chips on the table before taking a handful.

"I noticed that…" he trailed off, and I looked at him expectantly.

"Noticed what?" I asked when he didn't say more.

"It seems like—like maybe you don't drink," he finally said. "You've come by Luna a few times, and you've never gotten anything other than a mocktail or a soda."

"Yeah, it's not really for me." I grabbed some chips and set them on a napkin in front of me. "It's kind of embarrassing, but it gives me the worst heartburn, so I've never really developed a liking for it."

He smiled at his feet. "That's not embarrassing. That's endearing."

"Oh yeah, real endearing. A girl in her twenties who has to carry Alka-Seltzer in her purse in case she has two sips of beer." I winced at how boring and pathetic that sounded.

He was quiet for a minute.

"I-I don't drink at all anymore," he finally admitted.

My eyebrows shot up, surprised that he seemed vulnerable and that he felt the need to share this with me.

"Well, that's not a problem," I said.

He looked out the window and chewed the bottom of his lip. "Except I did kind of have a problem."

"You don't have to tell me if you don't want to," I said hurriedly.

"No, I want to." He drummed his fingers against the table. "You know how I told you I fell in with a bad crowd after high school? Well, pretty much all we did was drink and party. I worked as a bartender then, too, at the local dive bar one of the guys owned." He looked at his hands.

"My life had no direction then. I would go work at the bar, drink, get into fights, and hang out with these guys who had lived in this town their entire lives and had no intention of ever leaving. My mom was worried about me. She begged me to move away. Start over. But I was content just pissing my life away." He hesitated. "But it all went to shit one night. I-I had been sleeping with the girlfriend of the guy who owned the bar."

My mouth hung open at his revelation. It was almost impossible to picture Jared—this nice, fun-loving guy—being so reckless.

He eyed me anxiously before looking back out the window. "Anyway, we got caught at the bar, and he started beating the shit out of me, so I had to fight back. I did some damage before the cops finally showed up and carted me off to jail. Thank god my mom called Dean. He drove down there immediately, packed a bag, and bailed my ass out of jail. He drove me to his place, and I've been in Chicago ever since."

"Wow," I managed to say when he was done. "That's a lot."

"I know," he looked ashamed, so I reached across the table and placed my hand over his. "I still drank for years after that. I had it under control for the most part. But recently, with the band taking off, I decided to quit cold turkey. I didn't want all of these late nights at bars to get the best of me again."

"I'm proud of you for turning your life around. You didn't let your past stop you from pursuing your dreams."

"I wish I didn't have all that baggage following me around, though. It's like every time I tell someone I don't drink, it's this whole thing where I have to explain everything."

"No, you don't," I insisted. "It's no one's business but your own. Telling someone 'I don't drink' is a complete sentence. You don't have to justify anything."

He glanced at me and smiled. "Thanks for saying that."

"Of course," I bit my lip. "So, what was it like that day? After the fight."

He blew out a breath, and his jaw twitched. "Honestly? It felt like rock bottom."

"It's hard to picture you like that," I admitted.

"Oh, I'll be the first to admit, I was a total piece of shit. I deserved to get the crap beaten out of me. Sleeping with my boss's girl was so stupid. I didn't even have feelings for her. She was just there. I didn't think things through at all back then."

"Was it hard to get your act together when Dean brought you here?"

Jared looked down at the table and chuckled. "Not really. He told me he would be done with me if I didn't shape up. He informed me I'd be starting at his new restaurant the next day, and if I screwed it up, that was it for us."

"Tough love," I said.

"I needed it. Once I was out here, away from all those guys and that town, it was a lot easier to start over than I thought it would be."

"I'm sure it helped having Dean."

He nodded. "Definitely. I owe him everything."

We sat in silence for a moment.

"What was it like for you?"

My eyes widened when I looked up at him.

"When I left home?" I asked.

He nodded.

I chewed my lip. "I told you how I didn't last much longer after they found my bank statement. What I didn't mention was that I only lasted hours. That night I packed a bag, and I left before sunrise. Cam and I weren't even that close back then, but his was one of the few numbers I knew by heart. When I called him from a payphone in town, he dropped everything to come pick me up."

"Wow," Jared whispered.

"He was a freshman in college then. I wasn't even technically allowed to stay there, but nobody said anything. I crashed on his floor for months trying to figure out what to do with my life."

"You went from being stuck at home all the time to a college dorm? That sounds like an intense transition."

I laughed. "Oh my god, it was. Cam could tell you so many funny stories. I almost passed out from an anxiety attack when he took me to a frat party. Of course, he thought I should dive headfirst into the experience and practically forced me to do a keg stand."

Jared tossed his head back and laughed. "I would pay money to see that."

"Let's just say it didn't go over well. My acid reflux kicked in almost immediately, and I puked on the floor. We didn't go to many parties after that."

"How did you get from there to here?"

"My videos had already started taking off, and my account was growing like crazy once I could dedicate time to it. I think I watched one too many romantic comedies during that time because I decided that I absolutely *had* to go to New York."

Jared raised his eyebrows. "Damn. You really went from zero to one hundred."

"I guess you could say all those years feeling stuck finally caught up to me. After I left for New York, I haven't stopped moving."

"Damn, Evie. You've got some major guts."

Heat flooded my cheeks. "Don't give me too much credit."

"That would be impossible," he said, leaning forward and staring at me.

The timer went off on my phone, causing us both to jump.

"Oh, it's time to rinse." My voice shook after that heavy conversation. I never opened up to anyone like this. I took a few deep breaths as Jared followed me back into the bathroom.

Thankfully his shower had one of those heads that disconnected, so it would be easier to rinse.

"Um, do you want to go first?" I asked.

"Will you do it for me?" He handed me the shower head before dropping a clean towel onto the tiled floor. He ripped his shirt off, and I raised my eyes at him in confusion.

"What? It's just going to get wet."

He slumped down and wasted no time tilting his head back.

"Um, sure. Of course." I didn't want to seem nervous at the idea of running my hands through his hair, but it did feel a little too intimate.

Jared closed his eyes and settled into the side of the tub like he was at a salon. Bringing the nozzle to his head, I began to rinse. He gave an exaggerated sigh.

"Stop it, or I'm splashing you," I informed him.

He chuckled. "You'll pay if you do that."

Purple water splashed into the tub. I combed through his hair and squeezed until the water ran clean.

"All set," I squeaked, cringing at how my voice cracked.

He opened his eyes, and before I could think twice, I moved the sprayer and got the side of his cheek.

"Oops," I said.

His grin grew bigger. "You couldn't resist, huh."

He grabbed the sprayer from my hand and gestured for me to take his seat. "Your turn," he said.

My heart felt like it was beating inside my throat.

Just pretend like this is normal, I told myself as I lowered slowly to the floor.

My mind screamed at me that this was anything but normal. That this certainly wasn't typical friend behavior. But all I could do was ignore the warning bells blaring in my head.

I tilted my head back and closed my eyes.

When Jared's hands touched my hair, I held my breath. He massaged his fingers over my head with one hand while the other held the sprayer. I wanted to melt into a puddle with how good it felt. I concentrated on taking short breaths through my nose while he worked, counting down the seconds until this was over. I contorted my face to a neutral expression that ensured I wasn't showing any sign of pleasure at his touch. After the longest two minutes of my life, he finally removed his hands.

"All done," he said.

I opened my eyes to find him hovering inches away from me. My heart skipped a beat at his proximity.

"What are you—"

Jared cut off my sentence by pointing the sprayer straight at me.

"Jared!" I screamed and jumped to my feet.

I shoved him and raced out of the bathroom.

He turned off the water and followed me into the living room, laughing. My face and shirt were soaked.

"I can't believe you did that," I said, pushing him again.

"I can't believe you didn't see it coming." He pinched my side, and I squealed. "I told you you'd pay."

I pinched his side in return, and he yelped. "Don't I'm ticklish."

A devilish grin formed on my face. "Oh, are you?"

"Evie, don't." He warned.

But it was too late. I pinched both of his sides, causing him to yelp again.

"Oh, you're dead for that."

I laughed and ran toward the couch, but he was faster than me.

He grabbed my sides and pulled me back before I could use the piece of furniture as a barrier.

He spun me around and wrapped one of his strong arms around my waist, effectively pinning me to him. With the other hand, he tickled my neck.

"Jared, please stop." I screeched with laughter. "Truce, truce."

He took his hand away from my neck.

We were both breathless from laughter. Now that we were still, I realized my soaked T-shirt was the only barrier between my body and his bare chest.

I looked up to meet his gaze. His eyes darkened as they moved from my eyes to my mouth.

I licked my lips, unable to move from this spot. Heat built between my legs, and *nothing* about Jared felt friendly in this moment.

He hesitated, his gaze locking on me. Then he tightened his grip around me and pulled me even closer. His eyes flickered to mine one more time before his mouth dipped, capturing my lips.

The kiss was slow and sweet at first, but his lips quickly grew hot and demanding as they moved over mine. I opened my mouth, and he took the opportunity to slip his tongue inside. I hoped he couldn't feel my heart racing against his chest.

Before I could think twice about what was happening, he backed up a few steps and fell onto the couch. His lips left mine for a moment before he grabbed my sides and pulled me down on top of him. Now that I straddled him, I could feel just how much he wanted me.

What are we doing?

My brain tried to reach through for a moment of clarity, but Jared started trailing kisses down my neck. I gasped as he sucked on my collarbone, and all sensible thoughts were driven out of my mind.

His fingertips moved underneath my loose T-shirt until they brushed against the bare skin above my pants. I shivered at his warm touch, and tremors of pleasure shot through my body.

I should have stood up and rushed out of there. I should have pushed him away and told him this was a bad idea. But instead, I grinded against him and arched my back, giving in to the sensation.

"Fuck, Evie," he said in a voice so gruff I barely recognized it.

His hands roamed up my body as his lips resumed exploring mine. I grabbed onto his wet hair and tangled my fingers through it to bring his mouth closer to mine.

My mind screamed at me that this was dangerous territory, but my body had completely betrayed me. I was lost in his touch and frankly wouldn't care if he took me right here and now on this couch.

I rolled my hips forward, desperate for more.

Jared groaned and, in one swift motion, swung me off of him and had me on my back. He moved on top of me, pinning me beneath him. His hand moved over my stomach. He slipped his hand underneath the loose band of my pants, and I thrust my hips up toward him, eager to give him a better angle.

At that moment, to my misery, a phone started to ring loudly. Jared's dark eyes blinked, and it was like cold water had been splashed on his face. He jerked up and wrenched his hand away from me.

I scrambled to a seated position. We were both breathing heavily.

He glanced around the room and snatched his phone off the coffee table.

"Hello," he barked, getting up and pacing the living room.

I smoothed down my wet hair and pulled down my T-shirt that had ridden up in our frenzy.

What the hell was that?

My brain yelled at me now that my composure had returned.

Jared was my friend.

I was helping his band.

I was leaving soon.

I let my head flop into my hands and shook it pathetically.

"Really?" My head sprang up at the sound of Jared's excited voice in the kitchen.

I craned my neck to find him grinning from ear to ear. It was hard to believe that shirtless body was just on top of mine. My cheeks reddened at the thought.

"This is seriously awesome," he said and walked over to me. He grabbed my shoulder and shook it excitedly.

"What?" I mouthed.

"She's with me now. I'll ask her."

He hung up the phone and launched himself over the back of the couch, plopping down next to me.

He grabbed my shoulders again and gave me a shake. "You're a genius, Eves."

"What?" I asked again.

"That was Max," he explained. "That video you just

posted—of the new song—it already has, like, one-hundred-thousand views."

I raised my eyebrows. "That's amazing." I tried to inject enthusiasm into my voice, but my mind still reeled from thoughts of what we were doing on this couch thirty seconds ago. Jared, on the other hand, seemed to have forgotten entirely already.

He leaped up from the couch again and paced around the room.

"Do you think that means it's going to go viral?"

"Um," I stuttered. "It definitely could. That many views in this short of time usually means it's gaining momentum."

"This is amazing." His body looked like it couldn't contain his energy until he glanced back at me. He must have seen something in my eyes because his smile dropped.

He ran his fingers through his hair. I caught sight of his new subtle purple ends.

"Shit, Evie. I'm sorry."

I held my breath, waiting to hear what he was sorry for.

"I shouldn't have turned this"—he gestured between the two of us— "into that." He pointed to the couch where we had nearly ripped each other's clothes off.

"It's okay." I wanted to tell him it was more than okay, but I was too chicken. Plus, did I really want to risk losing the best friend I had made in years over something like this?

Yes, you do.

He chewed his lip and looked back at me sheepishly. "You're, like, my new favorite person. I love hanging out with you. I never meant to fuck it all up like this."

"You didn't," I said quickly.

"Are you sure?" He cautiously sat back on the couch, this time giving us some distance.

"Of course. We both got caught up in the heat of the moment."

I gulped, praying my words sounded calm and collected—the exact opposite of how I felt right now.

He scratched the back of his neck and eyed me uncertainly. I gave him a small smile in return before standing.

"I should probably get going."

"You don't have to," he said.

I shook my head. "No, really, I should. I told Cam we could have a movie night."

Jared's eyebrows pulled together, but he nodded.

I stood and grabbed my sweater, pulling it on over the shirt Jared had loaned me despite it still being damp. Moving to the door, I could feel Jared at my heels, but I waited until I was safely outside his apartment before turning around.

"I have to work tomorrow night, but do you want to get breakfast in the morning?" he asked.

I bit my lip and scanned my brain for excuses. Tonight had turned me into a flustered mess, and I desperately needed some space to regroup and regain my bearings.

"Um, tomorrow? I don't think I can make it." I hoped he didn't ask for more details because I couldn't handle making something up right now.

Jared nodded. "No worries."

I breathed a sigh of relief. "Goodnight."

He gave a small wave as I backed away.

It was only later, safely seated on the train, that I allowed my hand to brush my still-tingling lips.

SEVENTEEN

Jared

The Friday night crowd always made for a busy shift at Luna. Dinner would turn into drinks, and soon enough, the place would be packed well past midnight. Before the rush ensued, I busied myself putting away glassware and wiping down the bar top.

It was admittedly tough to focus on work lately. The video Evie had posted of my new song had already reached over one million views. Since then, she had posted a few times about our show this weekend. They were all getting a ton of local engagement. If this video had given us any sort of edge, we would know for sure by how many people showed up on Saturday. It seemed like investing in Evie was about to pay off big time.

My thoughts shifted from the band to Evie. Evie in her crazy sweaters and wild hair. Evie and her kind heart and genuine zest for life. I dragged one of my hands over my face and shook my head.

What the hell had I been thinking?

I met this amazing girl who wanted to help my band and had been nothing but supportive. Of course, I had to go and screw it all up by putting my hands on her.

The reality was I hadn't given a second thought to my actions in the moment. The way my fingers grazed her skin felt instinctual—a magnetic pull I couldn't resist. Yet, as I thought back on it, my mind and my desires were clearly at odds. I hoped things wouldn't be awkward between us. I really couldn't stand the thought of losing her.

"Dude, hello?" Dean waved to get my attention.

I blinked a few times to clear my head. "Yo, D, sorry about that. What's up?"

"What were you so distracted by?" He narrowed his eyes and gave me a once-over. "And what's up with the purple hair?"

"Just—" I wracked my brain for an excuse that didn't involve him giving me a hard time about Evie. I eventually relented and pulled out my phone instead. "This video Evie posted of me has gotten a shit ton of views. This could be great for the band."

His eyebrows shot up as he grabbed my phone. He watched the video before looking back at me. "Damn, this is awesome. Nice song, by the way." He looked from the video back to me. "Evie recorded this, huh?"

"She came by last night so I could play her the song."

"She came to your apartment?"

"That's what I just said."

"That wouldn't have anything to do with your new look, would it?" he asked, pointing to my hair.

I shrugged. "You know I like to switch things up."

"It's funny." Dean had a shit-eating grin on his face that

I wanted to wipe off. "When you were deep in thought, you looked awfully concerned about something. The Jared I know would be smiling like an idiot and talking my fucking ear off about this video as soon as I walked in the door."

Damnit.

Having a best friend who had known you your entire life had its drawbacks. One of them being that you couldn't hide anything from them.

I ignored him and continued working.

"That distracted, far-off look in your eyes wouldn't have anything to do with Evie, would it?"

"Drop it, Dean," I warned. I did not want to share what had happened with Evie last night and have him read too much into it.

At that moment, Dean's business partner, Eric, and his wife, Tiff, plopped down in front of us.

"You two look deep in conversation," Eric said. "What's the deal?"

"Hi guys," Tiff smiled at us, and I set down a water with lemon slices in front of her before she even asked.

Eric was probably Dean's closest friend aside from me. And Tiff was an absolute sweetheart. They were both great people, but that didn't mean I wanted to be grilled about my personal life in front of them.

I shot Dean a warning glare to drop it. But Dean, being Dean, barely acknowledged me before turning to Eric.

"Jared is having girl problems."

I rolled my eyes. "Dean is lying to you."

But Tiff's interest had already been captivated, and she leaned in. She wanted everyone to have a happy ending, the kind that involved love at first sight and wedding bells.

When I told her about my breakup, I think she had been more upset than I was despite hardly knowing Janelle.

"You met someone?" she squealed. "I'm so happy for you. Tell me more."

I sighed. "Dean is stirring the pot. It's just a new friend who happens to be a girl. She's helping with band stuff, but that's it."

Eric lowered his eyebrows. "A friend? You don't have female friends."

He echoed the same words Dean had spoken to me the other night. What was with these guys and not minding their own business? I was thirty-one years old. I could have a female friend if I damn well wanted to.

Tiff swatted Eric's arm and glared up at him. "Stop giving him a hard time. If Jared is taking it slow with someone, that's his business."

"Oh yeah, when Al and I first got together, Jared *really* minded his own business." Dean laughed.

I smiled despite my irritation. "I had to make it my business because you were being an idiot."

"Maybe I'm trying to save you from the same fate," Dean challenged.

"Dude, I promise. If something was going on, you'd be the first to know."

"So, you haven't slept with her?" Eric asked bluntly.

My eyebrows shot up into my hairline, and my moment of hesitation was all Dean and Eric needed. They shot a glance at each other before turning back to me, smirking.

I held up my hands defensively. "I didn't," I insisted, but it was too late.

"You're lying," Eric said.

I relented and dragged my hand over my face. "Fine. Fine. I didn't sleep with her, but—something might have happened at my apartment last night."

"Knew it," Dean said victoriously.

"But it was a mistake. We both agreed it wouldn't happen again. And that's that."

"That's that?" Tiff repeated. "That's *never* that."

"I don't know why you're bothering with these excuses," Dean continued. "You know you can't hide anything from me."

I threw a bar towel at him and told him to shut it.

He was right about not being able to hide anything, but he was wrong about there being anything to hide. Just because we shared a fleeting moment last night didn't mean anything in the long run.

Our connection was more than physical—I couldn't talk to anyone like I could talk to Evie. She made opening up and being myself easy. I wanted to be around her all the time. She understood me on a deeper level. It was almost as if the universe conspired to bring us together. I wanted to—

Shit.

I hated when Dean was right.

"Did you see all those people waiting outside?" Drew said, his face beaming with excitement.

"The bouncer I talked to said it was a full house. They're having to turn people away," Max said.

"And cover is fifteen dollars. That's way more than people normally have to pay to see us."

"I think they upped it when they saw how many followers we have," I said, checking my phone again.

I had told Evie to swing by before the show, and I didn't want to miss a text from her.

I turned expectantly at the sound of footsteps, only to see a mess of black waves and tattoos standing a few inches taller than me.

"What's up, Dean," Max greeted.

I grinned at him. "Did ya see that crowd out there? It's all for me. I told you I could do it. I don't know why you ever doubted me." It was laughable because Dean was my biggest supporter, and everyone knew it.

Dean rolled his eyes. "Hope this isn't all going straight to your head."

"His head couldn't get bigger even if we were nominated for a Grammy and got a world tour," Tyler said.

"My blind confidence is what brought you all here, and don't you forget it." I grinned.

"Hey, Jared." A quiet voice behind me caused my heart to jump into my throat as I turned my head.

Evie wore a tight, plunging black shirt, revealing more skin than I was used to seeing on her. It was tucked into faded ripped denim. My pants tightened at the memory of her underneath me a few nights ago.

"Hey," I said, wrapping my arms around her. She smelled good. I resisted the urge to inhale her hair and released her. "Our savior is here."

The rest of the guys greeted her. Max even pulled her into an awkward hug. A big deal for him, considering his typical reserved demeanor.

"Hey Evie," Dean said. He smirked, looking from her fresh purple locks to my hair. I ignored him.

"Are you going to get some more videos tonight?" Drew asked.

"Definitely. We need to get one of you all playing the new song live as a full band."

I nodded. "That's perfect. We've got that one down now. I think we'll play it fifth, right in the middle of the set."

"Great." She waved her phone in one hand. "I'll be ready."

"How should we introduce ourselves?" Max asked. "We've been trying to bounce around name ideas more seriously now that we're getting followers, but we're still stuck."

Evie winced. "I hate to break this to you guys, but you can't change your name."

"What are you talking about?" I narrowed my eyes.

"You have over one-hundred-thousand followers now and growing. People recognize your name. The venue even wrote it on their website for tonight. You can't change it and risk losing all of this exposure you've gotten."

Max and I exchanged glances, still confused. "But we've never had a real name," I said.

"Oh, but you do." She shifted and scrolled through her phone before showing us the event page for the show.

There the four of us were. Standing in front of Lake Michigan, a name written in bold font above us.

The Wedding Band.

"Are you serious?" Drew groaned.

Dean chuckled.

I flinched at the name but quickly shook it off and clapped my hands. "Hey, it's no big deal. At least they know us by name. That's something."

Evie nodded. "Exactly. And it isn't so bad. Maybe it could be ironic or something."

"How could it be ironic?" Drew asked in a snarky tone.

I whipped my head around and glared at him, daring him to speak to Evie like that again. He raised his hands in surrender and backed off.

"Look," I continued. "We were never going to get off our asses and come up with a name anyway. The universe forced us into this. It's better this way. Now let's move on and go out there and play as The motherfucking Wedding Band."

Max nodded, and Drew and Tyler grumbled in the background.

I looked back to Evie, but she had her body turned away from me, talking to Dean. The sight of the two of them together spiked my anxiety. I hoped he wouldn't say anything stupid to her. Or reveal that I had told him about the kiss. The last thing I wanted was her thinking I ran my mouth off to everyone about that.

Before I could think too much about it, an older woman dressed in a black T-shirt and jeans stepped backstage. Her graying hair pulled back into a low bun was the only sign of her age. That and the smile lines she had earned through decades of laughter. My lips turned up as I raced over to sweep her into a hug.

"Mom!" I exclaimed. "You made it."

"I wouldn't miss this."

We embraced for a moment longer before I stepped back and held her at arm's length, taking in the sight of her. Even though my hometown was only hours away, we both worked a lot, and it was hard to find time for either of us to make the drive.

"Mrs. Parker," Dean said, hugging her too.

"For the last time, Dean, call me Monica."

"Old habits die hard."

"I told you to text me when you got here," I said. "One of us would have come out and walked you in."

She laughed. "As if I'm incapable of walking into a bar by myself."

I introduced her to the rest of my band before getting to Evie. Before I even said anything, my mother opened her arms and pulled Evie into a hug.

"Oh, Evie. It's so good to meet you. Jared talks about you all the time."

My eyebrows shot up, and I cleared my throat. "I wouldn't say *all* the time."

"Hopefully, it's all good things," Evie said.

"Oh, of course. He told me all about everything you've done for the band." My mom looped Evie's arm through hers and patted her hand. "You're sitting with me, right?"

"We can all sit together," Dean said. "I've got us a spot reserved by the bar."

"You should probably find your seats," Max said. "We'll be going on any minute."

"Break a leg out there," Dean said, already turning away.

"You're going to be amazing," my mom said, walking away with Evie in tow.

As I watched my oldest friend and my mother lead the girl I may or may not be infatuated with away, nerves crept into my gut.

What were they going to talk about? What would they say about me? Would they embarrass me?

Forcing the thoughts from my mind, I chose instead to focus on the only thing that mattered—killing this set.

I shot one last look toward the three of them, disappearing into the crowd.

That situation would be fine.

Hopefully…

EIGHTEEN

Evie

"I love your hair," Jared's mom said.

"Thanks, um…"

"Call me Monica."

"Right, Monica. It's so nice to meet you."

"You too." She squeezed my arm. "Is that the same color Jared had in his hair?"

"Oh uhh…yeah, i-it is," I stammered, blood rushing to my cheeks.

Her lips formed an amused smile, but she didn't ask any follow-up questions. The two of us were seated at a table with an unobstructed view of the stage. Al and Dean had gone to the bar to retrieve drinks for us all.

"It's amazing you came all the way out here tonight to see Jared play," I said, hoping I could come across as charming. Meeting mothers was not something I did often. Honestly, Cam's mom, my Aunt Renee, was the only one I knew well besides my own.

"I wouldn't miss this for the world," she said. "I'm so

impressed by everything he's doing. Can you believe all these people are here to see his band?"

As I watched Monica watch Jared set up on stage, I couldn't help but feel a pang of jealousy. I wished I could bottle the admiration and unconditional love that poured out of her gaze. Then I could save it and open it anytime I felt a wave of self-doubt.

What must it be like to have the unwavering support of a parent?

"Jared told me you make videos for a living. How exciting. I'm glad he's found a fellow creative to spend so much time with."

"Oh, my videos are nothing like what he does. He's the creative one."

She leaned over, squeezing my hand in a maternal way that felt foreign to me. "Don't sell yourself short, sweetie. You've got talent. He told me everything you've done for the band. You're the reason all these people are here."

Her eyes were so sincere I found them hard to look at. Accepting praise was challenging for me. Probably because I hadn't heard much of it my entire childhood. I had only been commended when I managed to follow orders perfectly—which admittedly wasn't often.

"Well, maybe I posted the video, but it was Jared's talent that got people here."

Her smile widened as she spun around and took in the crowd again.

"I always knew he was special. From a young age, he had so much life in him," she said. "I'm so glad he's surrounding himself with good people now. Dean has always been such a good friend to him—and now you.

Sometimes he finds people that try to dim his light. Those guys from back home—that ex of his—anyway, I can tell you're a good one. You're special."

Her blunt statement took me by surprise. I didn't feel worthy of her approval. All I did was show up and post a few things online. Jared was the special one.

"Um, did you meet his ex?" I felt guilty for asking, but my curiosity got the best of me. I still couldn't picture Jared with someone that would stifle his energy like that.

"Just once," she said. "When I came out here six months ago. They were supposed to visit me a few times, but she usually came up with an excuse."

The look she gave me told me she hadn't bought any of them.

"She was the first girl he ever introduced me to. I was excited to get to know her. But she was just fine. Perfectly polite to me, but I couldn't see it, y'know? You want to see your kid with someone that complements them and loves them for who they are. She just wanted to change him. If it were up to her, he wouldn't be playing right now."

"Anyone that thinks Jared needs to change needs to have their head examined. Your son is a great guy—he's the best."

She smiled and nudged my shoulder. "See? I knew I liked you."

"There you are. I've been looking all over for you." Cam slipped into the seat on the other side of me.

"This place is a freaking zoo. I can't believe all these people. Have you noticed it's all women in the front row? Probably hoping to get a piece of Jared after that video. You better hop on that and claim your territory—"

"Cam!" I shouted, my eyes wide with panic. "This is Monica, Jared's *mother*."

His eyes moved past me. Recognition flashed across his face before he put on his best dazzling smile and extended his hand.

"Hi Monica, I'm Cam. Evelyn is my cousin. It's so nice to meet you."

"He's the only one that calls me Evelyn," I explained.

"So nice to meet you," she said. If she had heard his comment about her son, she didn't mention it.

"Here you go," Dean said, handing Jared's mom and me a drink.

Al squeezed in on the other side of Cam as Dean and Monica caught up.

"Wow, meeting his mom already?" Cam whispered in my ear.

"Shut it," I hissed. "She came to the show, and I just happen to be sitting next to her."

"Dean did say she seems to know all about you," Al said.

I glared at her. "How is that helping?"

She shrugged. "Sorry. I was just saying. It's none of our business what's going on between you and Jared."

If only they knew that no one wanted to know what was going on between the two of us more than I did. Had Jared told Al and Dean about our kiss the other night? My cheeks burned at the thought. Cam didn't even know yet. I was too embarrassed to tell him. It didn't stop him from being suspicious, though. I looked like a disheveled mess when I arrived home from Jared's house that evening. Needless to say, he gave me quite the interrogation. I had held strong and insisted nothing happened. Whether he believed me or not was beside the point.

"I still can't believe all these people are here to see Jared's band." Al surveyed the room.

"The Wedding Band," I corrected.

"What?" Cam looked at me with a blank expression.

"That's their name. The Wedding Band."

"That's a stup—"

"Stop." I raised my hand, silencing him. "Nothing can be done about it now. And if Jared ever asks you about it, you better say you love it."

"I was going to say that's a clever name," Cam said, correcting himself.

"I love it," added Al.

I rolled my eyes. "You're both terrible liars."

"Speaking of terrible liars, are you going to tell me what *actually* happened the other night when you were at Jared's?"

I scoffed at him. "It's unbelievable that you won't let this go."

"It's only because I know you're hiding something. I know all of your tells."

My mouth hung open in offense, but he might be right about that. My voice tended to crack and shift up an octave whenever I wasn't being truthful.

Cam could probably smell the lies—and Jared—wafting off of me that night.

"Can we talk about this later?" I whispered, jerking my head to my left to remind him that Jared's mother was still seated directly next to me. Thankfully, the music blared so loudly that I doubted she could hear anything with her back facing us.

Cam grinned. He knew he had me. "I knew. I knew it."

"What did you know?" Al asked as she looked between the two of us.

"Nothing," I hissed.

"Evie and Jared," Cam said nonchalantly.

A knowing look flashed across Al's face before she adjusted it back to neutral.

Had Jared told Dean and her? And if she knew about it, how many other people had Jared told?

"What do you know?" I asked, already dreading the response.

She bit her lip and looked at me apologetically. "I'm sorry. I didn't want to know. Dean tells me everything, even when I don't ask."

Cam looked at her as if she had just committed an earth-shattering betrayal. "What do you know that you haven't told me?" he demanded.

"It's not for me to tell." She raised her hands defensively.

I groaned. "Jared and I kissed. It was nothing. And you freaking out like this is exactly why I didn't want to tell you."

"I can't believe there is this huge secret, and I'm the last one to know."

"It wasn't my business to share. Plus, Jared told Dean it was nothing," Al insisted.

Even though she was only confirming what I had said, her words still felt like a punch to my gut.

Although I said the kiss was nothing, my brain had other ideas. I hadn't been able to stop fantasizing about the night in question and what would have happened if we weren't interrupted.

But I would never admit that to anyone. Not Jared. Not Cam. Not even myself. I would die of embarrassment at the possible rejection. He did tell Dean it was nothing after all.

The crowd grew louder as Jared appeared on stage.

Monica nudged my shoulder. "He looks great up there," she said.

"Truly a natural," I agreed.

Jared shared his perfect grin with the crowd, and everyone on the floor screamed—mostly women.

"Oh great, just what his delicate ego needs," Dean said.

My lips turned up. He was right. This would surely turn the already confident Jared into a nightmare. An adorable, cocky, endearing nightmare.

Jared found our group in the crowd and nodded his head. Maybe it was my overreactive imagination, but I swear he locked eyes with me and winked. My cheeks reddened, and I ducked my chin, grateful there was no way he could see me blushing from the stage.

As the band started and the crowd's energy rose, I let myself get lost in it. My eyes drifted shut as I felt the bass reverberating off of every surface.

When Jared started to play his new song, I ripped myself back into reality and grabbed my phone to record it. His voice moved beautifully over the lyrics as the whole crowd dipped into silence. Every time he glanced in my direction, my stomach did a little flip. I told myself he knew I'd be recording, and that was the only reason he kept looking at me.

With barely an interlude, Jared played the last note of the original song before launching into an upbeat cover. Cam and Al grabbed my shoulders and started jumping around, singing loudly.

By the end of their set, I was breathless, and my whole body felt animated.

Even after countless cities, new faces, and experiences, this was the most fun I could ever remember having.

NINETEEN

Jared

I ADDRESSED MY APPEARANCE IN THE BATHROOM MIRROR. Dark circles had made permanent residence underneath my eyes, and my hair stuck up in that unruly way it always did. I turned on the faucet and splashed cool water against my hot skin, trying to feel a bit more human before the band had to go on.

These past few weeks were a whirlwind of new followers and larger venues. The band was gaining momentum faster than a runaway train. We had been invited to open for a band passing through on their tour tonight. Shadow Banned was huge nationally, and this was by far our biggest opportunity yet.

I grabbed a fistful of paper towel to dry my face. While the band's success had me absolutely elated, these long nights of consecutive shows, and relentless practice, were wearing me down. Finding time to sleep had not been a priority.

A knock sounded at the door.

I heard the click of the knob before turning around to face Evie.

Anytime she walked into a room, my lips turned up like a magnet. She came to all of our shows, and finding her face in the crowd always gave me a surge of energy. After I almost blew it kissing her, we haven't had another…incident.

Unfortunately for me, just because it hadn't happened again didn't mean I hadn't stopped thinking about my mouth on hers. It was the first thing that flashed through my mind every time I saw her.

"Hey." She smiled at me, and I pulled her in for a hug. "This is so official. They even gave me a backstage pass and everything." She held up the laminated badge with pride.

I chuckled and ruffled her hair. "You would get excited over that."

"You're telling me you're not excited? You're opening for a freaking nationally touring band. This is amazing."

I shrugged, pretending to be nonchalant. My smirk gave me away, though. I was indeed extremely pumped to be here tonight. If only my teenage self could see me now. He wouldn't believe it.

"Are you going to watch from backstage?" I needed to make sure I knew where to find her in the crowd.

"I think so. I'll be able to get some good shots back here." She held up her camera.

"Perfect." I nodded. "After the show, we can go out and celebrate."

"I heard Max say something about hitting up a bar."

I shook my head. The guys had been going out a lot lately. I couldn't blame them, especially since they weren't overdoing it. I enjoyed going with most of the time, but tonight I needed a break.

"Let's go someplace, just the two of us. I can't deal with the bar scene tonight."

"Of course. We can do whatever you want."

"Navy Pier?" I teased. "Or something equally cheesy."

She laughed. "I was thinking maybe the top of the Willis Tower."

"Sears Tower," I corrected her.

"That's not the name."

"Yes, it is." I pinched her side, and she yelped with laughter right as Max walked in.

"Oh, sorry, man. Didn't mean to interrupt."

"You're not interrupting anything," I said.

"We're on in five."

I saluted Evie on my way out. "See you later, Eves. Take a picture that will make me look like a rockstar."

She rolled her eyes and followed us out to the main backstage area.

"We're up." Max smacked my back, and the four of us walked onto the stage. The hot lights beat down on my face from above as I squinted out into the sea of people. Cheers erupted when we picked up our instruments. Adrenaline ripped through me at the sound.

I glanced at Max, and we grinned at each other. To think we had only started playing together less than two years ago, and here we were. People knew us by name—albeit not a name we chose, but it still felt fucking incredible.

"Good evening, Chicago. You all look beautiful tonight."

More cheers. I smiled while they dissipated. It should

come as a surprise to no one that I loved flirting with the crowd.

"We're The Wedding Band. I hope you don't mind if we play you a few songs."

As soon as the cheers diminished, I counted down the guys before we launched into our first song.

"That was epic." Tyler all but bounced off the stage with glee.

Drew grabbed his shoulders, and they shook each other excitedly. "I can't believe they wanted an encore—we aren't even the headliner."

I used my T-shirt to wipe the beads of sweat off my forehead. We had sounded great up there, and we all knew it.

"Great job, guys," Derek, the lead singer of Shadow Banned, sauntered over to us. "That was a tight set."

"Thanks, man," I said. "We're excited to watch you guys play."

"We've got two more shows coming up in the Midwest in the next couple of weeks. Detroit and Indy. Wouldn't be too far of a drive for you guys if you would consider opening for us again."

"Are you fucking serious?" Drew looked about as eager as a dog that just had a raw steak set in front of him.

I smacked his chest and gave him a side-eye to be cool.

"That would be sick. Let us check our schedules," I replied.

Derek nodded at us all before leaving to prepare for his set.

"I don't know what's on my schedule, but I can tell you I'll clear whatever it is to play those shows," Max said.

"Same." I nodded. "I didn't want to seem too desperate, though."

Even though I had been playing music since I was a teenager, Max had been chasing the band dream a lot longer than I had. He had already been in a few failed groups before the two of us met. I'm sure being this close to success was tantalizing for him.

The bouncer approached me and leaned down. "This girl is trying to get backstage. She says she knows you."

Had Evie lost her backstage pass?

I glanced behind him and saw the only person that could wipe the smile clean off my face.

"Janelle?" I exclaimed.

She bit her lip and gave a small smile. I wasn't used to seeing her uncomfortable like this.

"Hi," she finally said.

"Shit," Drew muttered.

"We'll give you two some space," said Max, his eyebrows had almost completely disappeared into his hairline.

I pinched the bridge of my nose as the guys walked away.

A hand clasped my shoulder, and Drew whispered in my ear, "Don't let her drag you back down."

We exchanged a nod before I walked over to my ex. She wore a skintight black dress that hugged her in all the right places. The same one I had complimented her on a thousand times before. She knew it was my favorite.

"What the fuck are you doing here, Janelle?"

"Hi to you too," she said, folding her arms across her chest.

I sighed. "I'm sorry, I didn't realize we were doing the whole pleasantries thing."

Her bottom lip jutted out. "Please don't be like this, Jared. I just want to talk."

Shaking my head, I glanced back at the guys. I couldn't think of anything I wanted to do less than talk to my ex-girlfriend right after the biggest show we had played to date.

"Just give me a few minutes," she pleaded.

"Fine."

She looked up at me with darting eyes. It was clear she wasn't used to me being this short with her. When we were together, I was the definition of patience. Now that I didn't have to fake it, there was no point in being anything more than civil.

"Is there somewhere quieter we can talk?"

I gestured to the emergency exit that led out into the alley. "After you," I said.

"Jared?"

"What?" I snapped, turning around.

Evie's eyes rounded like saucers at my harsh tone as she glanced from me to Janelle. "Oh, I'm sorry I didn't mean to interrupt." She spun around and headed for the door.

I grabbed her hand to stop her. "Shit, I'm sorry." I dragged my other hand over my face. "I didn't mean to snap like that. I'm a little frustrated right now."

She forced a smile, but her gaze remained fixed on the camera she held.

"It's totally fine," she said in a shaky tone as she glanced up at Janelle before quickly lowering her eyes. "I actually think I'm going to head out. I didn't realize how tired I was."

"Aren't we hanging out after the show?"

"You seem busy," she muttered.

My eyebrows knit in confusion as I examined her face.

"Jared. Are you coming?"

I whipped my head around. "One second."

As I turned back to Evie's fallen face, recognition dawned on me. Had she thought I was leaving with some random girl?

"That's *Janelle*," I hissed, throwing my thumb behind me.

Her mouth hung open slightly before she snapped it shut. "Oh," she said.

"She wants to talk."

Evie nodded but didn't say anything.

"I'm just going to see what she has to say." For some reason, I felt like I had been caught doing something I wasn't supposed to.

"You should," she said.

"Will you stick around?"

She bit her lip. "I-I'm sorry. I really am tired." Her voice cracked as she forced the fakest yawn I had ever seen. "Can we catch up later this week?"

My chest tightened. Even though my head screamed at me to beg her to stay, I just nodded.

She gave me a small wave as she retreated. I turned back to Janelle, now finding her presence even more irritating than I had five minutes ago.

Walking past her, I shoved through the door and turned to her, raising my hands exasperatedly.

"Alright, Janelle. What's up? What have you come to say

—on a huge night for my band, I might add. Your timing is impeccable."

"Please." She grabbed my arm. "I didn't come here to fight. I just wanted to support you guys. When I saw—"

I laughed bitterly. "Now you want to support us? Now that we have a little bit of success, you figured you'd stop on by and—what? Congratulate us? Appreciate the thought, but it's really not necessary."

She shook her head. "It's not like that. When I saw that your video blew up, I was excited for you. I know how much you've always wanted this."

"And I know how much you never wanted me to have it."

Her eyes brimmed with tears, and I sighed. It wasn't like me to lose my cool, but seeing her here after such a high point in my life had completely killed my buzz. I wanted to go back in there and be with people who actually supported me.

"I-I'm sorry. I know toward the end, maybe, I was a little fed up. But you can't say that I wasn't supportive. I used to go to all your shows."

I crossed my arms and shook my head. "Yeah, when we were brand new, and you wanted me to like you. As soon as we got serious you stopped showing up."

"I just—"

"You begged me to quit the band every chance you got. It's literally why we broke up."

Her tears began to fall, and I had to turn away. How was it possible that, even after being apart for months, she still found a way to ruin this moment for me?

"I messed up, okay?" She wiped her eyes. "You were

such an amazing boyfriend. I should have realized it when I had you."

"Yes, you should have."

She took another step forward and grabbed my arm—a move that used to work on me but now caused the hair on my arms to bristle.

"Please give me another shot. I'll never bring up you getting a real job again. I'll go to all of your shows. I'll never start a pointless fight."

I shook my head, still in disbelief she had the audacity to come here and throw this all on me. She must have taken my silence as hesitance because she stepped even closer so that our bodies were touching.

"I love you," she whispered. "Please give us another chance."

I tilted my head up and looked at the sky. It took everything in me not to laugh in her face.

"Frankly, Janelle, I can't think of anything I want to do less than get back together."

My words caused her mouth to hang open as she stumbled backward.

"But—"

"But nothing. We were shit together. The only reason you're even here tonight is because you saw my band was doing well, and you—I don't know—wanted to jump on the bandwagon. *Literally*."

"That isn't it." She shook her head rapidly.

"Well, whatever it is, it doesn't matter. Us ending was the best thing that could've happened for me."

She opened and closed her mouth a few times before sniffling.

"Is that it then?" I asked in a tone that didn't hold any sympathy.

"Why are you being so cold?" she whispered.

"Because I'm not the pushover you think I am," I scoffed. "You could have tried to talk to me at any point since we've broken up, but you haven't. You chose the biggest day for my band, and you waltzed in here wearing some dress you thought I would like to try to manipulate me into feeling something. Sorry to break it to you but you have no effect over me."

"Jared, I—"

"Can you please just go?" I asked, my voice completely defeated. "I want to go back in there and be present, not sit out here with the past."

She choked out a goodbye as she spun on her heel and hurried away down the back alley.

The night air felt less suffocating after her departure. I sucked in a breath, relishing it. Closure hadn't been on my mind before our conversation, but it had been liberating to get that off my chest.

To finally let her know how I really felt.

I clenched my fist, thinking how I wished it could have happened on any other night. It pissed me off even more that her presence seemed to have scared away the one person I wanted to celebrate with the most.

TWENTY

Evie
___

Don't cry. Don't cry. Don't cry.

The train car bustled with people heading out for the night. Meanwhile, I couldn't get home fast enough.

I felt stupid for these emotions that coursed through me. Why was I even upset? Because Jared was talking to his ex-girlfriend? He had every right to do so, and he certainly hadn't seemed pleased about it. His pained expression flashed through my mind. I had absolutely no reason to run off or be upset right now. Still, seeing his ex—how gorgeous she was—immediately triggered my inferiority complex.

I pinched the tight gray shirt I had carefully picked out for the evening. It was a far cry from my typical brightly colored wardrobe. I had hoped Jared might think it looked nice, but after seeing Janelle, I realized I could never compete. That wasn't—and would never—be me.

I would always be the type of girl who crocheted her sweaters and didn't care that nothing matched. Pretending to be someone I wasn't just for a guy made me feel uncomfortable and dirty.

God, I felt like such an idiot.

A few tears escaped, and I wiped them away.

Jared didn't owe me anything, and it was completely irrational to feel this way.

All the logical thoughts buzzing inside my brain were doing nothing to quell the pit in my stomach.

The train finally screeched to a halt at my stop, and I bolted out of the car. A light, brisk wind whipped through the warm night. I wrapped my arms around myself as I walked as fast as my legs would carry me. Two blocks and one elevator ride later, I unlocked the door to Cam's apartment.

Cam looked up from the couch, and my face crumpled as soon as we locked eyes.

He jumped up, his eyebrows knit with concern. "What's wrong?"

The kind tone of his voice caused the dam blocking my tears to burst.

"I'm such an idiot," I said, wiping my eyes.

"Here." He reached onto the counter and grabbed a few tissues before handing them to me. "Sit and tell me what happened," he said, guiding me to the couch.

"Nothing happened."

He dipped his chin and raised his eyebrows. "Obviously not. Tell me."

"No, seriously, nothing happened. I'm so mad at myself for crying right now."

"Fine, then describe the night to me, and we can get to the bottom of why you're upset."

I took a deep breath. "Jared s-said he wanted to hang out with me after the show. Their band killed it, and I took some awesome pictures. After their s-set I went backstage to talk to Jared, but…"

"But what?" he encouraged.

"But he was talking to his ex," I spat out. "Who—thank you for telling me—is absolutely gorgeous."

Cam rolled his eyes. "I've only met her in passing, but I know she's got nothing on you."

I gestured to my flat chest. "I can promise you she's got a lot on me."

"Oh, whatever." He waved off my concern. "What happened next?"

"I left."

His face hardened. "Because they looked like they were getting cozy?"

"No, Jared looked pretty annoyed she was there."

Cam sat back and stared at me. "Did he ask you to leave?"

"He asked me to stay."

"Then why are you crying right now?" Cam asked, clearly exasperated.

"You should have seen how good she looked." I sniffed.

"Oh my god. You're impossible. So, you let your self-consciousness get the best of you, and you just left?"

I curled my legs underneath me and pulled a blanket over the outfit that wasn't at all me. "I felt stupid," I whispered. "For thinking I fit in with them—with him."

"Evelyn, look at me."

I sulkily lifted my chin to meet my cousin's eyes.

"There's no such thing as fitting in. All you can do is be yourself and stick with people that mesh with you—and let me tell you, you mesh with Jared. Whatever this weird thing the two of you have going on, it works. Don't let any feeling tell you otherwise."

"We're just friends." The words tasted sour in my mouth.

He gave me another look. "Would you really be this upset right now if you just thought of him as a friend?"

"We can't be anything more," I whispered before blowing my nose loudly into the tissue. "Ugh, what's the matter with me? I never get like this with guys."

"No offense, but the guys you normally gravitate toward want to go out for dinner at four pm and then go home and play a rousing game of Rummy. They've been dull, forgettable, and replaceable. Exactly what you prefer so you don't miss them when you inevitably decide to move on."

I leaned my head against his shoulder, hating that he was right.

"Jared is different," he continued. "He's exciting, fun, adventurous. His personality is electric. You're drawn to him, and maybe it started out as a friendship, but you're definitely feeling more now."

"Shit." I groaned. "What am I going to do?"

He shrugged. "Tell him?"

"Cam!" I balked. "I'm obviously not doing that."

"Why not?"

"Because I'm not a masochist. He's focused on his band right now, and I'm not here for much longer. Why would I put myself out there just to get rejected? I can already picture that look in his eyes when he lets me down gently. I basically already saw it after we made out. I am not going there again."

Cam shrugged. "Maybe you'll get over it then. It's just a crush, after all."

"Right. It's just a crush. I can get over that."

"Of course," Cam said in a tone that implied he didn't believe me.

"I can," I insisted.

"Not if you keep hanging out with him the way that you have been."

"Then I won't," I resolved. "I'll help out with stuff for the band, and that's it. No more hanging out just the two of us."

"If you say so."

RAP RAP RAP

"Who is knocking at this ungodly hour?" Cam poked his head out of the bedroom and glared at the door. "And how did they get past the doorman?"

I yawned and stretched my arms over my head. We never did get around to buying an air mattress, but Cam's couch was oversized and comfortable.

"Maybe it's the neighbor."

"I don't talk to my neighbors." Cam stalked through the living room and toward the door before glancing through the peephole.

He spun around and crossed his arms. "It's for you."

My eyes went wide. "Me?"

"So much for keeping your distance," he grumbled before storming past me.

I jumped off the couch. "Who—"

"Tell him never to knock at this hour again," Cam said before slamming his door.

I winced at the bang before swinging the front door open. Jared stood there in a gray sweatshirt. A backward baseball cap sat on his head, and the ends of his hair by his face curled up underneath it. How did he look perfect despite what must have been a late night after his show?

Looking down, I realized I still had on my rattiest pajamas. My hand jumped to my hair to smooth it down as much as possible. As I stood there, growing increasingly flustered, he just grinned and leaned against the doorframe.

"Morning, Eves."

"What are you doing here?" I asked.

He shrugged. "Can I take you to breakfast?"

I peeked my head around the person in front of me to count the number of bodies in this line.

"There's no way these donuts are worth it."

He smiled. "They aren't."

"Then why are we here?"

"Are you saying you're too good for something touristy?" He clutched his chest. "You're breaking my heart."

I laughed despite my grogginess. "Oh, I'm sorry, I didn't realize that's what this was. That changes everything. I must have one of these donuts."

We shuffled as the line moved forward. Jared swayed next to me with his hands buried deep in his pockets.

"So, I was hoping after this you could show me the photos from yesterday."

"Oh—uh, sure. If you want to."

"I do." He glanced over at me. "I wanted to see them last night, but you ran off so fast..."

I gulped as his voice trailed off. "Sorry about that. I was exhausted."

"You mentioned that."

Glancing up, I was met with his hazel eyes staring back down at me. Something about the cloudy day and his gray sweatshirt made them appear an almost sage color.

"Well, it's true."

"It wouldn't have anything to do with Janelle, would it?"

"Of course not," I scoffed a little too quickly.

He blew out a breath. "It just seemed like you ran off in a hurry last night. I was worried you were upset."

I shook my head rapidly. "No, of course not."

Hopefully, Jared couldn't detect my lie. There was no way in hell I could admit that seeing him with his ex had affected me so much.

"Just so you know, that's completely over. She showed up out of nowhere."

Hearing the edge in his tone caused the sick feeling in my stomach to fade away. He really hadn't been happy about seeing her.

"You don't have to talk about it. It's none of my business."

Jared fiddled with the back of his baseball cap as we moved forward a few paces in line.

"I like talking to you, though."

My heart did a little backflip at his simple, sincere words.

"Something else happened last night," Jared continued. "That band asked us to play a few more shows with them."

"Jared!" I exclaimed, turning to face him. "That's amazing."

His smile widened. "It is, right? We talked some more after the show and got most of the details worked out."

"Oh my god, you deserve it. That set was perfect last night."

He smirked. "You like watching us play, eh?"

I lightly shoved his shoulder. "Don't let it go to your head, but yes, you guys are great."

"I was hoping you'd say that because I wanted to ask you something."

I raised my eyebrows.

"Any chance you'd be down for a one-night trip to Indy next week?"

"Indy?" I chewed my lip. The excitement I felt for him had quickly dissolved into nerves. Going on an overnight trip with Jared's band wasn't exactly keeping my distance.

"Please, Eves?" He clasped his hands together and looked at me pleadingly. "The band needs you."

I couldn't help but laugh at his dramatics. "You guys hardly need me."

"We do, though."

Technically I had never been to Indianapolis, and it would be absurd for me to turn down a trip to a city I had never been to.

"I guess I can make it work."

He grinned, grabbing my shoulders and squeezing. "You're the best."

We took a few steps forward in line. Even though there must have been fifty people in front of us when we arrived, the line moved quickly. We were already almost at the door.

Jared whistled to fill the silence. "So, what's new with you? I feel like all we ever do is talk about some jackass's stupid band."

"Nothing, really. I'm a little behind on posting videos, so planning to crank out some editing this week."

"I watched your latest video. Really liked what you did with the yard."

My cheeks flushed. "Th-thanks. I didn't realize you were following me now."

He chuckled. "I may or may not have watched all of your videos."

"All of them?" My heart skipped as I snuck a glance at him. "That's impossible. There are hundreds."

He just shrugged. "What can I say? I can't get enough of you."

His comment had me completely tongue-tied. I remained silent as I tried to do the mental math of how many hours he would have had to spend to watch all of my videos. Thank god I had archived some of my older, more embarrassing ones.

We finally approached the counter, which saved me from responding. Donuts every color of the rainbow lined the glass display cases.

"Whatever your heart desires. It's on me," Jared said.

"I'll have a pistachio."

Jared ordered one with chocolate frosting. The worker handed us the pastries and two coffees before we stepped away from the counter.

"I can't believe you had all those delicious options, and you chose a green, nut-flavored donut," Jared said, holding open the door for me.

"Pistachio is the best flavor." As if to demonstrate, I took a giant bite. My eyes drifted close as the sugary donut melted in my mouth. "Okay, this might be a silly tourist trap, but it's freaking delicious."

"Even more delicious when you get a good flavor."

I rolled my eyes. "Have you ever even tried pistachio? You must not know what you're missing."

Jared leaned down and took a bite of the donut in my hand before I could protest.

"Hey!" I shouted, laughing.

He chewed and shifted his narrowed gaze to the sky as if deep in thought. "Hmmm. You might have been right about this one. Not the best flavor"—he held up his chocolate one—"but still pretty good."

I leaned forward to try to sneak a bite of his, but he pulled away.

"Hey, no fair. A bite for a bite."

He chuckled and held out his donut. "Fine, but only because it's you."

TWENTY-ONE

Jared

THE LAST OF THE PATRONS LINGERED BY THE FRONT AS THE cool air rushed through the open doorway of Luna.

"Have a good night," I called to them as they waved goodbye.

Dean came around from behind the bar where he was wiping down glasses.

"Feels like forever since I've had a closing shift," I said as I finished cleaning the last table.

"You've been busy."

The kitchen door flung open, and the chef for the night stuck her head out.

"You two want any pasta to take home?"

"Yes, please," we both replied simultaneously.

She retreated back into the kitchen, and I sighed. "I feel bad I haven't been here, though. I'm hardly pulling my weight as the lead bartender."

Dean arched an eyebrow. "That's not a real title."

"Everyone looks up to me."

"Do they?"

"Yes. I know it's been hard on morale with me never here anymore."

Dean rolled his eyes. "I think everyone is doing just fine."

"If you say so." I paused. "For real, though, man. I'm sorry I haven't been around much. I don't want you to think I'm blowing this job off."

Dean waved off my comment. "Don't even worry about it. I'd much rather your band blow up, and you never have to work here again."

"Wouldn't that be something?"

"You're on track. Doesn't seem so far-fetched at this point."

My lip turned up. "I guess you're right."

He clasped his hand on my shoulder. "I'm happy for you, man. You deserve it."

"Thanks, D."

I took a seat at one of the tables while Dean moved to the register to close it out. He had always been there for me. He had seen me through my absolute worst times and hadn't given up on me. Now I owed him everything, and he couldn't care less. Instead of making me feel guilty for neglecting the bar, all he wanted was for me to succeed. It truly was an unconditional friendship. To think we had once been kids together, riding our bikes and dreaming about the day we'd finally grow up and escape. If it wasn't for Dean I never would have.

I flashed back to that day Dean had bailed me out of jail. Still drunk and coming down from a high, I had groaned when the bailiff told me he was there to pick me up. Dean had been vocal in the past about not liking the path I was headed down, and I dreaded the impending lecture. Instead of yelling, I was met with silence and a hard expression. We didn't speak at all as I followed him to his car. When I got in, I immediately noticed piles of shit in the backseat.

"Are you moving or something?" I had asked.

"No, but you are," he said, already driving away in the opposite direction of my mother's house.

"What the fuck are you talking about?"

I still remember the glare he leveled me with.

"You're staying with me. You're going to work in my restaurant. You're going to get your shit together." His cold tone had left no room for arguing, but I still tried.

"What the hell are you talking about, man? I'm not moving to Chicago. I live here."

"Right. Seems like you've got a lot going for you."

"You don't know—"

"Jared, shut the hell up. I just bailed you out of jail. You're still drunk, and you look like shit. You're moving in with me. End of discussion. I'm not watching my best friend piss his life away anymore. You're better than this."

Even though he had said those words to me many times before, and after that car ride, I had never believed him. But now I knew them to be true.

Dean stepped in front of me, shaking me from my memories. He stuffed his hands in his pockets and shuffled his feet. His mouth parted before he snapped it shut again.

"What?" I narrowed my eyes.

"Nothing. Nothing." He sucked in a breath. "I was just going to ask how it's been being around all that partying."

It was almost as if he could read my mind at this point.

"It's fine," I said.

"Really?" I didn't appreciate his unconvinced tone, but I knew it came from a place of concern.

"Yes, really. I haven't been drinking, if that's what you're asking. And me being out with my band is hardly the same as the crowd I used to hang around with. This is harmless compared to that."

"I know it's not the same but…" His voice trailed off. "I just don't want you to get caught up in old habits."

I rolled my eyes. "I appreciate the concern, but it's not necessary. I'm the best I've ever been."

He nodded before throwing out casually, "Evie seems to have had a pretty big effect on you."

"What's that supposed to mean?"

"I just noticed that you aren't bringing a new girl home every night anymore."

"That has nothing to do with Evie," I snapped. In truth, it had everything to do with her. I hadn't realized I wasn't bringing girls home because I didn't even think about other girls with her around.

"Come on, Jared, I'm not an idiot."

I sighed. "Look, we've talked about this. I've got my hands full with band stuff, and she's leaving soon. We don't make any sense."

"Just because you don't make sense doesn't mean you can turn off your feelings."

My stomach felt hollow. I knew he was right, but what could I do about it?

Nothing. Nothing was the answer.

I would just enjoy her friendship while she was still here. Unfortunately for me, the thought of her leaving weighed on me like a thousand pounds.

TWENTY-TWO

Evie

I pursed my lips and looked down at my phone. Jared had texted me again. We were still communicating about band stuff, but I was trying to keep it as quick and casual as possible. He had asked me to hang out twice this week, and I had blown him off. I felt guilty for making up an excuse both times, but I feared the more time we spent together, the harder it would be to bottle up my true feelings.

> Jared: You busy tonight?
>
> Evie: Yep! Bad TV night with Cam, Al, and Nora.
>
> Jared: Hang out after?
>
> Evie: Need to catch up on editing, sorry!

Ignoring him made my stomach turn over, but what were my other options? Clearly, I had little self-control where he was concerned.

"What's that pout for?" Cam asked as he flung himself onto the couch.

"Nothing," I said before stashing my phone in my pocket.

"Can we start the show?" Al asked. "I need to see how the fight over that guy pans out."

As Cam switched on the TV, we nestled comfortably into the couch, our eyes glued to the cheap entertainment. A wave of contentment washed over me.

Meeting new people throughout my travels had never been an issue for me. I enjoyed the casual friendships I got to try out in every new city. But now—surrounded by my closest family member and his friends—I felt a sense of belonging that I hadn't felt in years. Maybe ever. To have friends with whom I could share moments like this. To simply call them up and unwind on the couch together, watching silly movies. I hadn't even realized my life was lacking this.

I had to admit I liked this comfortable feeling. Maybe even more than traveling.

We continued to watch the show, laughing, and talking through most of the episode.

"That was so good," Nora said when it ended.

"I can't stop watching," Al agreed.

"Couldn't convince Sean to come watch with us like old times?" Cam asked.

Nora laughed. "I think he was always too afraid to admit this to you, but he hates these shows."

Cam gave a look of mock horror. "I feel betrayed."

"Dean is the opposite," Al said. "I think he's gotten so into this show that whenever I come here to watch it, he's disappointed we're not watching it together. I swear, when I left earlier, he and Jared were on the verge of asking if they could join."

My ears perked up at the sound of Jared's name, but I tried my best to keep my face collected.

"Speaking of Jared, it's unbelievable how big his band is getting," Cam said.

"He's so pumped about it." Al nodded. "I swear, Evie, all he does is talk about how great you are and how happy he is that the band has you."

"Oh, really? That's nice." My cheeks flushed. "I'm sure they would have gotten here eventually without my help."

"No way," Al insisted. "You were helping them for two seconds, and now they're opening for a nationally touring band. That's huge."

"Yeah, don't sell yourself short, Evie." Nora squeezed my arm. "You're crushing it."

"Okay, okay." I grinned. "Thank you. I'll take the compliments. Anything else you want to say about me? Do you like my style? My winning personality?"

"I did want to tell you that I like your new hair." Al smirked.

Cam chuckled. "It's weird. It kind of seems like it's the same color as Jared's new purple ends."

I glared at him and Al.

Nora raised her eyebrows as she looked between the three of us. "Why does it feel like I'm missing something?"

"You're not," I said hurriedly.

"Jared and Evie are a thing," Cam said. "She dyed his hair."

"Oh, how cute," Nora gushed at the same time I told Cam to shut up.

Al and Nora shot each other a knowing look.

"It isn't like that," I insisted.

"He does talk about you a lot," Al said.

I shook my head. "We're just friends." The words felt robotic and forced coming out of my mouth.

"You sure you don't like him?" Nora asked.

"Come on," Al encouraged. "We're your friends. You can talk to us. I swear on my life, none of this will get repeated to Dean or Jared."

My heart swelled a little at her words. I hadn't talked with friends over boy troubles since—since ever. While I absolutely did not want to discuss our confusing situation, the thought of telling them exactly how I felt without holding back sounded absolutely cathartic.

"I like him." I groaned. "I don't want to, but I do."

"Obviously." Cam rolled his eyes. "Have you seen him?"

"It's not just that." I chewed the inside of my cheek. "He's so endearing and full of life. It feels good to be around him."

Al nodded. "That's Jared. He's got a way of making everyone he cares about feel special."

"Exactly, and I know I'm leaving soon and that he just sees me as a friend, but it's hard not to have a crush on him when he's being all flirty and easy to talk to all the time."

"Right, and him making out with you on his couch didn't help anything," Cam added.

Nora gasped. "What? I'm behind a few chapters."

"We kissed once at his apartment before we both agreed it shouldn't happen again. But of course, I haven't been able to stop thinking about it."

"Who could blame you," Nora said.

"But it's pointless," I insisted. "We would be fated to

end things in a month. Why ruin what could be an awesome friendship? If we started something and ended it before I left, there's no way I could go back to just being friends with him."

Al smiled at me sympathetically. "That is complicated, but if it makes you feel any better, I think this whole thing is torturing Jared too. He obviously can't stop thinking about you. When I told him I was coming here tonight, he tried to be casual, but he kept asking me how you were doing and if I knew what you've been up to this week."

"Ugh, I've been avoiding him. I tried not to make it obvious."

"Oh, he's definitely noticed, and he's sweating."

Al's admittance caught me by surprise.

"See? I told you he's got it just as bad as you." Cam sat up and leaned in closer to us. "No offense, Al, but if you blew me off for a week, I wouldn't give a shit."

Nora laughed. "Yes, you would."

"Okay, you're right. I would. But Jared and Evie just met, and it's not like she hasn't been texting him about the band."

"It doesn't matter." I got up from the couch and started to collect the bowls and glasses we had been using. "It's just a dumb crush. It will pass."

"Well, your dumb crush won't stop texting you." Cam held up my phone, and I dropped the dishes back onto the coffee table.

"Give me that." I snatched my phone away and glared at him.

> Jared: Are you still coming to Indy? We really need you there.

I groaned. "I told him I'd go to their Indianapolis show."

The thought of going with them had been stressing me out ever since Jared mentioned it. I would have to drive up with the band and stay at the same hotel as them. It would be more time than I'd spent with Jared in a week.

Cam shrugged. "At least you get to check out a new city."

"You were the one that told me to avoid him!" I exclaimed.

"What can I say? I thrive off the drama."

I rolled my eyes. "Whatever, I'll just avoid any alone time with Jared, and this should be no problem."

TWENTY-THREE

Jared

I drummed my fingers on the steering wheel and snuck another glance at Evie. Her window was down, and she leaned against the frame with her head resting on her arm. We were forty minutes into the drive to Indy, and she hadn't said much. She seemed closed off for some reason. I never found myself at a loss for words, but at this moment, I couldn't come up with anything.

"We got an email from this pretty big indie record label," I finally said.

She looked over at me with wide eyes. "Seriously? What did it say?"

"They want to talk to us about recording our songs."

She smiled and leaned over the center console. "Jared, that's amazing. Why didn't you tell me earlier?"

"I've been dying to tell you, but I wanted to do it in person."

Her smile faltered. "I'm sorry. I guess I've been a little busy this week."

"Haven't been avoiding me, have you?" I grinned and

looked over at her, fully expecting her to laugh at the ridiculous notion.

"W-what? Of course not." Her voice cracked, and my smile dropped. My forehead creased as I stared at the road ahead.

Why did it sound like she was lying?

The thought of her purposefully ignoring me stirred something deep inside my gut. Frustration ripped through me, and I wrapped my hands tighter around the steering wheel.

"What have you been up to this week?" I asked. I kept my tone even, trying to pretend there wasn't a war raging inside my mind.

"Oh-um. Just a few things here and there. Did a lot of filming and editing. I want to build up my backlog so I can take a small break when I start my trip. Oh, and I crocheted a new cardigan too." Her voice sounded shaky as she rambled on.

I bit the inside of my lip harder as each excuse floated past her mouth. I wasn't an idiot. None of those things would keep her so busy that she couldn't hang out with me at least one of the times I had asked her.

Why would she be avoiding me?

To distract myself, I snuck a glance at her. Her purple hair was pulled back into a ponytail, and she wore a cream long-sleeved sweater with brown and red leaves patchworked haphazardly onto it.

"That it?" I asked. My voice came out gruff, so I cleared my throat.

She raised her eyebrows. "What?"

"The sweater?"

She looked down at herself. "Oh, yeah, it is. I totally forgot I put it on."

"Nothing says 'I'm traveling with a band' like a freshly crocheted sweater."

Her face fell. "I brought something else to wear to the show."

"Shit, sorry. I didn't mean it like that. I love all your clothes." I mentally kicked myself for sounding like such an ass. "You wouldn't be you without them."

I fidgeted with the radio dial, trying to find some music to distract me. Being alone with Evie had never felt awkward like this. Typically, I couldn't stop talking in her presence. Now it felt like everything I said was wrong.

"Is everything okay?" I asked.

"Yeah. Why wouldn't it be?"

Her gaze was fixated on the passing landmarks outside her window.

"You just seem a little quiet is all."

Please talk to me, Eves.

"I'm just tired. I think I'm going to nap the rest of the way if that's okay."

"Of course," I mumbled.

A solid knot had formed in my stomach. She closed her eyes, and I tried my best to keep my mind on the show tonight.

I untangled a particularly challenging wire as Drew and Tyler jumped into the van to grab pieces of the drum kit.

"Can I help with anything?" Evie asked.

Max grabbed a box out of his car. "Actually, yeah. We ordered some T-shirts like you suggested. I brought a small table we can use to set them up on and have a little merch stand. Would you mind working it after you get a few shots of us?"

I whipped my head around and narrowed my eyes. "The shirts were Evie's idea?"

Max had told us he was going to order shirts, but I hadn't realized it was a group effort.

She blushed and looked at her feet. "Cam's friend Nora designed them, and I knew of a shop that was running a printing deal."

"Why didn't you talk to me about it?" I felt like an oaf for feeling jealous of my bandmate.

Max scratched the back of his neck and looked around as if desperate to escape.

"I-I just thought I heard Max mention shirts before, so I texted him. You gave me everyone's number."

"Max has never mentioned shirts before." I didn't know if this was true, but the unfamiliar rage bubbling in my gut wouldn't let me shut my mouth.

"Yes, I have," Max muttered.

I glared at him. "Well, I'm the one in charge of handling marketing. Just talk to me next time."

Max and Evie shared a confused glance. The fact that they looked at each other like they were in on something I wasn't pissed me off even more. I didn't want Evie texting Max, especially when she had been so clearly avoiding me.

I grunted, lifting a heavy amp. "Let's get the rest of this stuff inside."

"I'll go set up the merch," Evie said, grabbing the box

from Max. She scampered away, likely eager to get away from my strange attitude.

"What was that all about?" Max asked as soon as she was out of earshot.

"Nothing."

We walked through the back doors, up some stairs, and onto the stage we'd be playing in a couple of hours. I set down the amp and tried to ignore Max, who still followed me.

"Yeah, right. You all but yelled at Evie for no reason."

"I never raised my voice."

"You didn't have to. Your tone said it all."

I crossed my arms and surveyed the large venue before turning back to him. "It's just kind of weird that she would text you, right? Why wouldn't she talk to me about the shirts."

Max looked at me like I had grown a second head. "Dude, listen to yourself. Is this really about the stupid shirts?"

"Yes," I said stubbornly.

"Really? Because you sound jealous."

I rolled my eyes. "I'm not. It's just—she clearly distanced herself from me this week, and it's annoying. I'm allowed to be irritated that my friend is avoiding me."

"I'm so ready for this 'we're just friends' narrative to be over," Max said as he set his guitar on its stand.

I clenched my hand into a fist. "I wish people would stop saying that."

"Whatever, forget I said anything. Just squash whatever issue it is you have going on right now. We don't need this energy when we're on stage."

I closed my eyes and sucked in a breath before opening

them and plastering on a huge grin. "It's already squashed."

Max mumbled something inaudible and walked back to the van.

Now alone, I surveyed the venue again. It felt expansive and even larger than the last spot we played.

Any irritation I felt dissipated as adrenaline coursed through my veins.

"Do you want to hear one more?" I screamed out at the audience.

Beads of sweat dripped down my face.

The packed audience cheered back at me, begging us to play another one.

I grinned and looked over at the rest of my bandmates. We had killed our set. We played almost all original songs, and the crowd ate it up. The people standing up front even knew the words.

I struck the opening chord to our viral song and sang into the mic. My eyes scanned the crowd in front of me. A few girls screamed, pleading with me to make eye contact. But I hardly noticed them. The entire set, I had been searching the crowd for Evie, but I hadn't been able to find her.

Just too dumb to get it right
Too young to realize
It was never worth the fight
Try as I might
You would always villainize me

I'd yell out of spite
You were never contrite
Now you can't stand the sight of me

Almost the entire crowd sang the lyrics back to me.

I played the last note, and the crowd cheered.

"Thank you, Indy. You're beautiful."

"That was incredible." Max raised his hand for a high five, which I slammed excitedly.

I would never forget the high that I felt out there tonight. Everything felt electric. Never in my wildest imagination had I thought I could make something of myself. Growing up, I used to dream of writing and playing music, but I was too much of a coward to admit that dream to anyone. If only that kid could see himself now.

Once all our equipment was off the stage and loaded into the van, I looked around for Evie.

"I'm going to see if Evie is up front!" I shouted to Max as the next band's first song reverberated through the building.

Not wanting to walk through the crowd of people, I hurried down the emergency exit hallway. When I entered the front of the venue, twenty or so people were hanging around. I spotted Evie immediately. She sat behind a folding table. A small line had formed in front of her.

"Hey!" I shouted. She looked up and waved.

I sauntered over and crouched down next to her chair.

"Did you see us?"

Before she could respond, the guy at the front of the line interjected. "You were great out there. Love the songs."

I stood up and smiled at him. "Thanks, man. I appreciate it."

I chatted with him for a minute before he bought a shirt and walked away.

The next fifteen minutes were spent mingling with potential fans while Evie collected cash and distributed T-shirts.

When the line finally dissipated, I resumed my crouched position next to her.

"This is insane. I can't believe people actually want to buy shit with our name on it."

"Believe it. You guys deserve it." Her smile felt genuine now, unlike earlier. I couldn't stop myself from reaching out and grabbing her knees for support. The physical touch sent a jolt of energy through me.

"Did you watch us?"

"I snuck out for a second, but people kept coming to the booth. I didn't want to miss out on any sales."

My heart sank a little that she hadn't seen most of the show. She must have clocked my disappointed look.

"Don't worry though, the other band has a photographer, and she said she'd email me some pictures she took of you guys."

"Great." I smiled and pretended my change in demeanor was due to her missing out on taking pictures and not her missing my performance.

Evie shifted underneath me, and I realized my grip on her knees had tightened. Spotting another chair, I grabbed it and put it behind the table, straddling it so that I could face her.

"You don't want to watch the other band?" she asked. A blush crept across her cheeks.

"I've already seen them. I'd rather hang out with you. I feel like I've hardly seen you lately."

She winced. "Sorry, I really have been busy."

"Yeah, you keep saying that." I drummed my fingers on the back of the chair.

Someone approached the table to ask where the bathrooms were. Evie stood up to point them in the right direction, and I took the opportunity to stare at her. Was it my imagination, or did she look even cuter tonight? She had changed into tight jeans and a black and white top she must have crocheted herself. I could make out patches of skin where the holes in the pattern were.

"Jared?"

My eyes moved from her chest back to her face. The person had left, and I was caught openly gawking at her.

"I like your shirt."

She glanced down and then back at me. "Oh, thanks."

"It looks perfect on you."

Her eyes went wide, and her cheeks reddened further. "Oh-uh, I made it forever ago," she muttered.

A grin spread over my face. Maybe it was wrong, but I liked that my comment flustered her. It meant she felt something. Flirting might be playing with fire, but I couldn't help myself.

I leaned in and brushed a lock of her hair away from her face, my fingertips grazing her bare shoulder in the process. Small goosebumps rose where I had touched her.

"What are you doing?"

I ignored her question because there wasn't a good answer.

"We're going out to celebrate after," I said instead.

She bit her lip, and I tried my best to keep my eyes off them. "I'm pretty beat."

"Please, Eves? Just for a little bit."

"It's been a long day."

"Even longer for me," I pointed out. "Come on. Please?" I gave her my best puppy dog eyes.

She sighed. "Fine. But just for a little."

I grinned. "You won't regret it."

"Jared, get your ass back here and finish loading the van. I want to leave as soon as the set is over." Drew poked his head through the doorway and glared at me.

"Better head back there. I'll see you soon." I gave Evie a half-wave as I moved toward the door, following Drew backstage.

"Is this it?" I asked when I saw the few pieces of equipment that remained.

"The rest of us got everything else. You need to do your share," Drew said.

I rolled my eyes. "Fine. Fine. Like I've never picked up the slack for you before."

I hauled a few things to the van before coming back for more. By the time I had loaded everything, the other band was coming off stage after finishing their set.

"You guys were incredible," Derek said. "We gotta celebrate."

Before I could even process what was happening, a tray of shots started making its way around the room.

"Fuck yes," said Drew, grabbing one.

Tyler and Max followed suit.

He passed it to me, and for a split second, I hesitated. "Nah, I'm good. Thanks, man."

"Dude, you have to. You just rocked it out there. You deserve it."

I knew I shouldn't, but part of me just wanted to celebrate this moment and ride out the high. One drink wouldn't kill me. It's not like I had a serious problem. One drink would be fine.

"Cheers, buddy." I raised the shot toward Max. He eyed me warily but then smiled and clinked his glass against mine.

The tequila burned as it traveled down my throat. Maybe it should have disgusted me after all this time, but instead, I just felt alive.

My ears still rang from the show as we entered the bar. People were packed in almost shoulder to shoulder in some spots. Evie shrank into my side as she looked around and fidgeted with her hair.

Strange. She wasn't usually a nervous person. I grabbed her hand and squeezed it. The drink had dampened my inhibitions.

She looked up at me with a weak smile.

What was going on with her?

"I'm going to find the bathroom!" she shouted.

She disappeared through the crowd, and I signaled for Max to follow me to the bar. Drew and Tyler were already there, talking to two girls.

"Four shots of tequila, please," I said.

Drew smiled. "Hell, yeah."

"Finally. I feel like Jared never goes out with us," Tyler said.

Max glanced from me to the bartender.

"You sure you don't want to slow down," he whispered.

Of all the guys, he seemed to be the only one observant

enough to notice that I didn't drink. Drew and Tyler were far too self-absorbed.

I brushed off his concern. "It's fine. I typically don't drink to keep fit"—I flexed a bicep and winked at him—"but one night off won't kill me."

The bartender placed the shots in front of us, and we raised our glasses.

"To us," Max said.

"The Wedding Band," Tyler added.

"To fame," Drew said.

I smirked. "To feeling like a fucking rockstar."

We all clinked our glasses before slamming them onto the bar top and knocking them back.

TWENTY-FOUR

Evie

I glared at myself in the mirror. Being this close to Jared all day had me on edge. I groaned and closed my eyes. Ignoring my feelings was impossible when he looked at me the way he did. I thought about texting Cam, but I'm sure he would either pester me for details or say, "I told you so." Neither of those things would be helpful at this moment.

A girl in a short black dress stumbled through the threshold, jarring me from my thoughts.

"Excuse me," she slurred.

I pushed away from the sink and braced myself to return to the bar. After hiding out in here for at least ten minutes, I'm sure Jared was probably looking for me by now.

The loud music and smell of stale beer hit me as soon as I opened the door. Pushing my way to the bar, I spotted the guys through the crowd. As I got closer, I realized that they were all downing shots, including Jared.

What the hell?

"Jared? What are you doing?"

"Eves!" he exclaimed before throwing an arm around my shoulder and squeezing. "You want a shot? We're celebrating."

I threw a questioning stare at him. "Uh, no. I'm okay. Are you drinking?"

My concern must have been written all over my face because he leaned down and put his mouth right up against my ear. The hairs on the back of my neck bristled as I felt his breath on my neck.

"It's just a few drinks. It's fine."

"I might head out." My discomfort grew by the second. It wasn't my place to tell Jared what not to do, but I had a feeling this wasn't going to end well.

"No, Eves, you can't." He grabbed my shoulders tighter. "I've been waiting to hang out with you all day. And I've hardly seen you this week. Please stay. Max, tell her she has to stay."

Max glanced over from his huddle with Drew and Tyler.

"You have to stay," he confirmed.

"Yeah, Evie. Celebrate with us. You're the reason we're here." A clearly tipsy Drew threw his arms around me and swept me into an embrace.

I gasped at the shock of it but patted his back lightly.

"Yeah, Evie." Tyler reached around and joined our embrace. "You're the best."

"Am I high, or are you two hugging?" Max asked.

Jared laughed.

"It doesn't count if it's through Evie." Drew glared at him before they both let me go.

I held up my hands to avoid any further attempts at affection. "Don't thank me, guys. It was all you."

Jared wrapped his arms around my waist, causing my mind to go on high alert.

"You look so cute in this shirt."

My body went hot as I tried to pretend like his touch didn't affect me. Someone bumped into me as they tried to get the bartender's attention.

"Uh, should we go find somewhere else to stand?" I asked.

Jared released me and scanned the bar before motioning for us to follow him.

"We'll catch you guys later," Drew said, pointing to two girls at the bar and winking.

I nodded and joined Jared and Max at a high-top table. I opened my mouth to say something but was cut off by a man moving to stand directly in front of me. I recognized him as someone that bought a T-shirt earlier.

"Dude, great show tonight. Let me buy you a drink," he held up a glass, offering it to Jared.

I winced as he accepted, and the two of them launched into a replay of the set.

Frowning, I turned my attention to Max, who had also been left out of the conversation.

"He's got quite the star power, huh?"

"He's had that even before we started a band."

"His charisma bugs me," I muttered.

Max chuckled. "It's part of his appeal, I guess."

"Unfortunately for us," I joked. But seriously, if he wasn't so damn charming it would be a lot easier to pretend that I didn't like him.

"Why aren't you over there?" I nodded to Drew and

Tyler as they slung their arms around the two girls at the bar.

"There's kind of someone in the picture," he said.

"What's the story there?"

He looked at his feet, so I nudged him.

"Come on. I've been told I'm a great listener."

"I guess…I've known her my whole life. We were childhood friends. She just moved to Chicago a while ago, and we've been trying to figure out if something is there. She has a lot of trust issues, though, so it's hard for her that the band is getting bigger and that we're playing shows all the time."

I bit my lip. "That's tough."

"It is. And she's been pushing me away more and more lately. She's barely spoken to me in weeks. It's been killing me."

"Does she know how you feel?"

"I think so."

I laughed. "You *think* so?"

"I mean, I think I've made it pretty obvious."

"There's no such thing as obvious when it comes to relationships and communication. She isn't a mind reader."

He sighed and took a sip of his drink. "Maybe I should talk to her."

"You should definitely talk to her." I smiled up at him.

"What are you two talking about?"

I jumped, startled that someone hovered so closely behind me. Jared had walked up without me noticing.

"Nothing," Max muttered.

"Please tell me. It seems like you guys are smiling, so it must be amusing as shit." Jared's tone was friendly, but his eyes darkened as he glared at Max.

"Seriously?" Max narrowed his eyes and tilted his head. "It's nothing. We were just talking."

"Right," I confirmed.

I looked on as Jared glared at a confused-looking Max.

Max finally blew out a breath. "I think I'm going to go home and make a call." He nodded at me before starting for the door. He patted Jared's shoulder as he walked by. "Great show tonight, man."

"Damn right, it was." As soon as Max retreated, he leaned into me. "Okay, seriously, what was that about?"

"It really was nothing." I didn't want to disclose Max's personal life if he didn't want me to, but Jared's insistence unsettled me. He wasn't being his usual self.

He pinched the bridge of his nose and looked pained. "Seems like you've been talking to Max a lot lately."

My eyebrows scrunched together. "Is this about the shirts? I'm sorry about that, but I—"

"It's not about the shirts," he huffed.

My eyes widened at his short tone, and his face filled with regret.

"Shit, I'm sorry. I'm being such a dick. I just don't get why you've been avoiding me lately. And then when I found out you've been talking to Max—I thought we were friends."

Genuine hurt flooded his voice, and my chest grew heavy with guilt. My stupid crush had interfered with our very real friendship.

I reached out and squeezed his arm.

"I'm sorry. We can hang out this week. I promise."

The corner of his lip turned up, and his infectious smile spread to my face too.

He drew me into a hug and kissed the top of my head.

I leaned into the hug, and warmth surged through my body. Suddenly the proximity had me wondering if it would be the worst thing in the world to tell him how I felt.

Before I could even think it through, Drew appeared and tugged on Jared's sleeve. "Come to the bar with us. These girls want to meet the rest of the band."

"I'll be right back." He grinned at me before allowing himself to be pulled away.

I tapped my fingers against the dirty table, my eyes darting around the room. The crowd had gotten even thicker. The blaring music and sticky floors reminded me just how much I didn't want to be here. As soon as Jared came back, I would say goodnight and leave.

After a few minutes of reading the various raunchy things etched into the table, I glanced up. Jared, Drew, and Tyler were still standing around the bar talking with a group of people.

Screw it.

It sure didn't seem like Jared would notice if I left. I pushed off the table and headed for the door.

"Where you off to so early?" A massive guy with a buzzcut and a beer belly stood in front of me, effectively blocking my exit.

"Excuse me," I muttered and tried to slide by.

He grabbed my arm. I winced as he leaned in close. I could smell the whisky on his breath.

"Don't be rude. I was just tryna talk to you."

Alarm bells sounded in my head as I tried to extract my arm from his grip.

"I'm not being rude. I'm trying to go home."

"Why don't I walk you?"

I tried not to laugh in his face. "I'm good," I said before trying to yank my arm away.

He held on tight, and I could feel bruises forming.

Strong hands on my waist pulled me back. I barely registered what was happening before Jared inserted himself between me and the creep.

"Get your fucking hands off her," he growled, shoving the man backward in one swift motion.

"Hey, mind your own business."

"She. Is. My. Business." Jared seethed. His jaw locked, and his eyes looked like they wanted to rip the guy's throat out. I took a shaky step back. I hadn't even realized it was possible for him to look this angry.

"Is that right?" The other guy took a step toward Jared until their chests were practically touching.

"Jared," I hissed and tugged at his arm. "Let's just get out of here."

But his murderous gaze didn't move from the guy.

"Come on," I begged, pulling on him.

He looked down at me and back at the guy. His eyes didn't soften, but he nodded and took a step back.

He had finally turned away when the guy said, "You're just mad your girl wanted me to—."

Jared instantly spun around and smashed his fist into the side of the guy's head.

"Stop it!" I screamed, but it was too late.

The guy staggered backward before Jared swung and hit him again. Another guy tried to get in the middle and shove Jared back, but Jared's fist connected with his stomach and sent him stumbling backward too.

The first guy was back in his face, and he punched Jared in the side of the head before he could react.

"Come at me, you piece of shit."

"Gladly," barked Jared before he wound up and socked the guy right in the middle of the face, knocking him to the ground. The other guy bent over to make sure he was okay as he writhed on the floor.

"What's going on?" Tyler exclaimed, now at our side.

"Do you need backup?" Drew asked.

I glanced around to see the bartender on the phone.

"Shit. Shit. He's probably calling the cops."

"Go, get out of here," said Drew. "We'll deal with this."

"Jared, let's go," I hissed.

He stood there in a haze, glaring at his fallen opponent.

"Jared, let's go now!" I screamed and grabbed his arm.

He spun around at my connection, and his dark eyes cleared a little when they took in my panicked expression.

"Come on," I begged.

He finally nodded, and we raced out the back door.

"Where do you think you're going?" someone shouted from behind us. But it was too late. We were already sprinting out the door into the cover of the dark evening.

We ran through the street, past the bustling restaurants and bars. After a few blocks, the city quieted down. I hadn't run like this since childhood. The cool air whipped around my body as my legs started to burn.

I glanced to the right before grabbing Jared's hand and pulling. I led us across the street and into a small park before we stopped and leaned down to catch our breath.

Jared whistled. "That was a close one."

"What the hell was that?"

His eyebrows shot up as he ran a hand through his disheveled hair.

"He put his fucking hands on you, Evie. If you thought I was going to let that slide, you're out of your mind."

"You didn't have to fight him. He had already backed off by the time you hit him."

His jaw locked. "I wasn't going to let him talk about you that way."

"This must be a glimpse into the old Jared," I muttered.

Despite my anger, I felt sad. Sad that I didn't even recognize this person.

He sighed, the silence weighing heavily in the darkness between us.

"Hey, I'm sorry about tonight," he whispered.

I glanced over to see a pained expression on his face. "Don't worry about it." My tone came out harsher than I meant it to.

"What do you want me to say? I can't go back and unfight that guy."

"You also can't go back and drink less either."

Tears burned at the back of my eyes.

Jared dipped his chin to get a better look at my face, but I turned away.

"I'm sorry—"

"Don't worry about it. You don't owe me anything."

I snuck a glance at him. His eyes were clearer than they had been all night. The run—or the fight—seemed to have sobered him up.

"I do owe you, though. A lot. I know I fucked up back there, but you know that's not me."

I shook my head. "I guess I don't know you as well as I thought."

He groaned in frustration.

"We should get moving," I said before making a beeline back to the street.

"Fine, but you aren't walking away from this conversation." He fell into stride beside me.

We walked in silence for a few beats before I finally spoke. "It's like you were a different person back there."

He winced. "Fuck," he muttered. "It would have hurt less if you slapped me."

Despite my anger, my lip twitched as I forced back a smile. "That might have made me feel better too."

We fell into a silent walk with no clear destination. The streets were clearing out, but crowds of friends still lingered underneath bar signs as they spilled out onto the sidewalks. Jared's arm brushed mine as we walked around a large group. Trying to ignore the way his skin felt on mine, I took a deep breath in, savoring the slight chill in the air.

When Jared still said nothing after two blocks, I peeked up at him and frowned when I saw a somber expression on his face. His eyes were hard and focused on the ground—like his mind was trying to work through something. My heart cracked at the sight.

A neon open sign hung a few doors ahead, and I grabbed his hand. He jerked his gaze away from the sidewalk and looked from me to the diner I pointed at.

"I think you could use a coffee."

Once inside with our coffees and a plate of fries, Jared finally looked me in the eyes.

"I'm sorry, Eves," he said again, his voice thick with regret. "I was being stupid. I shouldn't be drinking. It's just —when Derek insisted, I kind of froze. I told myself I could be in control of it."

"It was weird to see you that way," I admitted. "You always seem so in control and sure of yourself."

"I am." He raked his fingers through his hair. "I guess I wanted—I guess I just saw everyone else drinking to celebrate, and I told myself I could do that too."

"Jared, you're more fun than any person I've ever met. You don't need anything to help with that."

He smirked from behind his coffee mug. "I know."

I shook my head, biting back my smile. "You're impossible to stay mad at."

"So don't."

I looked down into my mug and sighed. "I'm not really. It's just—you have this way of making anyone you talk to feel special. You're a light Jared, and you lost that spark a little bit tonight."

"Ugh, I'm sorry if I made you feel anything other than special. I never want to be that guy again," he muttered. "But trust me, seeing that guy put his hands on you sobered me up real fucking fast."

I winced. "I also hated seeing you in a fight."

His eyes darkened. "I know, but I can't apologize for that. That guy was a creep. Nobody touches you like that."

My heart sputtered at his defensive tone.

"I know you said you used to get into fights, but I guess I never pictured it. You're so easygoing. You never seemed like the aggressive type."

"I'm not," he said simply. "When I saw him with you, I only saw red."

"You should work on that," I said, reaching for his arm.

He stared at me. "I don't think it's going to be a long-term issue unless you plan on frequenting more dive bars filled with scumbags. Then I'll be forced to protect your honor."

I laughed. "You definitely do not have to worry about that."

"So, are we good?"

I nodded. "Of course."

"Good." He blew out a breath. "Because it already felt like you were drifting today, and I hated it."

"I'm sorry. I promise I'm right here."

For now.

I couldn't even think about how it would feel not to see him every day. And I still couldn't admit to him the way I felt—why I had been drifting.

I couldn't ruin this moment.

BACK IN THE HOTEL LOBBY, I HELD UP MY KEY CARD. "I better get some sleep."

"Right—shit." Jared patted the pockets of his jeans.

I raised my eyebrows. "What?"

"I don't have a key, and I don't know the room number. I just dropped you off and went straight to the venue to start setting up. Max checked us in."

"Try calling him," I said.

He fumbled with his phone. I heard the sound of ringing on the other end followed by Max's voicemail.

I sighed. "Maybe the concierge can help you."

We approached the counter as an older woman looked up from her magazine.

"Hi there." He threw on his best charming smile. "My

friend has the key card, and he isn't answering his phone. Can I get another key?"

"What's the room number?"

"I don't actually know. See, it's under my friend's name. Max Mason."

She raised her eyebrows. "I can't give you a key without an ID that matches the confirmation."

"But it's my room too."

"No can do."

He knocked on the desk defeatedly.

"Guess I'm sleeping in the van."

"Do you have the keys?"

He dug his hands into his pockets before throwing his head back and groaning. "Nope. Sure, don't."

There was really only one viable option here, and I didn't like it.

"You can crash in my room," I offered.

It'll be fine.

"You're a lifesaver."

As we walked down a hallway toward the room, I tried not to show any outward signs of panic. Internally, though, my heart raced a mile a minute. I was about to be alone with him—this supposed friend I hadn't been able to stop thinking about for weeks. It didn't help that with each step, Jared seemed to move closer to me. Now our hands kept brushing.

Opening the door to the room, my heart sank as my eyes darted around the small space.

"Shoot," I muttered.

"What?"

"There's only one bed."

He walked inside and sat on the fluffy white bedspread before kicking off his shoes.

"I can sleep on the floor," he offered, but even as he suggested it, he ripped his shirt off and started to snuggle into the covers.

I sighed. "Don't be ridiculous. There's plenty of room." I unzipped my duffel bag and searched for my toothbrush. "You want to use the bathroom first?"

"Nah. I'm just going to pass out."

I collected my toiletries and retreated to the bathroom. Once inside, I gripped the side of the sink and stared at my reflection.

This is fine. You're fine. Nothing is going to happen with Jared.

My thoughts continued this way while my body grew hot at the mere thought of climbing into bed next to him. I took my time changing and brushing my teeth, hoping he'd be asleep by the time I got back. Unfortunately for me, he was still awake, sitting up shirtless in bed, when I walked in.

"Nice shirt," he said, laughter in his voice.

I looked down, and my cheeks reddened. Why I had decided to bring my oversized shirt covered in rainbow kittens to an overnight with a band was beyond me.

"It's cute," I muttered, moving the covers and slipping into my side.

"It's ridiculously cute."

I felt my face turn an even deeper shade of red as I fiddled with the light switch. A dim glow from the window illuminated the room. Although I was pushed as far to my side as the bed would allow, I could still feel the body heat radiating off Jared.

"Hopefully, I don't hog the covers." My voice came out shaky.

My mind drifted back to him on top of me on his couch. How good his hands felt on my body...

I squeezed my legs shut to fight the tingling sensation forming there.

"Evie?" His voice sounded close—a lot closer than the other side of the bed. Goosebumps pricked the back of my neck.

I turned to find him staring at me less than a foot away. "Jared?"

His eyes darkened. "Do you think men and women can be friends?"

"I'm not sure. I haven't had all that much experience if I'm being honest."

"I think you're my best friend."

My breath caught in my throat as he shifted so that he was even closer to me on the bed. I gasped as he moved again, causing his body to brush up against mine. I remained frozen where I was, unable to tear myself away from the connection. He raised his hand and cautiously moved it to my cheek before lightly tracing my cheekbone. It seemed like he was waiting for me to tell him to back off. My mouth parted, but I couldn't find the words.

"I really can't lose you as a friend," he whispered.

I bit my bottom lip. Friendship was the last thing on my mind.

He moved his hand down my neck and drew a line all the way down my arm, underneath the sheets. He went past my hips and gently touched my thigh. I stiffened.

"Is this okay?" he whispered.

I nodded. All rational thought escaped my brain at his touch. His fingertips traced my upper thigh, nudging my baggy T-shirt out of the way. When he touched my bare hip and the flimsy fabric of my underwear, my eyelids fluttered closed. Heat pooled between my legs, begging him to continue his exploration.

He slowly moved from my hips to the inside of my thigh. I sucked in a breath, anticipating his touch. He hesitated for only a moment before caressing the pulsing spot between my legs. Fireworks went off in my body as soon as he touched me there. I had been thinking about this ever since that night on his couch. How badly I wanted to feel his hands on me. I had tried to deny it, but the fantasies that had invaded my dreams didn't lie.

"Fuck, Eves," he said as he felt my underwear. He shifted them to the side, and I shuddered as he ran his finger along me.

I let out a small moan in response and lifted my hips slightly, begging for more before crushing my mouth onto his. I licked his bottom lip before coaxing them open with my tongue.

My tongue explored his mouth while his fingers explored my body. He slid his fingers inside me, and my hips bucked in response.

"Do you like that?" he asked against my mouth.

I nodded.

"Let me hear you say you like it."

"I-I like it." My voice came out breathless.

He used his thumb to rub circles against me while his fingers moved in and out, building the sensation. He pulled his face away from mine and watched as I lost control. I bit my lip to keep from moaning and closed my eyes as he continued to touch me. The feeling was almost too much to bear. I reached for his arm and squeezed it as he pumped his fingers in and out of me.

"I want to hear you scream my name."

My eyes opened wide with surprise, and my mouth hung open. He took this opportunity to slide his tongue inside and envelop me in another deep kiss. His fingers moved with even more urgency.

"Jared, s-stop. I c-can't—" My voice was cut off by a loud moan.

He stilled. "You want me to stop, baby?"

"I-it's too much."

He smirked. "You're about to come all over my fingers Evie."

I clutched his arm so tightly I was sure to leave a mark.

"But I can stop if you want me to…" he started to withdraw, but I shook my head.

"No, please—I—"

"You what?"

"I need it." I licked my lips and searched his face.

"Fuck," he said before sliding back inside. He used his other hand to prop himself up so that he could hover over me.

The blankets had been ripped off of us at this point, and I lay splayed beneath him. My T-shirt had ridden halfway up my stomach.

"You're so sexy."

Without warning, he moved away, and my eyes snapped open in surprise. Every part of my body protested his absence.

"Don't stop."

He removed his boxers. "I want you to come with me inside you."

The thought excited me even more. I had been thinking

about this moment for longer than I would admit to anyone.

He fiddled around with his wallet before discarding a foil packet and hovering over me. He ripped my shirt up, and I helped him pull it over my head. My nipples were peaked on each breast, and they tingled with pleasure as he slid his hands along my sides and pressed his bare torso against mine.

He groaned as I grabbed his length and moved it to my entrance. His tip slid in easily with no resistance. My body begged for more. I was so ready for him. As he slowly inched in, I whimpered. This felt too good. I wanted it all. I hitched my hips upward, causing him to slide the rest of the way in. I rolled my head back and moaned as he filled me.

He groaned as he thrust his hips back and forth, allowing the friction to bring us both to the edge.

"Do you like that?" He asked before taking one of my hard nipples into his mouth. He bit it softly and rolled his tongue over it. I moaned in response, tangling my fingers in his hair, forcing him to keep his mouth there. I could feel him smiling against my breast.

I angled my hips and wrapped my legs around him, taking him in even deeper than before. The pleasure was building, and I felt lightheaded from the sensation.

I cried out his name, and he thrust once more before we both came undone.

TWENTY-FIVE

Jared

The sound of muffled footsteps on the carpeted floor stirred me from a dead sleep. My head throbbed. I reached up to pinch the bridge of my nose as my eyes drifted open. Evie wiggled into a pair of jeans as she looked around the room.

"Are you trying to hit it and quit it right now?"

Her eyes went wide as she glanced at me. "Oh, um. No, of course not."

I raised my eyebrows and sat up.

She sighed and fell back onto the bed.

"I just thought I could sneak a cup of coffee in before you woke up. Last night was a lot to process without caffeine."

"Tell me about it." I groaned and shut my eyes. "This is a great reminder of why I never drink. Even just a couple and I get a headache."

We both sat there in silence for a few moments. I could hear the soft sounds of her breathing next to me.

"I got a little carried away last night," I finally said.

She snorted softly. "Me too."

I sat up more so that I could see her face. "I'm sorry, Eves."

She stared at me. Her eyes might as well have been giant question marks. "What are you sorry for exactly?"

I ran my hands over my face. "Just…everything. I was drinking, and I never meant for it to go that far." In truth, my judgment hadn't been clouded at all when I reached for her last night. I just couldn't keep away from her any longer.

"Are you serious?" She shot off the bed and paced across the room before spinning around and pointing a finger at me. "You're seriously trying to blame this on your alcohol consumption? You were sober by the time we got back here."

I shrugged defeatedly. "I know it's no excuse, but—"

"I don't want an excuse." She shook her head, her eyes shifting to the ceiling.

She looked sad. Did she regret what we did?

"Then what do you want?" I asked.

"I want you to admit you have feelings for me."

My mouth hung open as my brain tried to process her words.

She shook her head at my stunned silence. "What I don't want is you blaming the amazing night we had on alcohol. And pretending we haven't been tiptoeing around how we feel about each other since basically the moment we met."

Her words hit me like a punch in the gut. Of course, I had feelings for her, but I hadn't realized she wanted me to admit it. I thought I was doing her a favor by keeping them to myself.

"I just thought…I thought it was better that way."

"Better for who?" She frowned. "Maybe you can't admit it to yourself, but I can't sit around here while you apologize and tell me last night was a mistake." She grabbed her duffel and moved to the door.

"Wait." I sprung from the bed, but she was already through the threshold.

"I'm going to see if I can get a ride back in the other car," she mumbled before taking off down the hallway.

"Evie, wait!" I shouted. I was two steps out the doorway when I realized I only had on boxers. "Shit," I muttered.

I raced inside to throw on pants and a shirt. I tried to get my shoe on, but after fumbling with one for a minute, I gave up and tore out of the room barefoot. I ran down the hallway, straight for the stairs. Taking them two at a time.

I raced through the lobby, jerking my head in every direction. My eyes caught a glimpse of purple hair exiting through the front doors. I moved quickly and was outside behind her in five seconds.

"Evie, stop." I grabbed her arm and forced her to turn and face me.

"What?" she asked. Her eyes were wet. I reached up to cup her chin in my hands.

"You're right, okay? I'm sorry. Last night didn't happen because I was drinking. It happened because it's all I've been thinking about since the moment I met you. It wasn't a mistake."

She sniffed.

"And I do care about our friendship. But I don't think I'm going to be able to keep my hands off you if we're in the same room together."

"Me either," she said.

I cupped her chin in my hand before leaning down and kissing her, savoring the way her soft lips felt against mine. I pulled back after a minute.

"Maybe we both have a lot going on, and I know you're leaving, but it doesn't matter. Let's enjoy the time we have together."

She bit her lip and nodded. "Right. Why waste any more time?"

"Exactly." I tucked a piece of her hair behind her ear.

"And we can still keep in touch after I leave," she added.

"Who knows? Maybe I'll even visit you when I get a chance."

She smiled. "I wouldn't say no to that."

I dipped my head again and pressed my lips against hers. My hand moved to her hair as I held her there. She tasted amazing. I couldn't believe I had been denying myself this for weeks.

Someone cleared their throat behind me. I turned to see my bandmates with their luggage, smirking at us.

Drew elbowed Tyler. "Called it. You owe me twenty bucks."

I rolled my eyes and slung my arm around Evie's shoulders. "Shut up."

Max laughed. "Glad you found somewhere safe to sleep last night."

I grinned. "Thanks for locking me out. Worked out a lot better this way."

"Jared," Evie hissed and pinched my side.

I kissed the top of her head in response.

"You guys almost ready?" Max asked.

I nodded.

"Oh, by the way," Tyler said. "Nothing happened at the

bar after you left. The guy stood up and stormed out of there. They didn't even end up calling the cops."

Max's eyebrows shot up as he looked from Tyler to me. "Sounds like I called it a night at the right time."

I sighed. "I'll tell you about it later."

Drew glanced down at my feet. "Where the fuck are your shoes?"

TWENTY-SIX

Evie

I CLOSED THE DOOR BEHIND ME AND THREW MY BAG ON THE countertop.

Cam glanced up at me from the kitchen island. "Wow, so nice of you to stop by. I forgot you lived here."

"Ha. Ha." I moved to the fridge and grabbed a glass of water.

"You've been at Jared's—what—three nights in a row?"

"Are you keeping track or something? I would have thought you'd be happy to have your apartment to yourself."

"Just an observation." He turned in the chair as I passed him to collapse on the couch. Jared and I had breakfast this morning and hit up a local art fair before he had to leave for band practice.

"I like being over there. What do you want me to say?"

Cam eyed me, a mischievous glimmer in his eyes. "I'm sure you do like being over there."

My cheeks reddened, and I threw a pillow at Cam's face. He dodged it and laughed.

"It's not like that."

Well, it was kind of like that. But I liked being at Jared's for many reasons other than just sex.

Cam came over and joined me on the couch. "So, what's the deal with you two anyway?"

"No deal."

Cam shoved me lightly. "Come on. It's me you're talking to. Give me the details."

"We're just having fun."

"Fun," he repeated.

"Right. We like each other and got tired of trying to fight it."

"Doesn't seem like you two will be having much fun when you have to say goodbye in a couple of weeks."

I shrugged. "We both know that's coming, but it's fine. We already agreed to stay in touch."

"Uh-huh." Cam didn't sound convinced.

"You're impossible. Why does everything have to be this big thing with you? Jared and I like each other, but our paths are inevitably diverting. It doesn't mean we can't enjoy this time together now."

"Whatever you say. I'm glad you two are being so mature about this."

"We are," I said.

"You know, you could always stay."

I glared at him. "Be for real, Cam. I'm not going to not go on this trip that I've been planning for years."

"My mom is pretty bummed she won't be in town to see you before you go," Cam said, changing the subject.

It was a bummer. Aunt Renee had decided to become a flight attendant a few years ago. After she completed her training, she moved down to Orlando where she was now stationed. She and Cam got together on trips frequently, but I hadn't been able to join them yet. And I guess it would be quite a while before I would be able to if I was going to be international for the next couple of years.

"Maybe I can come back for a holiday." I smiled sadly.

"It would be expensive."

"It would," I admitted.

"You know, if you wanted to make a trip down to the old hometown before you go, I'd be happy to go with you."

"Why would I want to do that?" I snapped, jerking up to stare at him. He seemed to have this demented idea that I needed to have a conversation with my parents. Like it would heal me somehow.

"I just think it could be healthy. It feels like you try to pretend that part of your life doesn't exist."

"It might as well not exist."

He sighed. "You've got a lot of baggage that's still back there."

"No, I don't. I don't need to see them to move on with my life."

I couldn't even imagine driving down that main road into town again. My throat constricted at the mere thought of it.

"Hey, don't jump down my throat. It was just a suggestion."

We sat in silence as Cam let me cool down. One of the advantages of being with someone who knew you well was the ease with which you could transition from a tense moment.

"Do you want to get dinner with Nora and me tomorrow?" he asked after a few minutes.

I winced. "I can't. Jared and I already have plans."

He huffed. "Fine. Fine. I can see that I've been replaced as the most important man in your life."

I tilted my chin and shot him a look.

"Want to hang out right now, then?"

I sucked in a breath. "I really need to catch up on recording. I'm behind on posting a video," I said guiltily.

Cam sighed and settled into the couch. "Can I at least watch?"

"Fine, but only watch. No commentary on my decorating choices."

"No promises."

"Here we are," Jared said, a huge grin on his face.

"The lake?" I asked.

"Not just the lake."

I looked around at the park that met up with the concrete that lined Lake Michigan. There were people running along the trail and a few people lying in the grass.

"This is where we came for the photo shoot," I said.

"Exactly." Jared plopped onto the ground and patted the spot next to him. He produced two sandwiches from his backpack and handed me one. "I wanted to take you back here in honor of the most epic first date ever."

"No way. That doesn't count as a first date."

He smirked and tilted his chin down. "Now that we're sleeping together it counts."

I laughed. "You can't retrospectively count that as our first date just because we're dating now."

"Why not?"

"Because you just can't."

"I prefer to make my own rules." He slung his arm loosely around my shoulders. "And I'm counting it because it's the spot I first realized I liked you."

I shoved him in the chest. "You're so cheesy. It is not."

His eyebrow ring glinted in the sun as a playful look crossed his face. "Are you calling me a liar?"

"Yes, there's no—" I squealed as Jared grabbed me around the waist and rolled me onto my back, pinning me against the soft grass. He leaned down and touched my nose with his.

"No one calls me a liar."

"Let me up," I said, laughing.

He planted a kiss on my lips before releasing me.

"There's something I want to tell you."

I looked at him expectantly.

"We have a meeting with that record label I was telling you about. They want to finalize the contract and schedule us time to record."

"Oh my god, Jared. That's incredible." I snaked my arms around him.

"Right? It's hard to believe we're actually going to record an album. Well, EP more likely, but still. It's all I've ever dreamed of. Hell, it's more than I ever dreamed of."

"You deserve it."

"It's all thanks to you."

"You give me too much credit. You're seriously so talented."

"Oh, I know."

I rolled my eyes. "There's the Jared I know."

"Are you calling me cocky?"

"Maybe."

Instead of denying it, he placed his hand on the back of my neck and pulled me in for a slow kiss. I returned it, getting lost in him once again. Any onlookers might think we were a happy couple without a care in the world.

No one would suspect that we were only temporary.

TWENTY-SEVEN

Jared

"Hey, man." Dean greeted me from the couch as I took my shoes off at his door.

"Alone tonight?" I asked, taking the seat next to him on the couch.

"Al is at Cam's for reality TV night—but I guess you probably already knew that."

"I tried to crash, but Cam said no significant others allowed," I said.

"He's a tyrant. I'm never invited."

I put my feet on the coffee table as Dean pressed play on the show he was watching.

"Good thing Evie was busy, or I might never have seen you again."

"You're exaggerating."

"Barely. You haven't stopped by in days."

"Is this your way of saying you miss me?" I wiggled my eyebrows.

"Nah, it's been nice to get a break from you."

"Liar."

"Even when you were with Janelle, you still spent more time here than your own place."

I grimaced. "Evie and Janelle could not be more different. I actually like spending time with Evie."

Dean laughed and stood up, moving to the kitchen. "Want anything to drink?"

"Soda water if you have it."

He tossed me one, and I caught it.

"Hey, before I forget, we're doing a new menu tasting in a couple of days at Luna. Want to come? You can bring Evie."

"Definitely."

A soft lump poked my back when I shifted on the couch. I sat up and felt around behind me before producing a sock. Scrunching my nose, I handed it to Dean.

"Gross, D."

Dean grabbed it and threw it in the direction of the open bedroom door. "Sorry. It's Al's. She's always leaving them everywhere."

"How has cohabitation been, anyway? Everything you thought it would be?"

"She's messy, hogs the TV, and is constantly spilling her food and coffee on every surface." He smiled. "I love it."

"You're so obsessed with her it's disgusting," I joked.

"Maybe…" he hesitated. "I was thinking…I was actually thinking I might propose."

My mouth hung open. While I knew Dean loved Al, he had never said one positive thing about marriage. I had always assumed he would never bother with it. "You? Mr. Fear-of-Commitment? Mr. Anti-Marriage?"

He shrugged. "I know what I said. But it's different now.

I'm in love with her. She's my family. I just want to make it official."

Evie's face flashed through my mind at his sentimental words.

"That must be a good feeling," I muttered.

"It is." Dean eyed my sullen expression. "You okay? Evie's leaving kind of soon, isn't she?"

"Yeah, she is." I bit the inside of my lip. "I knew it was coming."

"Doesn't make it easy."

"It's fine. I've barely even thought about it."

Dean chuckled. "I can tell when you're lying."

I sighed. "Fine, it fucking sucks, okay? Is that what you want to hear? I haven't been thinking about it because the thought of her leaving makes me sick."

"Have you told her that?"

"What's the point? Why should I make this harder than it already is?"

"You should still put it all out there."

"What—like ask her to stay?"

Dean nodded. "You'll probably regret it if you don't."

I shook my head. "I could never ask her to give up her dream."

"Dreams can change."

TWENTY-EIGHT

Evie

"I can't believe she's taking him back after all that," Cam said.

"She can do way better than that guy," Al added.

Nora nodded her agreement.

With a heavy heart, I cast my gaze around the room and felt a pang of sadness wash over me. I would miss these moments—curled up on the couch, eating junk food, and watching bad TV with friends. I had never had nights like these before, and I wasn't sure when I could expect to have them again. A nomadic lifestyle didn't exactly lend itself well to close friendships.

I'm sure I would meet other travelers, but it wouldn't be the same. I couldn't imagine finding anything that would match the warmth and familiarity I felt now. It was uniquely comforting.

"Look at this date he set up for her," Nora's words ripped me from my thoughts and brought me back to the show. "I mean, how cheesy could he get."

"Speaking of dates, how did yours go last night, Cam?" I asked. "It was the third one, right?"

Al sat up. "What? You're dating someone, and you didn't tell us?"

"We need to know everything," Nora demanded.

Cam glared at me, and I pretended to look innocently unaware, satisfied it was me bringing to light his dating life for once instead of the other way around.

"Thanks so much for bringing that up, Evelyn." His voice dripped with sarcasm. "I wasn't going to mention anything. I don't want to jinx it."

"Jinxes aren't real," insisted Nora.

"Yeah. Tell us."

He huffed a sigh and crossed his arms. "Fine. If you must know, we met through my coworker, and things have been going well. He hasn't started annoying me yet which is huge for me." Cam tried to sound tough, but I could sense his bottled excitement. "He invited me to a housewarming party the Friday after next. You two have to come and be my wingmen."

"Yes, I want to meet him!" exclaimed Nora.

My stomach dropped as I played with the frayed edge of the ancient sweater I wore. I wouldn't be here the Friday after next.

Al must have seen my face fall because she tucked her chin and knit her eyebrows together. "I wish you didn't have to leave. It's been fun having you in the group."

"Yes, please don't leave us," Nora added.

I tried to turn the corners of my mouth up into a smile, but my whole face felt heavy. "I'm sure I'll be back for a visit."

"Not soon enough," Cam said. "I'm going to miss my favorite cousin."

I rolled my eyes. "Your only cousin."

He shrugged and smiled. "Same thing."

As I struggled to focus on the new show Cam put on, tears pricked at the back of my eyes. The trip that used to feel like a once-in-a-lifetime opportunity had now morphed into a bittersweet experience. I couldn't help but wonder what was wrong with me. How could such a short time in one city have such an intense effect on me? The mere thought of leaving this place behind and getting on that plane felt like a punch to the gut. Even the prospect of landing in that first foreign city no longer filled me with the excitement and anticipation it once had.

Traveling and moving around had always seemed like the ultimate adventure, but the past few weeks had made me feel more alive than ever before. Also, there were certain people it was becoming increasingly harder to fathom saying goodbye to.

Staying in one place for friends—or a guy—wasn't right. Surely, I was just romanticizing it all.

Despite everything, I held onto the hope that the overwhelming sadness would soon dissipate. Deep down, I was a wanderer. Being stuck in one place with no hope of escape had been my reality for years.

I could never revert to that state again.

TWENTY-NINE

Jared

I SQUEEZED EVIE'S HAND AND BROUGHT IT TO MY LIPS, brushing them against her soft skin. Her time here was dwindling, and it had become completely unbearable to think about her leaving. Instead of facing that reality, I chose instead to spend every free second I could find with her.

I even skipped a band practice for her—something I vowed never to do for a girl.

"Navy Pier again?" She looked up at me with questioning eyes.

"I never got to walk you to the end of the pier. I still feel guilty about that."

Her eyes glimmered as she threaded her arm through mine and around my waist, squeezing tight.

Fuck. I would miss this.

"Thank you for always humoring the cheesy stuff for me," she muttered against my chest.

"Thanks for making the city I've lived in for years feel exciting again."

"It's a good thing I'm leaving soon. We're running out of tourist traps to check out."

Pain sliced through my chest at her casual words. I tried not to let her see it in my face.

"Speaking of you leaving, we just finalized the opening for that band in Detroit. It's a couple of days before your flight, but I really want you to come."

"I wouldn't miss it."

I leaned down and kissed the top of her head. Affection with her came easily. It felt like we had been doing this for years. For the hundredth time, I cursed my past self for not sweeping Evie off her feet the moment she arrived. We wasted so much time trying to be smart. In the end, it hadn't mattered. We couldn't stay apart.

We continued to stroll along the pier, settling into a comfortable silence. My arm slung around her shoulder—her hand in my hand—everything about this felt right.

As we approached the end of the pier, I looked out into the expansive water shaded by the gray sky. It was almost dusk.

I paused and glanced down at her.

"I wasn't going to say anything until it was official, but another band asked us to go on the second half of their tour with them—it's along the east coast for two months."

Evie's eyes lit up. "That's incredible." I would miss her unwavering support. "When do you leave?"

I hesitated. "Right after Detroit."

The same day as you.

"Wait—what about recording and the record label?"

"They said they'll schedule us when we get back. It's all pretty last minute, but the tour is too much good publicity to pass up."

"Wow, look at you. Getting an adventure of your own." Her voice shook.

I pinched her chin lightly between my thumb and index finger, forcing her to look at me.

"It isn't much of an adventure without you there."

She smiled, but it didn't reach her eyes. She turned back to the water, wrapping herself in her cozy gray sweater that I'm sure she made herself. We watched the waves for a while, just enjoying each other's presence.

"You know, there was a reason I wanted to come to Navy Pier that day," she whispered.

My eyebrows knit in confusion as I waited for her to continue.

"When I was a kid, Cam's mom took us to Chicago. It was pretty much the best day of my life up until that point." She went on to tell me how she got to wander the city streets freely. How she got to eat whatever she wanted. How she and Cam were dying to ride the Ferris wheel. How they were on their way there when her mom called. How she didn't get out much after that.

I wrapped my arm around her shoulder and pulled her into my chest, kissing the top of her head.

"It's kind of funny, but I feel like without even knowing all that you helped me relive that day."

"I wish you told me that story then."

"Why?" she asked into my chest.

"Because I would have tried to make it special for you."

She laughed softly. "It couldn't have been more special."

It was official. My heart was going to be absolutely wrecked.

BACK AT THE APARTMENT, I STARED AT EVIE WITH A NEW sense of longing. An unfamiliar one. Suddenly I felt like I had to be constantly near her—touching her. I wanted her to fill every space around me. I wanted to be completely consumed by her.

She looked up at me, and I saw my want matched in her eyes. Dipping my head, I planted kisses along her forehead, making a trail down her cheek to her neck.

I pulled my head back and stared into her eyes. "I'm going to miss this," I whispered.

She bit her lip. "Let's not talk about that."

She stood on her tiptoes to reach my lips and shut me up with a kiss. Her fingers tangled in my hair as she backed up, pulling me toward the bed.

A feeling like grief overtook me as I took in her perfect body. The one I had thoroughly enjoyed exploring and knew so many intimate details about. Details that now seemed cruel and pointless to know.

She felt like such a significant part of my life. The way she just crept in and inserted herself so perfectly. The unjustness of it all hit me like a brick wall. How could the universe gift her to me only to snatch her away so quickly?

I pulled away briefly to stare into her wide eyes. Three words crossed my mind and danced behind my lips. Something I wanted to say even though I knew it was too soon. Instead of letting them escape, I molded my mouth to hers, choosing instead to get lost in her.

"I can't believe I'm missing another one of your shows," Dean said, handing me a small plate that just came out of the kitchen.

I ate the stuffed mushroom in one bite. The restaurant closed early for the new menu tasting. There were just a few employees here, Dean, the other owner Eric, and some friends.

"It's hard to make it when they aren't local. I get it."

"You'll kill it in Detroit, and I fully plan to be at that New York show. Al and I already booked our flights."

"New York, huh?" I eyed him. "What a perfect place to get down on one knee and—"

Dean elbowed me in the ribs and jerked his head to look around the room. I choked on the bite I had just taken.

"Shut up. I don't know when I'm going to do it, and I don't need you going around and running your mouth. I want it to be a surprise," Dean hissed.

I mimed locking my lips and throwing away the key. "Who would I tell?"

Dean groaned. "I should have never told you. You're a liability."

"I'll be leaving for the tour soon enough. Can't tell Al when I'm not in the same city."

He sighed and ran his hands through his dark hair. "I wouldn't put it past you. You're always texting her about something."

I rolled my eyes. "I hardly text her. Just to ask about that dumb show or to send her a funny video."

Dean shot me a look. "You text her more than me."

I shrugged. "I like her better than you."

"Hah."

I grinned and searched the room for a head of lilac

waves. Glimpsing them outside, I saw Evie talking with Al underneath the patio's twinkle lights. She looked up at me and smiled, causing her nose to scrunch. I had to resist the urge to step outside that instant to kiss her.

"Is Evie going to Detroit?"

I glanced over to see Dean watching me watching her.

"Of course," I said simply.

"You planning on saying anything?"

"I'm not going to." I sighed and shook my head, not wanting to deal with this conversation—or my chaotic emotions.

As amazing as Evie was, and as strong as my feelings were, she was undoubtedly a free spirit. I couldn't be the one to hold her back. Plus, I had a lot going on with the band. Our timing just wasn't right. Maybe under different circumstances we could have worked out, but I was just happy to have met her.

"I just don't want you to regret any unsaid words," Dean said.

"I won't."

Maybe I would, but Evie was like an epic novel. Engaging, fascinating, impossible to step away from—but only half finished. She needed to close this chapter so she could move on and write the next one. Me keeping my mouth shut was the right thing to do. Her developing story was the reason I fell for her, and I couldn't be the reason she abandoned it.

THIRTY

Evie
___

"Are you ready for the big trip?" Al asked.

I nodded stiffly. "Of course."

Tiff, the wife of Dean's business partner, squealed. "Oh my gosh, how exciting. What kind of trip."

"I've got a one-way ticket booked to Bali. I'm going to backpack around southeast Asia for a few months—or a year—before I move on to Europe."

Tiff's mouth hung open. "That's amazing. Tell me all the details. What are you most excited for?"

I forced a smile and shared some of the few details I had planned out so far. Most of the trip was open-ended. I didn't want to be tied down by any kind of itinerary. As I rattled off the cities on my bucket list, I noticed something. The spark in my voice had died. When I had first decided I was going to go, I remember being elated. My heart had practically burst at the idea of exploring new countries for the indefinite future.

Now, my heart ached.

Tiff's smile faltered slightly at my flat tone of voice.

"Well, that all sounds amazing. I always wished I traveled more."

"Same," Al interjected, eyeing my crestfallen face. "I've never been further north than Canada."

Al and Tiff continued to talk about the cities they'd love to go to. I smiled and tried to nod at the appropriate times, but my mind zoned out.

The past few nights with Jared were all I could think about. His studio had become so comfortable to me. Just reading a book on his couch while he strummed his guitar. The way lines would form between his furrowed brows as he squinted in concentration from writing a new song. I hated that I wouldn't get to see that face every day. The face that felt a lot like home lately.

Home had always been a complex concept for me. The word held a lot of weight. My home my entire childhood had always felt more like a prison. As soon as I broke out, I vowed never to settle. To suck the life out of every experience I could fit into my short time on this planet. It overwhelmed me thinking of all the things I had yet to do.

Yet standing here on this brisk evening, thinking about all those adventures right around the corner, I couldn't help but feel like I was leaving the biggest one behind.

Suddenly it felt like I *was* settling.

"Babe," Tiff's husband, Eric, poked his head outside. "Can you come inside and try this new wine we just got in?"

Tiff excused herself. "I'll see you two back inside."

I watched her go, my eyes drifting to where Jared still stood with Dean. He threw his head back, laughing at something. I smiled as if I could somehow hear what was so funny.

"He's going to be a mess when you leave."

I tore my eyes away from the scene.

"Huh? Jared?" I gripped the glass in my hand, cursing my voice for shaking. "I'm sure he'll be fine."

I would be the mess.

THIRTY-ONE

Jared

"That was incredible," Tyler said, grinning from ear to ear.

Drew raised his hand and high-fived his brother. "I can't believe we get to do this full-time for two months."

"Think of all the new fans."

"Think of all the new girls." Drew smirked.

"Hell, yes."

Max and I exchanged a look as they walked ahead of us.

"Good to finally see those two not at each other's throat every second," he said.

"Amen to that."

I set my guitar in its case and glanced up at Max. "I'm surprised you're not more stoked. We're living the dream, after all."

Max stared off into the distance. "Right. Right."

I squinted my eyes in confusion. "What's up with you, man? Isn't this all you ever wanted?"

He jerked his blank gaze away from the wall and finally

met my eyes. "It is. It definitely is. Just some personal stuff weighing on me."

I tilted my head to the side, waiting for him to continue.

"I don't want to get into it. Just this girl from back home. Things have been going well, but she's got a lot of trust issues. Doesn't exactly bode well for me that I'm leaving for two months to go on tour."

"Can she come with us?"

He shook his head. "She's a nurse. Can't exactly drop everything."

"That's tough, dude. But she's going to realize that if she can trust anyone, it's going to be you. You're, like, the best guy I know."

He rolled his eye at my sincerity. "Whatever, don't get sappy on me."

"I just don't want any personal issues getting in the way of you celebrating what we're doing. I know you've been dreaming about this for longer than me. Enjoy it."

He nodded. "You're right. I earned this."

I smacked his shoulder. "Damn right, you did."

My voice held more pep than I felt. In reality, I should be taking my own advice because I knew exactly what it felt like to be consumed by personal issues. We had just killed our set, but the whole time I was out there, I only had one thing on my mind. Evie, and the fact that she would be leaving me in a few days. Less than seventy-two hours. The short countdown had my stomach turning over.

"You guys were amazing!" Evie exclaimed, entering the backstage area and throwing her arms around me.

I held on tight and tried not to think about how this would be the last time she congratulated me after a show.

"You guys want to get a drink and watch the set?" Drew asked, walking toward us.

I looked down at Evie tucked underneath my arm.

"I'm going to hang with her and sell some merch up front."

I wasn't about to spend a single second out of her presence if I could help it.

An hour later, Evie and I stuffed shirts back into tote bags.

"We sold so many," I said.

"What are you going to do without a photographer and a merch girl on tour?" she teased.

"Maybe we can get Drew to do it. His bass lines have been sounding sloppy anyway."

Evie tilted her head back and laughed. "For real, though," she said. "Are you sure you guys can handle the social media stuff?"

"I've got this, Eves. I barely have to do anything after everything you've done."

"You can always text me if you have any questions."

My eyes narrowed, and I quickly looked to the floor. The thought of texting Evie while she was thousands of miles away made me irrationally angry. I gripped the bag and stood, heading for the backstage door.

The guys were grabbing the last of the stuff, and they were already passing around a clear bottle.

"You guys ready to hit the town," Derek asked.

"Hell yeah," Drew said.

Tyler nodded, and Max shrugged. "Just for a little bit."

I cocked my head in Evie's direction. "I'm good. Evie and I already have plans."

Evie raised her eyebrows. "We do?"

"Obviously."

THE HARSH FLUORESCENT LIGHTS HIT EVIE'S SOFT PALE SKIN as we settled into the sticky booth. She glanced around the bustling late-night diner. Drunk people stumbled in and out, and loud conversations floated around the small space.

"This was the place you had to come to?"

I smirked. "It's world-famous. Didn't you see the sign out front? They don't just let restaurants put those up without fact-checking."

"Oh right, totally. I'm sure judges came in and everything to determine if this place warranted a sign."

"Exactly. They only ship those out to the best of the best."

She giggled, and my heart swelled. Making her laugh these past few weeks had become my new favorite activity. But the thought of not being able to do it anymore filled me with a sense of dread. How was I actually going to handle it when our time came to an end?

"Are you going to be okay?" she asked.

My spine stiffened as the shock of her question ripped through me. Did she know me so well by now that she could read my mind?

"With the tour," she added. "I know there will be a lot of temptations. I just don't want you to have another bad night again."

I let out the breath I held. "I'll be fine. You don't need

to worry about me. One night falling off the wagon was all it took to remind me why I'm on it."

"Promise?" she asked. Even though she was only across the booth from me, she felt small and far away in this moment.

I reached forward and grasped her hand. "I promise, okay? Max will be there too. He's responsible."

"You're responsible," she insisted. "I didn't mean to doubt you."

"I know you'd never doubt me." My lip tugged up as I ran my thumb across the back of her knuckles.

The waitress appeared and set down a plate in front of us.

Evie winced. "Another hot dog?"

"It's a coney dog," I said, grabbing a fry off the plate. "It's a Detroit thing, apparently."

She sniffed it before taking a bite. Chili dripped onto her chin, and I stifled a laugh. She glared at me before quickly dabbing her mouth with a napkin.

"Still not my thing, but sorry to inform you that's a million times better than a Chicago dog."

"Watch it. Those are fighting words," I said before taking a giant bite. I had to admit it was pretty good. "This is definitely inferior. Take it back now."

"Never."

I reached under the table and squeezed the spot right above her knee. She let out an involuntary squeal and swatted my hand away. The waitress shot us a look before attending to a different table.

"You're going to get us kicked out," she hissed.

I grinned. "Fine by me. I can't wait to take you back to the hotel anyway."

We paid our bill and emerged back into the crisp evening air. Summer had almost completely transformed into fall, and the evenings were getting cooler. I slung my arm around Evie's shoulders and rubbed my hand up and down to keep her warm.

As we strolled through the unfamiliar city, a comfortable silence settled between us, allowing us to soak in our new surroundings. A football game must have just ended. The streets bustled with fans chatting and laughing while making their way to nearby bars. For a moment, my sadness disappeared.

My dreams were coming true. I was going on tour. My band would record an album. The best girl in the entire world was tucked underneath my arm right now.

I spotted a storefront with a neon sign that said, "Walk-Ins Welcome" and dragged Evie to it.

"Come on," I said.

"Where are you going?"

"A surprise."

The bell above the door sounded as we stepped into the shop. Evie looked around, and her mouth hung open.

"A tattoo parlor?" she whispered. "What are we doing here?"

"I want to remember tonight."

I want to remember us.

Her eyes widened as she looked around the room. The shop was empty except for someone in a chair in the back corner getting a tattoo.

"You can't just get a tattoo without thinking it through."

I chuckled and gestured with one hand to my neck and

arms. "How do you think I got all of these? I can promise you, thought was not involved."

She crossed her arms. "Fine, but I'm not getting one."

"I never said you had to."

"Can I help you two?" A bearded man in a black sweatshirt walked over to us.

"Hey, man. Any chance you have availability right now?" I pointed to my left forearm, which still had some bare skin. "I'm just trying to get something small."

He nodded and waved his hand for us to come back. "Not a problem. What about you?" he asked Evie.

When I didn't hear her immediate rejection of the idea, I looked down at her, surprised to find her biting her lip.

"Are you considering this?"

"I don't know," she admitted.

"Well, it would definitely be a new experience," I joked.

"You're right."

"Evie, I was just kidding. You don't need to feel pressured into doing this."

"What if I want to?" She raised her chin defiantly.

This girl was full of surprises.

"What are you going to get, Ms. you-have-to-think-it-through?"

She nudged my shoulder. "Hey, I'm thinking it through right now."

"Let's surprise each other," I suggested.

THIRTY-TWO

Evie

Adrenaline coursed through my body as I stared at the bandage covering my wrist, still in disbelief that permanent ink lay beneath it. I had always been an adventurous person, but this kind of spontaneity was out of character even for me. The feeling of the needle pressing into my skin had been surprisingly thrilling. Amidst the recent haze clouding my mind, grounding myself in the present moment felt refreshing.

I peeked at the counter where Jared paid.

It was kind of comical, really. I always thought that adventure lay in whatever destination awaited me. When I used to lay in bed and fantasize about getting out of my hometown, I told myself I would never stop. Never stop moving. Never stop experiencing new things. Never stop living.

Jared could make anything feel like an adventure, though.

"You took that like a champ. I don't even think I heard

you whimper." Jared stepped out of the shop and drew me into a hug. "Let me see yours."

"You first," I said.

He pulled away his bandage. I leaned in to get a closer look before smacking my hand over my mouth and gasping.

"You did not do that."

He cocked his head and smiled. "Do what?"

"That," I said in disbelief, pointing to the small script "E" that was now etched on his forearm.

He looked down at it and pulled his eyebrows together. "What? My grandmother's name was Emily."

Heat flooded my cheeks. "Oh, right. I shouldn't have assumed anything." I cursed myself for being so stupid.

Jared threw his head back and laughed. "Her name was Mary. It's obviously for you, you dork."

"Jared!" I exclaimed, swatting his chest. "Who just goes and gets the initial of some girl they barely know permanently drawn onto them?"

He reached out and tucked a piece of my hair behind my ear. "Someone that really doesn't want to forget her."

My heart pounded so loudly that I feared he would hear it. I just stood there, blinking like an idiot. All coherent thought had left my mind.

Jared raised his eyebrows expectantly. "Are you going to show me yours, or what?"

"S-sorry," I stammered, pulling my bandage to the side.

The corner of his lip curved as he shook his head. "You're seriously going to tell me you didn't get that for me?"

I glanced down at the tiny line-drawn Ferris wheel.

"I told you the story. I have a lot of memories about this."

He smiled sadly but nudged my shoulder. "Pretty sure I was in the good one."

That night back at the hotel, Jared held me close. I laid awake next to him for a while, trying to memorize every detail of how his body perfectly enveloped mine. I breathed in his scent, already scared of forgetting it. I was fully convinced I would never feel like this again. No one out there could ever compare to Jared. He was truly unique.

I squeezed my eyes shut and forced the hot tears to retreat. I willed my heart to soar at the thought of my next adventure.

Instead, it just ached at the thought of losing him.

THE HOT ESPRESSO BURNED MY TONGUE AS SOON AS IT passed my lips. Sleep had never come last night, and now I could barely pry my tired eyes open.

Jared and I walked aimlessly down the river trail. We wanted to get an early morning walk in before we had to make the drive back. After a few minutes, he stopped to take in the view, tucking me into his side as he did so. I reached my arms around his middle and held on tightly, never wanting to let him go.

"Look, Eves." He pointed across the river to the Canadian side. "You don't even need to leave the Midwest to see another country."

I laughed softly and buried my cheek into his sweatshirt. "No offense, but that wasn't exactly what I had in mind when I thought about jet-setting around the world."

What had I thought? That it would be incredible? A once-in-a-lifetime opportunity? I couldn't even remember anymore.

"You all ready for the trip?" he asked.

I snuck a glance at his face to see his gaze still fixated across the river.

"I-I think so."

He stiffened in my arms. "You think so?"

I sighed and willed my eyes to remain dry. "I know it will be amazing once I get there, it's just hard to be excited about it right now. I just feel so hollow lately."

Jared still didn't look down at me. His eyes darted across the city skyline, seemingly processing my words. I held my breath, waiting for his response.

"How's your wrist?" he finally said.

"What?"

He pointed to my bandage.

"Oh, right. It doesn't even hurt."

He nodded. "Good."

The memory of Jared running into that tattoo parlor like a little kid already felt like a lifetime ago. His mood had darkened. The solemnity of it all made it feel like we were attending a funeral rather than standing on the precipice of grand, life-altering milestones.

I pressed my face into his chest. "I don't want to let you go," I muttered.

He remained silent for a few heartbeats. "So don't," he finally said in a voice so small I was sure I misheard him.

"What?" I pulled away from him so I could see his face better.

He ran one hand across his jaw before throwing both of them in the air.

"Fuck, Evie. I didn't want to do this."

"Do what?"

He gripped the sides of his head as if he was ready to tear his hair out.

"I need to say something."

My breath hitched as his eyes bore into me.

"Trust me. I know how unfair this is for me to say. To ask you to give up your trip—but fuck it. Stay. Stay with me."

"Jared, I—"

He held up his hand. "Let me just get this out, or I'll lose my nerve," he said. "I know it's completely ridiculous to ask you to choose me over this dream, but I'm asking it all the same." He gripped my shoulders, his stare intense. "Choose me. Come on tour with us. I can't even imagine how it's going to feel doing all this without you. I don't know when it happened, but you became my person. The one I want to share all this with. Hell, if this wasn't what I've been working toward my whole fucking life, maybe I'd just leave it all behind and go with you. But I can't. So, I know that makes me even more selfish for saying this, but please, Eves, stay with me. I can't stand the thought of you getting on a plane without me laying it all out there. I-I'm in love with you. I tried to fight it, I really did, but you made it impossible. Please come with me. I promise you it'll be an adventure too. I'll spend every day making sure of that. And as soon as I get a chance, I'll take you somewhere —wherever you want to go. Just please, stay with me."

Tears streamed down my face as he clutched my arms. My mouth hung open as a million responses crossed my mind.

Of course, I'll stay.

You already make every day an adventure.
I love you too.

Instead, a choked sob escaped my mouth. "I-I'm s-so sorry, I-I can't."

Jared sighed and closed his eyes before blowing out a long slow breath. He drew me into him and held me tightly, kissing the top of my head. My body shook as tears streamed uncontrollably down my face.

"Please don't cry. I never wanted to make this harder on you. I just—I just couldn't let you leave without saying it."

I held him close for what I feared was the last time.

THIRTY-THREE

Jared

Yesterday's events played on a loop in my mind. I couldn't stop thinking about the car ride home after I had mustered the courage to confess my feelings to Evie. The atmosphere had grown tense and uncomfortable to say the least. Once she had stopped crying, an impenetrable silence settled between us, heavy with unspoken words. I had poured my heart out, but in the end, it wasn't enough. The weight of my unrequited emotions lingered in the air, leaving an impassable void between us.

When I dropped her off in front of Cam's apartment, I got out of the car to hug her. We didn't say it, but I knew it was our final goodbye.

A cupboard closed loudly in the kitchen. I looked up from the couch to see Dean and Al tiptoeing around.

"I'm awake," I said without getting up. "No need to pretend to be quiet."

"Sorry," Al still whispered. "We didn't want to bother you."

I had crashed on their couch last night. Being at my studio without Evie had sounded too painful.

"I can't believe you're leaving tomorrow," Dean said.

"We'll really miss you around here," Al said. "I almost forgot you weren't our third roommate."

"Ha. Ha," I replied dryly.

Dean winced. "Come on, dude. You should be pumped. Your successful band is going on tour tomorrow. This is huge."

"I would be pumped if I hadn't just gotten my heart ripped out of my chest and stomped on. All because of your stupid advice."

Dean held up his hands. "I stand by what I said. You would have regretted not telling her."

Al gave me a halfhearted smile. "At least now you'll have no what-ifs."

I sighed. "Except that the what if would have been 'What if she loved me too and decided to stay.'"

"Wondering that would have been worse," Al insisted.

"Whatever. Just let me get my grieving out of the way before tomorrow."

As Dean and Al retreated to the patio with their coffee, their voices gradually faded into the background. They knew I needed space to wallow in my thoughts.

Dean's words still echoed in my mind—that performing on tour was my absolute dream come true. He was right. This opportunity meant everything to me. Yet, despite the outward appearance of success and fulfillment, my emotions remained conflicted.

Frustration seeped through my veins, directed not at Evie but at myself. How could I not be fully immersed in my journey? My teenage self would kick my ass for not being amped about this tour. Hell, myself two months ago would have kicked my ass for it too. I had made something of myself in an undeniable way. I had poured everything I had into music, and it paid off. Yet now, in this pivotal moment, nothing but emptiness consumed me.

Obviously, my source of discontentment wasn't lost on me. It wasn't even Evie herself, but her absence that haunted me. Evie—the one person who had captured my heart in a way I hadn't realized was possible. Even though she couldn't choose me, I felt no trace of anger or resentment. I completely understood why she couldn't stay, but thinking of her face, her eyes, her smile…my heart fucking ached.

My mind swirled with the memories we shared in our short time together.

But I couldn't let that cast a shadow over my aspirations. It wasn't as simple as moving on, but I still had to choose myself just as she had. She put her dreams and wants over me, and I had to do the same. As much as it killed me.

I owed it to myself to be present for this time in my life. Because while this heartache could last forever, who knew what my future held without her? I needed to compartmentalize the pain so I could focus my energy on celebrating myself—my wins. I deserved it.

As much as I wished I could change her mind, I couldn't. So, for today and today only, I would mourn what could have been.

THIRTY-FOUR

Evie

"You've got to stop crying."

"I can't help it," I sniffed.

Cam threw another box of tissues at me. "You've been like this since you got back. Shouldn't you be excited?"

I blew my nose in response. Leaving tomorrow felt physically painful. All I could see in my head was Jared telling me he loved me and me saying nothing in response. I could practically see his heart break through his eyes.

"You could always stay, you know."

My face crumpled. "This is my dream, Cam. I can't just give that up."

He sighed and crouched on the floor next to my open suitcase that remained unpacked.

"Evelyn, can I be real with you?"

I tilted my head. "Are you ever not?"

"Fair." He blew out a breath. "Look, you've been running away for years. Ever since you turned up at my college dorm that day."

"I'm not running away." Sure, I had technically run away from home, but that was it.

"Yes, you have. Because you feel like if you stay in one place it will somehow be the same as it was for you growing up."

"That isn't true."

He lifted his eyebrows. "Yes, it is. You're so desperate to leave that life behind you never stopped to ask yourself what you actually want."

"I want an adventure."

"Staying is an adventure."

"I don't want to settle."

"What part of staying, making lasting friendships, and being with the guy you're crazy about would you consider settling?"

I stuck out my lip. "But traveling is my dream."

He shrugged. "Dreams can change."

"How can I just stay?" I choked out.

He sighed. "I'm not saying a drive to our hometown would replace the years of therapy you might need, but it's at least a start."

My face paled as I rapidly shook my head. "I'm not going there."

"Look at you," he said exasperatedly. "You're a mess. You're so scared of staying in one place that you'd rather be miserable than address your fears. You're giving the place you grew up and your parents way too much power over your life. I know you think that moving constantly is you taking back control, but it's not. It has its own warped power over you. You're stuck in a different prison now, and you aren't going to break out until you confront your fears."

My mouth hung open as I tried to process his words.

Could he be right? Had I been so desperate to be free that I ended up overcompensating?

"Will you go with me?" I asked softly.

THE ROAD STRETCHED OUT BEFORE US WITH ONLY A FEW houses and buildings breaking up the endless fields of dying grass. It had been years since I last set foot in this place. Anticipation and dread consumed me the closer we got.

"How are you doing?" Cam asked, glancing from me back to the road.

"I'm fine," I answered.

"No, really. Tell me."

I kept my eye trained on a crumbling barn as it whizzed by us.

"I feel anxious."

He nodded. "I believe it. But I'm proud of you for coming. It's just a place. It has no power over you."

"What if…"

"What if what?"

"What if they aren't there?"

He shrugged. "Then they aren't there. Just being here is the first step."

As the familiar scenery rolled by, a wave of resentment washed over me. The landscape, once suffocatingly stagnant, now seemed to mock me with the memories I spent here under the watchful eyes of my parents. Each passing field reminded me of the constraints that had once felt unsurpassable, stifling all my hopes and desires. I despised the thought of being back here, of revisiting the ghosts of my past. But I now recognized the necessity of this journey

—a step toward forging my own path and embracing an authentic future without the irrational fear of settling. I thought I had freed myself back then, but what I hadn't realized was that leaving was just the first step.

I took a deep breath to steady my racing heart. We were quickly approaching the small main street my parents now resided on according to the address we had received from Renee.

I pulled out my crochet hooks and fiddled with the tangled thread in my bag.

"Evelyn put that away right now and focus."

I jumped at Cam's stern tone.

"I need a distraction," I insisted.

"No, you need to absorb this."

"What should I say?" I asked, setting the half-finished sleeve in my lap.

"What do you feel like you need to say?"

"I-I'm not even sure." For how much my past consumed me, I hadn't once thought about what I would say if I confronted my parents.

"I'm sure it'll come to you," Cam said, reaching over and squeezing my hand.

His touch grounded me, and a flicker of determination extinguished some of my anxiety. This town—my family—no longer possessed the ability to hold me captive and define me. I would turn around and drive out of this town just as easily as we had driven in. This was nothing more than a place that had haunted me for too long.

Cam pulled into a small parking lot lined with modest-looking brick condos.

"Here it is," he said.

My mouth hung open as I gawked at the buildings.

They were right off the main street. Walking distance to everything. The mother and father I knew thrived in isolation.

"Are you sure?"

"Yep, unit number two. This is the address they gave my mom."

We both exited the car cautiously. I stood at the bottom of the small staircase, willing my legs to move.

"Hey," Cam said, standing by my side. "You've got this, okay? I'm right here."

I took one last deep breath before I walked straight up to the door and knocked.

Only a few seconds passed before the door opened. My heart flew into my throat at the sight of my mother. She was dressed casually in a plain shirt and jeans. Her hair was longer than I ever remembered it being. She looked older yet the same. There were more fine lines by her eyes, and her lips were pursed in the manner they always were.

I saw a flash of confusion cross her eyes as she glanced from Cam to me before her mouth hung open.

"Evelyn." My name fell from her lips, but nothing else came after.

"Hi, Mom. It's been a while."

Cam waved awkwardly next to me. "Hi, Aunt Catherine."

"Cam," she said. "You've grown since I saw you last."

"Can we—would it be okay if we came in? Just for a minute. We can't stay long," I said hurriedly.

She looked at me and nodded slowly, as if hardly processing who I was. Stepping back, she gestured for us to enter her home. Once inside, I took note of the pristine white walls adorned with pictures of meadows and wildlife.

A small TV sat in the corner, a computer next to it. A far cry from the living room I had grown up in.

"Wow," I said. "Looks so different than the old house."

"Right, well. We decided to get something more manageable," she muttered, still staring at me. "Can I get you two something to drink? Lemonade?"

I shook my head. "I'm alright. We won't be long."

She nodded and sunk back into one of the floral armchairs in the living room.

Cam and I perched uncomfortably on the loveseat opposite her. Seeing her frail form enveloped by the large chair, it felt surreal that this woman once held so much authority over me.

"Where's Dad?" I asked, the word "dad" almost getting caught in my throat.

"He's out of town for a few days," she said. "A fishing trip with some of the men from town."

"Oh," I said. While I had been mentally preparing to confront them both, perhaps it was better this way.

"How fun," Cam said to fill the heavy silence.

She glanced at him. "Are you still living in Chicago?" She said it the same way you would a dirty word.

"Yes, Aunt Catherine, just living my best miscreant lifestyle." His sweet tone almost made me want to laugh.

"Mmmm." She pursed her lips and turned away from him. "I know your mother is still living in Florida. Sounds like a swinger's club."

"Just an apartment building with other vibrant individuals," he said. "She was dying to get out. After all, this town has become a little stale."

She ignored his comment and turned her attention back to me. "So, what made you stop by after all these years?"

I sighed. "I don't know, honestly. I guess I had been dreading this moment for so long I wanted to finally get it over with."

"Dreading?" Her brow furrowed.

"Yes, dreading." I laughed bitterly.

"That seems extreme," she muttered.

"You must know how much I hated it here—how stifled I felt."

I expected her to get mad or call me ungrateful. Instead, she just sucked in a breath and stared out the window.

"Do you hate me?" she asked quietly.

My mouth hung open at her unexpected question. I looked to Cam, who tilted his head toward the door—as if asking if he should leave. I shook my head. As strong as I wanted to be on my own, his support was the only thing keeping me grounded.

"Do you hate *me*?" I asked.

She crossed her arms in a defensive manner. "I just...I did the best I could. I thought we were raising you right. But then you up and left and became this whole different person. It wasn't a person we knew, and it certainly wasn't who we raised you to be."

I snorted softly. "Thank god for that. I became who I was always meant to be despite the way you raised me."

She nodded. "I guess it's a good thing you left then."

"You don't regret any of it? You can't see in hindsight how you could have done things differently?" I pushed.

She scoffed. "We did the best we could, Evelyn. We raised you how we thought was best. It isn't our fault you decided that wasn't what you wanted."

I sighed. Communicating with her was pointless. All of

the anticipation I had felt at the thought of coming here had completely dissolved by this point. This person in front of me was nothing to fear. She could hardly hold a real conversation with me. She couldn't control me, didn't understand me, and therefore pushed me away. It said everything about her close-mindedness and nothing about me as a person—as a daughter.

I would never get the resolution or true confrontation I needed from her—or my father. I would have to find that within myself. I knew one thing for sure. I would no longer let them hold any power over me. It might take a while to overcome this in full, but I knew I had already come a lot farther than I had even realized.

"You're right, Mom. It wasn't what I wanted," I said, standing. "We should probably head out."

"You're leaving already? Don't tell me you drove here just for that."

I nodded. "I think this was all I needed, actually. I'm ready to get out of here."

Cam stood and moved for the door. "Lovely to see you, Aunt Catherine."

"Mmmm," she said.

"Bye, Mom," I said, following him.

"Wait," she said.

I turned back, eyebrows raised.

She tore a piece of notebook paper and scribbled something before handing it to me.

"I have email now. Maybe you could send me one sometime."

"Sure." I wanted to laugh at the mundaneness of it all.

Back in the car, Cam had us on the road in record time. "That was fun."

My lips turned up. "So fun."

"I mean, it could have gone better, could have gone worse. Overall, I would call it a success."

Laughter finally bubbled over at his ridiculous comment. He started laughing too until we were both in tears. After a few minutes, we settled down, and I watched the same familiar scenery pass us as we left the town I had once so desperately escaped.

"I can't believe I built this up so much in my head for years. She's just—nothing to me anymore."

"It's healing," Cam said. "To realize your demons aren't as strong as you thought they were."

I nodded. "It is."

"I was serious about the therapy, though," Cam added. "You're still a mess."

A fit of inappropriate laughter hit us again as we passed the town sign.

Driving away, it felt like a hundred-pound weight had been lifted off my shoulders. Cam was right. I hadn't healed yet, but at least I had started. They were no longer my family. I had found my own.

We rode in silence for a while before Cam broke it. "Have you given any more thought to what you're going to do tomorrow?"

I bit my lip. After today I felt like I had permission to think about what I wanted to do, not just what I felt like I had to do.

Staying no longer felt like settling.

"I already bought the ticket," I finally whispered.

Cam scoffed. "You're going to walk away from the guy of your dreams because you were too dumb to buy refundable airfare?"

A wave of hesitation washed over me, leaving me momentarily frozen as I stood in front of Jared's apartment. My heart nearly stopped when I spotted him, already packing up his van. He looked up and paused when he saw me. A flicker of confusion flashed across his face as his eyes locked onto mine. But then, an easy smile graced his lips, and I breathed a sigh of relief.

"Have you come to say goodbye?" he called. "I was worried you might just take off."

I walked over and stood a few paces away, hating the distance between us and the sadness I could see in his eyes —hating myself even more for causing it.

"I'm sorry about the other day," I finally said.

He shook his head. "There's nothing to be sorry for."

I silently begged him to close the space between us, but I didn't want to push him. He had put himself out there, and I hadn't reciprocated. It was my turn to be vulnerable.

"Are you headed to the airport?" he asked, glancing down at my suitcase.

I searched my mind for the best place to start.

"I'm not sure. I mean, I don't think that trip was ever actually my dream."

He crossed his arms and tilted his head, waiting for me to continue.

"I was just scared," I said shakily. "Scared of staying in one place and feeling stuck again. When I ran away, I was so focused on the running aspect that I never stopped to determine what I wanted out of life. I had my online world and all these new experiences, and I thought that was enough."

"Evie, you don't have to explain yourself to me."

"I do, though. You're the only person I need to explain myself to. I-I went and saw my mother yesterday."

His eyebrows shot into his hairline. "What? Why didn't you tell me? I would have come with you."

I shook my head. "I know you would have, but I couldn't ask that of you. Not when you have so much going on and not after—not after the other day."

"You're still important to me, Eves. I would have made it work." He dragged his hand over his face. "I mean, how did it go? Are you okay?"

"I'm fine. Better than I have been. It was good to see her. I mean, it wasn't actually good. She just stood there and got defensive, but it was cathartic for me to realize I'm free. I don't have anything to run from anymore."

Tears brimmed my eyes.

"Come here," he murmured and pulled me to him. I held on tightly, breathing him in.

Too soon, he released me and grabbed my shoulders. His eyes took in every inch of my face as if he were trying to memorize it. Cupping my chin in one hand, he tucked a piece of hair behind my ear with his other.

"I'm going to miss you so much," he said.

I bit my lip, suddenly nervous for what I had to say next.

"Actually, I was going to see if you still had room for one more."

He tilted his head and scrunched his eyebrows. Recognition flashed across his eyes, but he still looked unsure.

"What are you saying?"

"That I'm in love with you t—"

Jared cut me off by crushing his lips onto mine. He

kissed me deeply for a moment, holding onto me so tightly that my feet lifted off the ground. When he finally released me, he had a grin plastered to his face. "Sorry, you were saying."

I laughed. "I was saying that I'm in love with you too. I should have said it before, but I was being an idiot."

"Does that mean—" he searched my eyes "—does that mean you aren't leaving."

"The only way I'm leaving is with you—if you'll still have me, that is."

His entire face lit up as he pressed another kiss to my lips.

"Hell yes, I'll still have you," he said. "If you're sure that is. I don't want you to regret this."

I nodded. "I'm so sure."

"Good, because I don't think I could handle saying goodbye to you again."

He spun me around in a circle as I laughed.

"Let's go before you change your mind." He grabbed my suitcase and threw it in his trunk. "Think you're ready to deal with the band twenty-four seven for two months? We can be pretty loud—and smelly."

I wrinkled my nose. "I guess I'll have to endure it for you."

He tussled my hair. "I love you so fucking much."

"I love you too," I said, beaming at him as I climbed into the passenger seat of his car.

I could already tell this would be my best adventure yet.

Epilogue

JARED

Cold winter air flowed through the cracked window as I drove along the dark highway. The heater in the van had broken a few weeks back. It was either max heat or off. Evie was the one that suggested just cracking the windows when it got too hot.

She slept soundly in the seat next to me as we finally headed back to Chicago after two months on the road.

The tour had been the experience of a lifetime. Our band had grown in popularity with every new city, and we had written quite a few new songs. I spent any free time I had wandering the streets with Evie, checking out every unassuming diner and tourist trap we could find.

I smiled as one memory of Evie running along a frigid beach on the east coast flashed through my mind. She had insisted on taking her shoes off and going barefoot, even though it was only forty degrees. Afterward, we had to rush home immediately so she could take a hot shower.

I thought of another memory where a girl at one of our shows had approached the band after our set. She seemed excited to talk to us before spotting Evie. It turned out she had been following her videos for years and fangirled hard over her. Instead of taking a picture with the band, she ended up asking me to take a picture of her with Evie.

I glanced over as she breathed softly against the window.

She brought so much joy to the trip that it was impossible for me to imagine what it would have been like if she had decided not to come. I shuddered at the thought and reached my hand over to hold her knee.

She moved underneath my touch, and her eyelids drifted open.

I squeezed her leg. "Sorry, babe. I didn't mean to wake you."

She reached her arms over her head and stretched, letting out a yawn in the process.

"That's okay. I should probably get ready for my shift anyway."

"Not tonight. We're only a few hours away. I can take us home."

She bit her lip and stared out the window.

"What is it?" I asked.

"Nothing, it's just…"

"Tell me," I said when she hesitated.

"I should have spent more time looking at apartment listings. Cam has a new boyfriend, and I highly doubt he wants me to keep crashing on his couch."

"Apartment listings, huh?"

"I know, I know. I'm stupid for putting it off. It just always felt like I had time, and then all of a sudden, here we are driving back. It really snuck up on me."

"I kind of thought you would want to stay with me." I smiled as heat rushed to her cheeks.

"Like live together?"

We hadn't talked about it, but I had assumed we were on the same page. She had basically spent every night at my apartment before we left anyway.

"Why not? You sick of me or something?" I teased.

"Of course not, it's just…isn't it a little soon?"

I pretended to sigh. "Shit, you're right. I forgot. Were we supposed to move in together before or after you came on tour with me, and we shared cramped hotel rooms for two months?"

She laughed. "Well—"

"Or were we supposed to do it before you canceled your dream trip for me?"

She swatted my hand. "I already told you. I did that for me."

I smirked. "I think I had a little bit to do with it."

I grabbed my phone off the dash and tossed it into her lap. "Speaking of dreams, why don't you check the latest email on my phone."

Evie gave me a puzzled look but grabbed my phone and scrolled.

"What is thi—oh my god! Jared, you didn't!" she exclaimed.

"I did."

"Thailand?"

"For two weeks. We leave as soon as we're done recording."

She snaked her arms around my neck and hugged me. I took one hand off the wheel and squeezed her arm.

"This is amazing, Jared. Thank you. I'm so excited!"

"I know it isn't your dream trip but—

"It's better," she said quickly.

I grinned. "Are you going to say it's because I'm there?"

She laughed. "Something like that."

She kissed my cheek. I stared out at the road ahead as Evie excitedly looked up an itinerary for our trip.

All of my dreams were coming true, and I hadn't even realized my biggest one was her.

The End

Review Settle Up

Thank you for reading Settle Up! As an indie author, I appreciate it so much! If you enjoyed this book, please take a few moments to leave a review.

Haven't read Comfort Zoned yet? **Check out Al and Dean's story!** *Available now on Amazon.*

Keep reading for a sneak peek of...

A small-town, enemies-to-lovers, snowboarding romance.

Key Ridge

"Seriously, Garrett, wake up! You're going to be late." I threw a pillow at my boyfriend's head and tried to coax him out of our bed for the third time that morning.

"What time is it?" he groaned.

"Seven fifty-five."

Even though we had been together for eight years and lived together for two, his inability to get moving in the morning still irritated me. He always slept through his alarm, so it was up to me to ensure he got up in time for work every day.

I was a morning person through and through and couldn't relate to his zombie-like demeanor. Waking up early to work out, read, or go for a walk was the highlight of my day.

Garrett finally spilled out of bed and went straight for the tiny bathroom the two of us shared. Once I heard the shower start, I breathed a sigh of relief and returned to the living room to savor one more cup of coffee. Settling into our sectional couch, I resumed working on my crossword puzzle.

A warm breeze hit me square in the face through the window I had left open. Now that it was almost October, the intense and humid heat had at last settled down in Florida. It was a luxury to go outside again and *enjoy* the weather without sweating through whatever shirt I was wearing.

"Hey, Mattie." A damp and shirtless Garrett poked his head out of our bedroom doorframe. "We've got dinner with the crew tonight. You'll probably have to head there straight from work."

My mind worked quickly, scanning through all my upcoming social commitments.

"Tonight? I don't remember you telling me that."

"It's kind of last minute. We're celebrating." Garrett looked at his feet sheepishly and rubbed his short brown hair with a towel. "Will and Lauren got engaged last night."

"What?" I exclaimed, springing up from the couch. Will was Garrett's best friend from the college we had both attended. "But-but they've been together for like five minutes."

"It's been a year, babe. Lauren was really riding on him to propose."

"I didn't know riding someone to propose was an effective strategy." I crossed my arms and glared at him.

"Don't even go there. You know how swamped I am with work. Once I make partner, I'll be able to think about marriage."

My chest tightened in that familiar way it always did whenever marriage came up. The subject of our relationship status was an ever-looming issue between the two of us.

I could recite Garrett's excuses by heart at this point. First, it was "But we're too young." Next, it was "We don't have enough money for a wedding." Now, he had moved on to the "Once I make partner" narrative.

"It's getting old watching friends who've been together a fraction of the time we have beat us down the aisle," I muttered.

He walked over to me and cupped my chin in his hand, attempting to get me to look at him. I relented and stared back into his blue eyes.

"I love you," he said and planted a kiss on my forehead. "I promise when I do propose, it will be the grandest gesture you ever saw. It will put everyone else's to shame."

"It's not just about the proposal. I want to get married to *you*. I want to start our life together."

"We already have a life together," he responded, turning away from me, and heading back to the bedroom to change.

It was pointless to argue with him anymore about this. I knew I was fighting a losing battle. I should have been more insistent earlier on in our relationship. Once a guy knew he could get away with not asking you after four years or six years, he certainly wasn't going to suddenly have a change of heart after eight.

I walked into our bedroom and shoved past Garrett to get into our cramped bathroom and closed the door. Gripping the side of the countertop, I took a deep breath and scrutinized myself in the mirror.

My long, wavy hair was thick and constantly trying to double in size with the Florida humidity. I fingered a blonde highlight that I had recently added to my light brown hair. I thought it popped against my tan skin, but Garrett had said it made me look high maintenance. My blue eyes were almost as light as Garrett's. When we met in college, I remembered thinking that our future children would look adorable with the blue eyes they were sure to inherit from us. Somehow the thought of children felt further away now at twenty-nine than it did back then at twenty-one.

A soft knock echoed through the tiled room. Sighing, I opened the door to face my boyfriend, or some would say, roommate. He met my gaze with pleading eyes.

"Please, let's not fight, okay." He grabbed my hand and pulled me into his chest. "I love you."

"Who's fighting? Not me." I gave him a weak smile, knowing the argument wasn't worth it. It never was.

"You're the best." He gestured for me to exit the room first and smacked my ass when I passed him. "We need to get going. How many times do I have to tell you we're going to be late?"

"I could use some help with the housekeeping team. They don't respect me and it's causing issues. I have to double-check every room they turn over to make sure they've done a good enough job."

I nodded sympathetically at a property manager I had worked with for years as she rattled on about the latest issues she was facing at one of our resort properties.

"Have you tried setting up a meeting with the owner of the company?" I asked her.

"He keeps giving me the run-around. It's useless. Our old company was so much better."

"Well, we have a contract in place with these new cleaners, so we need to make it work. Their rates were much better, and we're going to close out the year with huge savings. It looks great for our department."

She bit her lip and looked unsure.

"Trust me. It just takes time to build these relationships. You're doing a great job. Keep up the amazing work."

I gave her my brightest smile and continued to reassure her. By the time our meeting was over, I had hoped some of my optimism had rubbed off on her. I was known for my sunny disposition and positive attitude at Brook's Boutique Property Management Firm.

I swiveled around in my plush chair and surveyed the view outside my window. Our firm occupied the twenty-fifth floor of a high-rise. When I got my own office last year, I thought I would never get used to the fantastic view. Sometimes I had to pinch myself to make sure I wasn't dreaming. I had gotten a job here right out of college in operations and had risen through the ranks to Director of Property Management.

Despite my best efforts, my mind wandered back to my conversation with Garrett this morning. If only my personal life was on the same trajectory my professional life was on.

There was a knock at my door before it cracked open, revealing a tall redheaded woman looking disheveled.

"Hey girl, how was your weekend?" she asked, sitting opposite my pearly white desk. Sharon from the finance department was the only person I might consider a friend instead of just a coworker.

"Just the usual. Garrett and I went out to dinner, and I hit up the farmer's market on Sunday. What about you?"

"I went to this cute little pop-up bar on Friday and met the coolest guy. Very starving-artist vibes, but he was so hot.

Anyway, we ended up going out on Saturday, and you won't believe where he took me." Sharon rambled on about her adventurous weekend.

I felt a pang of jealousy. She was constantly trying new things and meeting new people. It made me feel like such a dull square. I had lived in Florida my entire life, and the only people I hung out with were my friends from college. I thrived on routine, and my idea of an adventure was trying the new sushi place that had just opened up on our block. I was twenty-nine going on fifty.

Actually, my parents were in their fifties and were more adventurous than I was. They had just gone on a two-week Alaskan cruise and snowshoed on a glacier. I hadn't even *seen* snow in real life before.

"Do you want to grab drinks after work?"

Sharon's question ripped me from my thoughts.

"Can't. Garrett and I have dinner plans." I chewed my lip before continuing. "His friend Will and his girlfriend Lauren just got engaged."

Sharon sat up straight at the news. "Excuse me. They met, like, fifteen seconds ago."

"I know."

"And didn't you tell me Will was a bit of a player?"

"Yep."

"What the hell."

"Trust me. I feel the same way."

"What did Garrett say about it."

"He said Lauren really wanted to get engaged." I wrinkled my nose as if there was a putrid stench in the air.

She scoffed. "And what about his devoted girlfriend of almost a decade? What she wants doesn't matter?"

"It's fine, really. We're just waiting until we're at a more secure point in our lives." My closed-lip smile felt tight.

Sharon rolled her eyes but didn't press the subject further. I knew that she knew what I was saying was bullshit, but she was kind enough not to point it out. I had cried one too many times over a bottle of wine with Sharon for her to fall for the same excuses I rattled off to everyone else.

"Are you ready for the new client pitch this afternoon?" she asked, graciously changing the subject.

"I was just about to go through the deck again. Did you see pictures of this property? It's gorgeous. It looks straight out of a movie. Almost makes me want to move out to the mountains."

She snorted. "Right, and give up your beach days? Not likely."

"Snow just seems so romantic, though."

I sighed and stared at the pictures of the property I had pulled up. It was located next to a ski resort in Colorado. The Key Ridge Ski Lodge. We managed resorts across the state of Florida and had recently opened our portfolio to other states. The prospective client's town was growing in popularity, but they were having trouble scaling. The property was large, and a huge potential money grab for the winter months. I had to nail this pitch.

"I can picture Mike in a Speedo better than I can picture you in snow."

"You're only saying that because he *did* wear a speedo at last year's holiday party."

We both doubled over, cackling, until a knock at the door interrupted our outburst.

"Mattie." My boss, Mike, stepped into my office. "Are you ready for the Colorado pitch? The clients just arrived from the airport. I know we scheduled the meeting for this afternoon, but they're earlier than expected, and I don't want to keep them waiting."

Just then, a gray-haired woman, maybe in her early sixties, and a thirty-something guy walked past my office. The guy was lean and muscular with dirty blond scraggly hair and stubble. He looked rugged and athletic. Although attractive, the scowl he was wearing and the hard set of his jaw were a turnoff for me. Mysteriously moody was not my type, but he was undeniably good-looking, nonetheless.

Sharon gasped. "Was that Giles Stone?"

"Who?" I asked at the same time Mike nodded.

"His family owns the property. He came with his aunt to hear the pitch." Mike made a move to follow them before turning back to me. "I'm going to go with them to the conference room. Meet us there in five."

With that, he rushed out of the room before I could object.

"Who is Giles Stone?" I asked again.

"He's a professional snowboarder," Sharon whispered despite the subject of our conversation being nowhere within hearing range. "Or was. I think he retired, but he was in the last two Winter Olympics. How have you never heard of him?"

"Oh right, *that* Giles Stone. I'm such a huge fan of snowboarding. I *totally* forgot I have his poster hanging in my room."

Sharon rolled her eyes at my sarcasm. "I'm not a winter sports fan either, but he's gorgeous. There's something extra attractive about a guy that does winter sports."

She came around to my side of the desk and pulled my keyboard toward her. She opened a search engine and typed his name in. Pictures of him filled my screen. They mainly consisted of him in winter clothes contorting his body into crazy positions high up in the air.

I stared at her. "Um, what's attractive about winter sports? You can't even see him underneath all those layers. I can't believe you even recognized him."

She clicked on a picture of him shirtless on the cover of a sports magazine to enlarge it.

"You were saying?" she asked.

"He's okay there, I guess."

"You should read up on him so you're prepared."

"By 'read up' do you mean stare at half-naked pictures? I only have five minutes." I closed the window she had opened. "I need to review this deck one more time. I'm sure snowboarding, or his career, is not going to come up in our presentation."

"If you say so." She walked back around toward my office door. "Hey, if it comes up organically, mind slipping him my number in case he's looking for something to do while he's in town?"

I laughed and tossed a balled-up piece of notebook paper at her.

"Out."

Sitting across from Giles Stone was different than looking at his pictures online. Sharon was right. He *was* gorgeous. And intense. From the moment I entered the room, his deep brown eyes hadn't stopped searing a hole right into me.

His aunt, Bev, seemed nice enough, but she had a slight edge to her. My hand was still throbbing from her firm handshake. All I could do to hide my nerves was plant a massive grin on my face and pretend I was completely at ease.

"Hello, I'm Mattie," I greeted them cheerily. "How was your flight?"

"It was fine. We appreciate you flying us out for this," answered Bev.

Giles just grunted in response.

I extended my hand to Giles, and he eyed it like I had an infectious disease. After a few heartbeats, he engulfed my hand in his and gave it a quick shake before dropping it. I noticed him flexing the hand that had touched me.

"So," I turned to Giles. "Colorado, huh? I've always wanted to visit. Must be a beautiful place to live."

"It is," he replied flatly.

His short remark and hard stare had me on edge. This was not the typical demeanor of potential clients.

"What do you think of Florida? It must be pretty different, huh?" I cleared my throat nervously.

He narrowed his eyes. "Obviously."

Bev nudged his arm before turning back to me with a smile. "It's lovely here. Always nice to be in a tropical climate, even if it is just for a quick trip."

Mike cleared his throat. "Well, Mattie is our director of Property Management. She's put together a great presentation for you. I think you'll find it all very informative."

"Thanks, Mike. I'll just get us started, then." I plugged in my computer and my slide deck appeared on the screen in front of us. "Feel free to stop me at any time with questions, but for now, let's just dive right in."

The first few slides outlined our basic structure. We would place a property manager on-site at their resort to handle all the daily operations. They would manage the housekeepers, order supplies, and go above and beyond to keep guests happy.

"And because your property hasn't been updated in a while, our team will make improvements as we see fit to make the space appealing to guests and ensure we capture as many new customers as possible."

Giles mumbled something under his breath. His presence made me uneasy.

"I'm sorry, what was that?" I asked, my voice dripping with politeness.

"I don't think you, or your team, has the first idea what would make us appealing to our customers," he spat. "Our customers *like* our vintage charm. None of them want to stay in a place with the same aesthetic as a sterile doctor's office." He gestured to the conference room we were sitting in.

My lip twitched as I tried to maintain my smile.

"Of course, sir. I didn't mean that the lodge didn't already possess a certain charm. And we would certainly work to create a feel that would appeal to your customer-"

"Please, spare me." He waved his hand as if to dismiss me. "You're so full of shit."

"Excuse me?" I choked out.

"What would a couple of suits that live in Florida know about running a ski lodge? Do you even ski?" He crossed his arms.

"Well, no," I sputtered. "But I know a lot about hotels and prop-"

"That's what I thought. I've heard enough."

He stood from his chair and circled around the table toward the exit.

"Giles, please sit down. You're being rude." Bev shot me an apologetic glance as she tried to talk down her nephew.

"No, I'm done here. I'll be outside."

With that, he stormed out, leaving me flabbergasted. While I didn't always nail every presentation, this was undoubtedly the first time I had lost someone's interest within the first five minutes.

At least Mike looked just as shocked as I felt. A sure sign that it wasn't my pitch that was the problem. Just that the person I was pitching to was an asshole.

"I'm sorry about him," Bev said, rising from her chair. "It's not you. He's got other things going on."

"It's not a problem," I responded through gritted teeth. It most certainly was a problem. I had spent days on this pitch, and he never intended to listen to it—the nerve of that jerk to waste my time.

"Look, despite that scene he just caused, I'm the decision-maker, and I'm drowning."

My ears perked up at her desperate tone. Was there still a shot of landing this?

"We would be happy to step in and take some of that burden off you," I chimed in. "Trust me. This is exactly the type of work our firm was made for. We'll step in and organize all your processes. When we're done, I promise we'll have your lodge running like a well-oiled machine."

I slid a packet of papers toward her.

"Maybe you and your nephew would like to review our numbers and mission privately to see if we'd be a good fit. I've outlined the details here."

She nodded.

"I appreciate a prepared woman." She winked at me.

Mike was sitting so far forward in his seat that I thought

he might fall out of it. I could tell he was eager to intervene, but he knew I had a way of reading people. Bev seemed like the type of person that valued her privacy and didn't like to make a production of things. The raw numbers and no bullshit information were precisely what she needed to make a decision.

She took my packet and paused in the doorframe. "I'll review this on our flight home and get back to you. Again, I'm sorry for the outburst and I hope we can move past this if we do decide to go forward."

"Of course," Mike and I said in unison. I'm not sure which of our smiles was bigger.

As soon as Bev was out of earshot, Mike raised his hand, and I gleefully high-fived it.

"What a save. I thought we were screwed when he walked out of here like that. Good job having that write-up prepared."

"We're not in the clear yet." I reminded him. While I was an eternal optimist, I did try to keep a realistic perspective on things.

"When she sees those estimated returns and reduced working hours, it'll be a no-brainer."

"Fingers crossed," I replied. "Let's just hope if we do land this account, there will be minimal interaction with that pro snowboarder asshat."

Continue reading!
Key Ridge **by Allison Speka available now on Amazon**

About the Author

Allison Speka aims to bring a refreshing blend of passion and authenticity to her writing. A self-proclaimed romance aficionado, Allison has been lost in the pages of love stories since she discovered the genre. She met her partner in Chicago before they both picked up and moved to Colorado five years ago.

Made in the USA
Middletown, DE
14 November 2023